"HOLD ME," SHE WHISPERED.

Her breath caressed his cheek, her legs spliced between his own. "Make me feel like I'm something more than a character in a thirty-second commercial."

He chuckled huskily, raising his head against her hair. "What? You don't like all this stardom? There're a thousand men who'd give their arm to be in my shoes right now."

"But there's only one I want," she said, tracing the line of his jaw. "The man who created that image."

Could he really be the only man in her life? Was he ready for that? He knew that's what it meant, especially with a woman like Kelsy. "You're making it hard for me to face that love seat tonight."

"Then don't." She ran her hands through the bristly ends of hair at his temple. "Without knowing it, you created a woman who isn't afraid to go after what she wants. Tonight, Tate Alexander, I want you."

DeANNA TALCOTT
Celebrity Status

ZEBRA BOOKS
KENSINGTON PUBLISHING CORP.

ZEBRA BOOKS

are published by

Kensington Publishing Corp.
475 Park Avenue South
New York, NY 10016

First Printing: March, 1993

Printed in the United States of America

*Dedicated to the memory of Kimmy Poxson
who loved Snuffy, Mickey Mouse,
and the color purple.
She fluttered through life
on the tips of angel's wings,
leaving hope and inspiration
in her wake.*

Chapter One

Kelsy Williams was being watched and it made her uneasy. She didn't know the man, but she recognized his intent. Maybe that was why she struck up a conversation with the woman standing next to her in the discount store. It was certainly a lot more comfortable than gazing back at the hunk standing at the end of the aisle; he was too tall, too dark, and far too handsome.

Everything about him carried warning signs — the pressed twill pants, the strip of leather binding them provocatively low on his hips, the dress shirt, and the double-breasted jacket. But the way that jacket was hanging open, with his tie loosely knotted and a few coarse hairs lapping at his throat, made him seem like a tease. A teal-colored pocket square drooped out of his coat pocket, looking as if he'd swiped it from his dresser and stuck it in his pocket as an afterthought. Kelsy seriously doubted that.

His haircut appeared to have been contoured with a scalpel, giving new meaning to the phrase "surgically precise." Sunstreaked, it was short over the ears and swept back off his forehead. Obviously he took great pains to keep it perfectly groomed, as if it was important to emphasize that his rugged build was housed in the kind of clothes, the kind of facade, of an ambitious builder of dreams.

Men, at least ones put together like that, rarely stared at Kelsy Williams for any reason. Unless maybe her slip was showing or she had a chocolate-milk mustache. No, she usually attracted the kind who grinned a lot, wore glasses, and sported generic haircuts given by the next available barber.

But this man's unabashed scrutiny sent a tremor through her knees and a tingling through her middle. Clutching the bottle of shampoo a little tighter, she leaned closer to the stranger next to her. Wearing a crisp lab uniform, one with a plastic name tag identifying her as Betty, the lady turned one bottle of shampoo after another.

"I've started using this for a little extra control," Kelsy said, running her fingernail over the label. "This stuff's the greatest. I swear by it."

Betty peered over the blue-tinted rims of her glasses to study it. "I don't know, I've never heard of it . . ."

"Try it," Kelsy encouraged her. "I know it's new. But, like I said, this stuff lives up to its claims. My hair's never looked better, never had more control." She skimmed a glance over Betty's shade of red hair. "Besides, I figure why not? Blondes have had their chance at lemon shampoos, brunettes get henna. It's about time redheads have something to call their own."

Betty lifted the bottle out of Kelsy's hands.

" 'Redheads Only,' " she said musingly, turning it over to read the ingredient label.

"It really brings out the highlights in your hair. You know—those gold tones. And there's another formula that's supposed to deepen the color." Kelsy pulled a second bottle off the shelf, suddenly aware Mr. Good-Looking had edged closer. Obviously listening to their conversation, he'd plucked a bottle of dandruff shampoo off the shelf, also pretending to read the label.

Dandruff? Hah! The man probably didn't even have one hair follicle on his whole head that had ever come in contact with a patch of flaky, dry scalp. Kelsy could tell he was the kind of guy who looked good without even trying. The kind who never got a runny nose when he skied, who never wound up with a spot of grease on his tie after eating in an elegant restaurant, which he doubtless did frequently.

"Have you tried the conditioner?" Betty asked.

"No . . ." Drawn back into the conversation, Kelsy realized she sounded apologetic. "My budget only stretches so far. I'm using up what I have. After that, I'm going to be a faithful user of Redheads Only products. I guarantee it." She grinned, adding, "I hate it when I look in the mirror and it looks like the fire died."

Approximately six foot two inches of trouble bit back a smile. Kelsy winced, wishing just once she could open her mouth and have something sophisticated come out. Instead, knowing she'd been overheard, she felt like a poor imitation of a sales-

9

man, one who was a bit unsteady on his soapbox.

Betty decisively threw the bottle into her cart. "I'll try it. I haven't been happy with the shampoo I've been using anyway. Oh — " surprised by Kelsy's empty hands, she pulled down a second bottle of shampoo, thrusting it at her " — sorry. And thanks for the tip, dear. We redheads have to stick together."

"No kidding," Kelsy agreed, wondering if the man was still eavesdropping. "Redheads are accused of all kinds of things — hot tempers, sexy body language, and flaming independence. At least now the manufacturers have given us a shampoo to package it all."

Betty chuckled and rolled her cart into the main aisle. Reluctantly Kelsy, too, turned away, consciously avoiding Mr. Good-Looking and telling herself his interest was only because of a redheaded wife — or, more likely, a girlfriend.

But her movement was abruptly stopped by the broad expanse of a white dress shirt that was pulled taut over a somewhat bulging belly. Tripping over his scuffed wingtips, she started apologizing. Older, heavy set, he filled the aisle, effectively blocking her. He caught her elbow and steadied her, asking, "Guess you didn't see me. You okay?"

"Fine. I . . ." Looking over her shoulder, Kelsy saw the hunk sidle up behind her. Sandwiched between two overly interested men, Kelsy hesitated, looking from one to the other.

The hunk paid little heed to her features, but seemed mesmerized by her hair, absently setting the dandruff shampoo between carefully stacked cans of mousse. The green and orange bottle of economy shampoo looked ridiculously out of place.

"So you like the shampoo?" the heavyset man beside her prompted. "Redheads Only, I mean."

"Yes, I-I use it." Kelsy sent a fleeting glance to the hunk. He was still transfixed by her hair. Did he have some kind of redhead fetish?

"Nice texture," he murmured to the older man. "Maybe a good layered cut?"

"Maybe." The man straightened his tie, then slid his hand into the inside pocket of his jacket and drew out a business card. He offered it to Kelsy. "Eugene Theis. Well, actually, everyone calls me Gene. We're, uh—" he paused, sailing a look over her head to his counterpart "—representatives for the Redheads Only shampoo. And we're just doing a little market research. You know, standing around the health and beauty aisles, watching what women buy."

Kelsy stared at him, wondering if he really believed she was gullible enough to fall for the line. Then she dropped her eyes to the card. It looked authentic.

"Oh. I was beginning to wonder. . . ." She shrugged. "I mean it's not every day a woman's approached in the middle of a discount store over a bottle of shampoo. I was beginning to think you guys were undercover agents for the FDA or something."

Gene smiled, cocking his head to one side to study her. It made the gray at his temples more

11

striking. He had a full face, one that looked as if he enjoyed home cooking, and his clothes were just rumpled enough to make you think his after-dinner activity was a romp with the kids. "Worse," he said. "We're businessmen. We're the guys who're looking for motive. We're the ones who try to figure out why you picked up that bottle of shampoo. That, and what it's going to take to make you buy it."

"Oh, I'm going to buy it all right. I think it's terrific. You just want to ask me a few questions about the shampoo? Is that it?"

"Mmm, sort of."

"Kind of like a questionnaire thing?"

"Nothing that formal. Just tell me why you like the product, how long you've been using it—that sort of thing."

"Oh, let's see . . . I discovered it about a month ago and I've been using it ever since. It leaves my hair soft and silky, and gives highlights, kind of burnishing the color rather than leaving it coated with something sticky. It's not drying, either."

"You blow-dry your hair?" the hunk asked.

Kelsy gave a start. As implausible as it was, she'd nearly forgotten him. "Usually. I don't have time for a lot of fussing. No perms or electric rollers. Fortunately, I've got all this natural curl, and—" She stopped, cautiously eyeing the hand creeping toward her shoulder, merely inches from her shoulder-length hair.

"May I?"

Apprehension shot through her and she stiffened imperceptibly.

12

Beside her, Gene laughed, breaking the tension. "You'll have to forgive Tate," he said. "The man just isn't happy unless he can have his hands in a woman's hair. Tate, meet the woman who is one heck of an unwitting spokesperson for Redheads Only."

A slow smile lifted Tate's lips, and Kelsy stared at the twin creases on either side of his mouth, guessing a pair of dimples lurked beneath the surface. His eyelids sank like a sunset, briefly blotting out lazy blue color and veiling his emotions. Still, it was a confirmation of how she viewed him. Leisurely, confident, self-assured.

"My friend and coworker, Tate Alexander, Miss . . . ?"

"Williams," Kelsy supplied automatically, falling victim to this Tate Alexander's oddly penetrating gaze. She extended her hand. "Kelsy Williams."

"I apologize, Miss Williams," Tate said smoothly, his voice as rich, robust, and distinctive as an early-morning cup of freshly brewed coffee. "It seems I get carried away when I find what I've been looking for. It's too bad you're not, well . . ." His gaze scoured her, taking in her persimmon sweater and the only pair of expensive jeans she owned.

Tilting her head, Kelsy waited for him to continue. But he didn't, and she was unaware that her movement had put her features at an inviting angle, the overhead light dusting her unfettered hair with golden sparkles, gilding the smattering of honey-colored freckles across the bridge of her nose.

"You see," Tate said, "Redheads Only shampoo was my idea. I've been intimately involved—" he paused as though regretting his choice of words "—involved in it from the beginning. And I have an extraordinary interest in how it's promoted. Naturally, seeing someone like yourself, someone who's so enthusiastic about the shampoo, makes me see all the possibilities." He grinned. "Honestly, I'm not trying to drag you off caveman style, just . . . feel your hair."

His gentle humor was infectious, and Kelsy grinned. She could see there was substance beneath his well-sculpted exterior. "Thank goodness. I *was* a bit worried."

Both men chuckled.

"I have to tell you, though—" feeling a bit more confident, Kelsy slipped the business card in her jeans pocket—"my customers all noticed the difference after I started using the Redheads Only shampoo. Everybody said, 'What'd you do to your hair? It's beautiful.' Two of my regulars even invited me out for dinner and a movie, another came up with concert tickets, and a fourth insisted we take in a baseball game. No matter how you figure it, that's a pretty swift payback for investing in your shampoo. If you could only convince the Redheads of America there's a direct correlation, you'd have a multimillion-dollar success story."

"How about you, Kelsy? Suppose you could convince a million potential customers of the same thing?" Gene asked, a twinkle in his gray eyes. "Infect them with some of your enthusiasm for the product?"

She laughed. "Honestly. I swear it's the truth. Four dates in four days." Kelsy raised her hand in a mock pledge, holding the shampoo aloft like Miss Liberty's famous torch. But then, looking into Tate's amused eyes, she wished she hadn't been so candid.

Sure, the guys who'd asked her out were sincere. They were also quiet, shy, and conservative. None would choose a double-breasted jacket or a flower-garden tie. They certainly didn't know what to do with a pocket square. They didn't know how to ski and they figured candlelight was something used only during a power failure. They weren't at all sophisticated. They were auto mechanics and accountants and insurance salesmen. They were good men, plain men.

Gene sighed. "Anyone with this much conviction ought to take a screen test.

"What?" Kelsy was jolted back to reality. Beside her, she felt Tate straighten.

"A screen test. We're looking for the perfect Redheads Only girl. As far as I'm concerned, Miss Williams, you fit the bill. You're enthusiastic, outgoing, attractive—"

"Inexperienced," Tate interjected firmly, warningly."

"No, I'm serious. She ought to take a screen test."

"Gene. . . ." Again, that warning.

"I can see her as the Redheads Only girl," Gene persisted, shifting his weight and leaning closer to Kelsy. "It's going to be a great campaign, a standard contract, and a lot of perks. A few free flights, some gorgeous clothes, and a salary that's probably quadruple the one you're making now."

Kelsy's jaw dropped. His words were going slow motion through her head. Flights. Clothes. Money. Contract. Perks. Lots of perks. Probably a lot more perks than she was getting now, owning a coffee shop with her sister. Now all she did was wipe up spills and harass the bakery for not delivering the Danish on time.

But Gene's proposition bordered on the ridiculous. Ludicrous. No one offered a job like that in the health-and-beauty aisle of a Minneapolis, Minnesota, discount store. Somehow, inexplicably, caution seeped in to temper her response. Any enthusiasm was significantly diluted. "Things like this just don't happen. I don't think—"

"Absurd, yes. Not impossible," Gene admitted. "You're a natural redhead, aren't you?"

Kelsy felt herself grow warm. "Of course it's natural!"

Gene winked at Tate. "And just the kind of spunk our redhead deserves."

"C'mon, Theis. Don't start making these impulsive moves on me now. We've got too much invested—"

"Who's got too much invested? I got there by trusting my instincts, something you could learn from. God knows, I'm trying to teach you." Slipping his hand into his pants pocket, Gene jingled his change. To Kelsy, the gesture was vaguely symbolic of the monetary opportunity he was offering her. "There's a downtown firm that'd be happy to do a little screen test for you, Miss Williams. We

16

can schedule one first thing tomorrow morning. Why not throw your hat in the ring and take a shot at it? I've got a sneaking suspicion you have what it takes."

Kelsy saw the skepticism in Tate's blue-clouded eyes. There was something honest about his reaction. She was both relieved and disappointed by it. Part of her wanted to show him, the other part was relieved she wouldn't have to.

But the whole premise was preposterous. Her? A model? A glorified salesperson, actually, one touting a haircare product.

"No. No, I don't think so," she said, shaking her head and sidling past Tate. "It all sounds too good to be true."

"At least she's got some sense," Tate said.

"It's a dream job," Gene wheedled.

When they were shoulder to shoulder, Tate seemed to focus on her face. "For a dream girl," he added thoughtfully, as if imprinting either her bone structure or the emerald color of her eyes in his memory.

Kelsy hesitated, her gaze locking with Tate's. Not only did she see trouble brewing in the depths of his eyes, but she saw ambition, determination. Fascinated, she felt herself gravitate toward him. For an instant she didn't know whether her response was triggered by welling curiosity or the mysterious lure of comfort. With a slight shake of his head, he was the first to break the inexplicable spell surrounding them.

"I heard you say you hadn't tried the conditioner." Reaching into his pocket, he withdrew

17

half a dozen sample sizes. "Take these. With my compliments."

Taking the packets from Tate, Kelsy was struck by their warmth in the palm of her hand. They had lain against his thigh, absorbing his body heat. Closing her fingers around the packets, she wished their provocative warmth could remain. For once cold, they would merely be a reminder of her brief exchange with Tate Alexander — cool, indifferent, and severed.

"Thank you. I will. Maybe I'll even save one so I can say I knew you when. A piece of American ingenuity from an infamous manufacturing company." The coy small talk earned her only a slight smile. She wondered what made a man like Tate Alexander tick. Was it the drive to succeed that made him so curt, so restrained? Whatever it was, it piqued her curiosity, made her want to win his confidence.

"Think about the screen test, Miss Williams," said Gene. "I'm sincere about it. I can't guarantee what would happen, but it could be worth your time."

"I'll tell you what," Kelsy answered, reluctantly dropping the packets into her shoulder bag. "I'll think about it, and if I change my mind I'll give you a call."

Moving away, she didn't look back. But long after she'd passed through the checkout and endured the cashier's idle chitchat, Gene's disappointment and Tate's narrowed gaze were firmly etched in her memory.

* * *

18

It should have been a quiet afternoon. But one obnoxious customer and a battle with the ice machine changed all that. The service repairman for the ice maker kept shaking his head and clucking his tongue against the roof of his mouth. For some reason Kelsy felt guilty, as if she had intentionally knotted the water lines into one expensive, and thoroughly incomprehensible, puzzle.

Wiping down the far end of the counter, she thought again of Tate Alexander and Gene Theis. She still experienced a thrill when she thought how she'd been asked to take a screen test. A screen test of all things!

The invitation fired her imagination with possibilities, all of them appealing and all of them a lot more glamorous than wiping up spills in a coffee shop. Trips, clothes, cars, a bank account. A bank account she could actually write checks on, one that might honestly balance instead of swaying precariously into the red. As for savings, all she'd seemed to do lately was pitch nickels and dimes into a mayonnaise jar.

Worse, the jar, nearly three-quarters full, was still a long way from paying for another semester of her sister Devon's tuition. Taking classes only as they could afford them was getting Devon closer to her master's in city management. But it was a long slow haul. Sometimes her limbs simply went through the motions, making her feel like a pet-store hamster on the monotonous grind of a tread-wheel.

"Miss?" The pinstripe-suited man at the end of the counter slid aside his saucer. "This coffee is cold."

"Oh? I'm sorry. Let me get you a refill." Outwardly, Kelsy sounded apologetic, but inside, she was annoyed. Her customer had become so engrossed in the stock market report, he hadn't touched his coffee for almost thirty minutes. "Sure you don't want some Danish with that?"

"Nope."

The answer was short and clipped as he rattled the paper. Seconds later, Kelsy put a second cup of coffee in front of him.

"Haven't you got the sports section?" he asked, waving the thrice-folded paper the restaurant provided for its patrons.

"Let me look." After rummaging through the magazine rack, she found it and brought it to him. For thanks, he grunted. It took all of her willpower not to wrinkle her nose and roll her eyes.

"Say, get me some change, will you?" he asked, reaching into his pocket as he scanned the headlines. "Ones, if you have them."

Kelsy blanched when he handed her a fifty. Coming back, she handed him twenty ones, four fives, and a ten. "It's the best I can do. I need to keep a little change for the customers." Smiling while gritting her teeth was an accomplishment she took pride in. Well, at least he'd probably leave a decent tip.

The guy laid down exactly ninety-five cents, enough for a cup of coffee and a ten-cent breath mint. It figures, she thought sourly, dropping the change into the till.

She was still stewing about being stiffed when

the repairman handed her an itemized bill. "You oughta have a service contract," he told her, tossing minuscule wrenches into his case.

"How much is that going to cost me?"

"More'n the machine's worth. But you can't afford not to. A new ice maker would really eat up a chunk of cash. Here." He tossed a service contract onto the counter, all of the appropriate blanks filled in with a ballpoint pen. "If you decide to take out a policy, keep the pink copy. Send the yellow and white ones back to us. I guarantee it's going to save you a lot of money in the long run."

Dismally, Kelsy picked up the document, silently comparing the fee to the price of one credit hour. The way things looked right now the return on either investment was about the same. "I'll send you a check," she muttered, taking the contract, bill, and receipt back to the cash register.

The phone rang just as she was debating about whether or not to sign the service contract. "Coffee 'n' More."

"Hi. It's Devon, Kels."

"Get registered?"

"Yeah. They're having that class on a Tuesday night. Ought to work out, huh?"

"Sounds good."

"But there's something else . . ."

"Oh?"

"They had an opening in Friedman's class, the one I've been trying to get into?"

"And?" Kelsy knew without asking.

"I went ahead and signed up."

"Of course."

"It's Wednesdays and Fridays. I figure we're going to have to push the Danish."

"Huh."

"Maybe hot dogs or nachos?"

"No more new machines. You're going to die when you find out how much the ice maker cost to get fixed."

There was a moment of silence. "I could drop the class. Pick it up later."

"Not on your life. If nothing else, I'll see you peddling Danish to your classmates to appease both me and our budget."

The mock threat at least wrung a titter from her older sister. "So, anything new happen this afternoon?"

Her encounter with Gene Theis and Tate Alexander darted through her mind. But Kelsy refused to talk about that. The whole thing was too much a dream, one that kept replaying through her head and tantalizing her imagination. Knowing Devon, she'd be skeptical. On the spur of the moment she could probably even grind out a very effective case against talking to strange men at the local strip mall.

"Not much. That jerk who sits and reads the stock report was in again. I'm sure he thinks we're running a nonprofit organization."

"The one who buys breath mints and doesn't tip?"

"The same. And I swear he believes Juan Valdez and his donkey deliver an endless free supply of freshly ground coffee beans to our doorstep."

Devon chuckled. "You need a vacation."

"Fat chance."

Kelsy thought about her sister's advice for several minutes after they hung up. The truth was she did need a break. Meeting her sister's tuition was like pumping up a worn tire, one with a leak. They never quite seemed to get ahead of the demand. They were always on the low side, their bank account always a little soft and typically unreliable.

Maybe what she needed was a working vacation.

The offer of the screen test popped into her head. Either that or she'd lured it there, hoping for the great escape of fantasy. It would be great to have a fun job and actually make money, too. What if the offer had been legitimate? What if she'd looked a gift horse in the mouth?

Digging the business card out of her pocket, she propped her elbows on the counter and studied it. Eugene R. Theis. Elsethe Industries. 5243 Arden Way, Minneapolis, Minnesota.

First, she pulled out the phone book, checking the address against the card. Then, before her mind could tell her fingers to stop, she was punching the numbers into the phone. Within minutes, she was talking with a secretary. It only took two phrases for her to learn Gene Theis was not just a representative of the company, he was its founder and president.

Suddenly she didn't really care how Tate Alexander fit into the picture. She only marveled at the fact she impulsively scheduled a screen test for eight the following morning.

Devon could handle the morning regulars.

Chapter Two

Kelsy arrived twenty minutes early. Tate watched her from across the room. She was perched on the edge of a vinyl-covered couch, picking at a loose thread. Out of her element, she looked as if she didn't quite know what she was doing—or why. Instead of the smooth catlike greeting he'd become accustomed to from other models, Kelsy sat meekly, one hand smoothing her skirt.

She had great legs, Tate observed. That was a surprise. He'd expected thick ankles and heavy calves. No one ever knew what to expect after a pair of designer jeans were peeled away.

"Ah, good!" Gene boomed. "You're early." Checking his watch, he seemed doubly surprised. Tate hoped he wasn't impressed. "We can get things set up right away. Tate wants to see that your hair's done before the shoot."

Kelsy flicked a startled glance at Tate. Obviously, she hadn't expected this. It didn't take much to see that the thought of being imprisoned in a hydraulic chair while someone towered over her with a blow dryer and a can of hair spray was already sending shivers through her. He was amused.

Reaching up, Kelsy crimped the ends of her hair, dragging it over her shoulder like a peace offering. "But I did my hair this morning."

Gene grinned. "Tate just wants to get a feel for it. To see how it responds. To see how *you* respond."

Tate guessed that if the surroundings hadn't been so legitimate, so professional, Kelsy would have fled after hearing Gene's suggestion. As it was, a pink stain crept over her cheeks.

She had pretty features, really. They were on the verge of delicate, with cheekbones just high enough, just pronounced enough to refute the description. The same with her mouth. She had a sweet smile, one that formed a perfect crescent, accentuating sculpted lips and even teeth.

In the past few months he'd seen plenty of models who had dozens of teeth crammed between the never ending slash of a too-wide smile. That, and eyes defined by heavy strokes of eyeliner. Kelsy, instead, simply wore a flattering brown mascara, her lids highlighted with a touch of taupe shadow.

Tate instinctively knew her eyes would look good on camera. They were clear, an emerald green shot with gold sparks. Slightly almond-shaped, any coquettish angle she threw the camera would be magnified, and her intent, either provocative or shy, would dazzle an audience. He already knew that; he only wondered if Gene did.

"So? Shall we get started?" Sweeping his hand toward the small dressing area and makeup room, Tate anticipated her reaction. The front of her cotton shell top vibrated, dipping into the hollow between her breasts as she took a cleansing breath. It was either a cleansing breath or a shudder, he wasn't sure which.

"I guess."

Kelsy allowed herself to be led. If she was surprised by the sparse surroundings, she said nothing, waiting only until the hairdresser, whom Tate introduced as Bruce, turned the vinyl chair for her to be seated. Bruce was a slight man, with a decidedly sallow complexion and an earring in one ear. The only exercise he appeared to get was wielding a hairbrush.

Tate waited, knowing from experience this was usually the chance for overeager models to come up with some interesting small talk. Kelsy didn't utter a word.

But her eyes said it all. They darted about the room, taking in stark walls, high ceilings, and the exposed wires and cables overhead. Bruce whirled her in the chair, and with the benefit of the mirror, her searching gaze collided with Tate's.

He was mesmerized. He saw honesty in their green depths, enthusiasm behind her control. The graceful arch of her delicate brows emphasized her awe and disbelief of what was happening. She possessed the wide-eyed look of innocence—

one most men found irresistible. One with which' the camera could do very provocative things.

He moved to her, intending to show Bruce the type of style he was looking for. But when his fingers brushed her shoulder, he felt her quiver. "Nervous?"

"Not too. I suppose I should be."

"Oh? Why?"

"Because it's not every day a girl finds herself having a screen test." Kelsy shook her head, smothering a smile as Bruce pumped up the chair. "My sister's worried sick, calls the whole thing a sham. She says if I don't phone her by noon she's calling the police." Consulting the wall clock, she added wryly, "You'd better hurry this up. She usually means what she says."

It wasn't easy to stop the grin from stealing onto his face. Tate compromised his reaction by experimenting with a lock of her hair, delving in near the scalp and pulling the length of red out over her shoulders. Twining a curl around a finger, he realized it was thicker than he'd first thought. "I figured we'd just wash your hair and do something simple. No cut, nothing extraordinary."

"Thank God. I've been sitting here thinking you might actually cut it."

"Hah. So much for the vote of confidence," Bruce said, obviously a little peeved as he whipped a fresh towel from the nearby stack. "But don't worry. You get the contract, I promise I'll be following you with a pair of scissors.

Tate'll see to it. By the time I'm finished we'll create a whole new dimension for redheads."

Kelsy, looking a little embarrassed about her unwitting remark, laughed. "Sorry. But there's something a little forbidding about having someone you don't know stand over you with scissors. I do hope you understand."

Accepting that, Bruce adjusted the towel and snapped the cape at the back of her neck. Knocking Tate's hands away, he lifted her hair to her crown, turning the chair slightly so Tate could see what lay beneath. "She's got an uneven hairline."

With the knuckle of his forefinger, Tate traced the two delicate, wispy vees creeping down the column of her neck. The flesh there was moist, damp. Touching her there made him feel a bit like a predator, one cautiously picking its way into a new lair. In an updo, he imagined the fine hairs would curl into spirals. On a practical note, if she sported a short cut, he'd have to have it razored. Pity.

Bruce let her hair drop, fingering through it. "Well, she hasn't ruined it with too much heat and she hasn't stripped it by using color. Thank God she hasn't got any home permanent damage, but this cut . . ." He actually sneered, and Kelsy looked as if she'd like to shrink-wrap herself into the hydraulic chair. Picking up a strand, Bruce waggled it under her nose. "Who did this?" he demanded.

Tate had to give Kelsy credit, she barely stirred,

and only one apprehensive breath rasped through her lungs. Then the single word popped out — as quietly and as inconspicuously as she could possibly utter it.

"Me."

"What'd you use?" Bruce groused. "Nail clippers?"

The look Kelsy shot him was positively murderous. Tate, buoyed by the implications, had a hard time quashing a smile.

"She really hacked it, huh?"

"Well—" Bruce sniffed "—these amateurs."

Kelsy's expression became fixed, the line of her jaw stolid. "I did not hack at my hair," she said clearly. "Hacking requires a butcher knife or a machete. I merely layered it with my mother's old pinking shears."

Tate's smile faded rapidly. Then he saw her smirk.

"Gotcha." She winked, unbothered. "The fact is the last time I got such a bad cut — for such an exorbitant price, I might add—" she paused just long enough to nail Bruce via the plate glass mirror "—I decided to do it myself."

Bruce shook his head, as if the mere thought of a woman cutting her own hair was nothing short of scandalous. "Well, I suppose it's not that bad," he finally conceded, "and there's enough length, so we've got plenty of room to experiment."

"Great," Tate put in without enthusiasm. All right, so he was cynical. He had a lot of misgivings about hiring an inexperienced model for this campaign. These jobs were filled with unexpected surprises—he'd come to learn the real treat was watching models react to them. Sure, Kelsy Williams seemed nice enough, but taking a chance on a virtual unknown was more of a gamble than he was ready for.

"So you just want me to play around with it or what?"

Tate found Bruce's choice of words annoying. "I want it swept away from her face. Feathered back, I guess. A little height on the crown and lots of body."

"Body? Huh, you won't have to worry about that, she's got plenty."

The unwitting choice of words jarred Tate further, and his gaze fell to her draped figure. She was shorter than he'd choose, but well-proportioned, her ankles dainty, her wrists looking like they deserved bracelets and bangles. For crying out loud, he reprimanded himself, this was not at all how it was supposed to be working out. He was supposed to be proving to Gene that taking someone off the streets and turning her into a model was a farfetched idea.

Still, while Bruce washed and dried her hair, Tate stayed in the room, hovering constantly, suggesting a lift here, a different stroke of the brush there. But it was uncanny. The more Bruce worked with her hair, the more pleased Tate felt, fiddling with a wisp near her temple, dragging his hand back to sweep the nape.

"Her hair's really quite glorious, Tate. Glorious. Tremendous amount of body, and just a hint of natural curl. With a good cut, she wouldn't even need a perm."

Tate frowned. "Is that a cowlick near her temple?"

"Mmm-hmm. And I've got just the perfect style in mind to accommodate it. If anything it gives her character." Bruce, finally finished, whirled her in the chair, stopping it short so she could see herself in the mirror.

Kelsy stared, her mouth forming a small "o" as she reached for the wispy ends brushing her shoulder. Like a child caught red-handed, she guiltily pulled back. "Guess I shouldn't do that," she said, reminding herself not to disturb a single strand.

"Well," Bruce said, airily lifting one shoulder, "we're not talking about a work of art here. Once under those hot lights, and with Chuck giving you all kinds of stage directions, your hair's going to look like a few hands have been through it."

"Still . . ."

Unsnapping the cape, Bruce swept it off her shoulders with the same flair he'd unveil a masterpiece, going back only once to fluff a wisp at her crown. Kelsy sat immobile, silently considering her reflection. "Tate?"

"Yes?"

"Is there anything I need to know?"

Why had he said what he did? He probably

31

shouldn't have. In fact, even though he was trying to be nice, the whole thing went against his better judgment. Kelsy Williams had no business taking a screen test or working as the model for Redheads Only. It would be a stretch of the imagination to think she could handle the job or any of its implications. She was attractive, but far from perfect. Had it been simply her distinctive features that snared their attention? Or her enthusiastic testimonial of Redheads Only?

No matter. He said it anyway. And for a second, when it sounded like encouragement, he really meant it. Maybe it was because it was impossible not to like her. Maybe it was because he sensed a quality in her that was genuine. "Just go out there and sparkle. Turn on every emotion you can summon and give each one to the camera like it was a gift. A special gift—a gift just from you, Kelsy."

To Kelsy, the camera offered an optical illusion. But she was absorbing the sensation—and relishing it. In her mind, it was like being on center stage. Everyone, the hairstylist, the makeup artist, the lighting experts, the sound people, the photographer, even Tate and Gene, were moving about her, the focal point. There were moments she felt as if she were a wax figurine, one being molded, and changed, by heat—and inclination.

Before any pictures were taken, though, the sound people experimented with her voice. They talked a lot about resonance and quality and inflection, and Kelsy was left with the strangest feeling that whatever could possibly be wrong with her voice, they would fix it. Finally she read some silly little nursery rhymes that had absolutely nothing to do with shampoo. When she finished, they turned to one another and smiled.

Wearing the same beige skirt and shell top, she was amazed at how the lighting experts changed her look and feel. Dropping colored filters over the lights, they created a mood or accented the action by bathing her in an incandescent glow, or wicked glare and shadow. She found there were colors she liked, the blues, the reds, but there were others, such as yellow, that made her feel brittle inside.

All the while the photographer talked to her. He became a director. An amazing metamorphosis took place within her as she worked. She began depending on his instruction, then she started to trust him. Chuck was the force that wheedled, cajoled, and coaxed her into the proper response.

Move here, place your arm there. Above your head, below your waist. C'mon, tuck your tummy in, he teased, we're not doing a maternity ad. Tilt your chin, arch your back. Drape the jacket over your shoulder. This time, fling it. Fling it, and throw your head back.

Smile.

Grin.

What'sa matter? Do I have to get the sound men to recite their repertoire of dirty jokes?

Giggle.

Take a break, change the pace.

Loosen your hair, blow it into tendrils. This time, stretch and arch, like someone's putting the palm of his hand between your shoulderblades. Be provocative. Seductive.

Why did her attention stray from the camera? To Tate, to the man who stood beyond the circle of lights and critically watched? To the man whose gaze seemed to smolder with a dark fire?

"Hey? Are you getting tired?"

Kelsy gave a start at the photographer's question. "No. I—"

"It's been three hours, Chuck," Gene interrupted from the sidelines. "Why don't we break? Tate says Kelsy needs to make a call anyway."

Someone threw her a towel. Kelsy caught it midair. Dragging it over her shoulders, she experienced relief, wondering if this was how a fighter felt when he sank back in his own corner of the ring. Before she could wipe her face, the instructions from Chuck's assistant registered in her saturated mind.

"Blot. Don't wipe, it ruins the makeup."

Carefully following his instructions, Kelsy wondered how much they'd invested in this filming session. She'd never expected it to be so time-consuming. Everyone was kind, but it was definitely business—no one seemed to be letting her off the hook because she was inexperienced.

"How's it going?" Tate asked, guiding her by the elbow to the nearest door.

"Fine. This is an incredible way to work—it's actually fun. Why, I can't believe it's almost noon already."

"It's nearly one," he said, leading her into someone's empty office and handing her the phone. "Here. Better call your sister before the cops raid the place. But don't take too long. I can see Chuck's getting impatient to finish."

Tate left, but the door to the office hung ajar. Rather than closing it, Kelsy turned her back and started dialing the number.

"Coffee 'n' More."

"Hi! How's it going?"

"How's it going for you? They don't have you taking your clothes off yet, do they?"

"Get serious. This is just a routine thing."

"Well, I don't mind telling you I've been more than a little bit worried. When I didn't hear from you by twelve, I called—"

"You didn't!" Kelsy gasped, anxiously moving to the window to see if any squad cars were in the parking lot. It would be just like Devon to do something like that.

"No. But I did call the Better Business Bureau. Elsethe Industries has a flawless record. Of course, anyone could pose as a representative of the company. You hear of these things all the time—"

"Devon!"

"So, unless they promise you the moon, don't sign anything."

"How about if they offer me a salary that'll

35

cover your tuition?" Kelsy waited, her question receiving a distinct pause.

"In that case, sign it in blood."

Kelsy was laughing when Tate stuck his head in the office. Holding up one finger to silence him, she said her goodbye.

"I heard some sirens off the interstate," he said. "Please tell me they aren't heading our direction."

"No. But my sister did call the Better Business Bureau."

"And?"

"And Elsethe Industries has a wonderful reputation."

"The president and his partner have one, too."

She grinned. "Yes, well, the way she was thinking . . ."

"Let me guess." Tate lounged against the door frame, his eyes boring into hers. "She figured this was one of those little productions where the model is scantily clad."

Kelsy tried to bite back the sarcastic quip hovering on her tongue. "Well, you did mention something about a swimsuit."

Tate didn't release her from his gaze. But his hands were working, drawing forth a scarlet garment and unfurling it before her eyes. He held the shapeless swimsuit by the shoulder straps and offered it to her. "Try this on. If it doesn't fit, well, let me know and we'll work around it."

"Around it?" Apprehension caused Kelsy's question to come out in a squeak. The wicked flash she saw in Tate's eyes unnerved her.

"Just remember," he said, "most models are a collection of salable body parts. I know one who has the most sought-after feet in the industry. She's either modeling high heels or Dr. Scholl's inserts. But the bottom line is that in this business it doesn't matter whether a model's wearing shoes or a swimsuit. Eventually they all shed their modesty. Get used to it, Kelsy."

"I see. Thanks for the tip. But under the circumstances I'll make every effort to see this fits."

But it didn't. Oh, it was the right size, all right. But the cups were a tad too small, making her bosom plump over the top. No matter how she pushed herself back down and pulled the suit up, everything seemed determined to spill over the edge. She didn't know whether the pink flush staining her throat and chest was due to embarrassment or her frustrated attempts to bind herself into Lycra and elastic.

When Tate saw her, his perusal was brief but thorough. "Terrific," he finally commented. Kelsy wasn't convinced. His voice was too flat, too strictly controlled. "We've got a couple of ideas we want to try for the shoot, then we'll be finished."

On re-entering the circle of light, she found a beach umbrella, a canvas deck chair, and a beach towel. Someone turned a fan on her, making the forced air whip through her hair like a Gulf Coast breeze.

"Don't squint!" the photographer directed.

"You're supposed to be having fun, not trying to keep the sand out of your eyes."

By the time they were done, her eyeballs felt as round as two golfballs and as dry as sandtraps.

Then they changed the lighting and carried in the Hollywood bed.

Gene sent her some lunch after she'd showered. Kelsy, still feeling a little amused—and unquestionably relieved—that they'd propped her up in that Hollywood bed with a terry-cloth robe, a book, and glasses, discovered the reason she was famished was that it was nearly three in the afternoon. Sinking onto the lumpy sofa in the makeup room, she devoured fresh fruit, crackers, and tuna salad. Suspecting the Coke they'd sent her was diet, she only sipped at it, regretfully longing for the real thing.

But she hardly had time to dwell on the matter because her hopes for the screen test were high—oh, so high. Every minute that passed encouraged her to think of the role she could have the chance to play. It was all an elaborate vision, drawn and created in the minds of an enterprising industry, and brought to reality by her face on a strip of videotape.

The Redheads Only girl.

From the talk she'd heard, she knew there would be TV commercials and a print-ad campaign. Both Gene and Tate were looking for an image—one that they both expected she could fill. She'd not only be a model and actress, but a spokesperson, a visible, touchable representative of Redheads Only. If anyone had asked her yesterday if she was a model, she'd have scoffed. Today she felt as if she'd accomplished an unexpected and remarkable feat. She could do it, she knew she could.

It was exhilarating, all of it. But the benefits would be extraordinary, and it was that she was hoping for. Sometimes she thought the last twenty-four hours had flown so quickly she hadn't had time to comprehend all the implications. It was truly a whirlwind of opportunity, financially and professionally.

Occasionally, when she realized this single screen test could change the entire course of her life, she shuddered. An assignment with Elsethe Industries could open doors she'd only vicariously passed through by way of magazines and the ten-o'clock news. This job could introduce her to people from all walks of life, the wealthy and influential to the hardworking and blue-collar.

Yet it was nothing but dumb luck that brought her to this unexpected crossroads. After all, being a redhead was the luck of the draw. It superseded socioeconomic boundaries, intelligence, and even the sexes. Neither of her parents were redheads. Her hair color was a throwback, skipping two generations entirely. The odds she'd inherit that particular gene must have been fifty to one. She hoped her chances at becoming the Redheads Only girl weren't as slim.

On this particular sunshiny winter day, in the sprawling city of Minneapolis, Kelsy Williams could wholeheartedly admit it was her own good stroke of fortune to be born, barely twenty-seven years ago, as a stride-stopping redhead.

How well she remembered being stopped as a child while admirers patted her head or rolled a curl between their fingers. In grade school she was teased mercilessly; in high school the boys accused her of having a red-hot temper to match her red-hot curls. Ha! If she landed this contract she'd get the ultimate revenge on those classmates and elderly curl tweakers alike.

"Kelsy? Mr. Theis would like to see you." The bespectacled secretary, Hannah, opened the door, her squarely set features betraying little emotion. The woman seemed to epitomize the executive's dream, a secretary who could stand her ground in the face of aggressive sales reps and whining consumers.

Kelsy saw her dreams dashed. Thank you, but no thank you. You see, Kelsy, it was a crazy, wonderfully brilliant idea to take a girl off the streets and mold her into the Redheads Only image, but . . .

In the stoic corner of her mind, the reasons multiplied.

Woodenly, Kelsy followed Hannah, silently speculating whether she wore steel-plated shoulder pads beneath her blue wool dress or copper-toed protection within in her patent leather pumps. When Kelsy stepped inside the office, she forgot the secretary. Kelsy hadn't gotten the job. Gene's too-friendly smile confirmed it.

She eased into a chair without being invited. When she realized Tate was sitting next to her, she felt like a fool, one who'd hung her dreams on a star and was simply waiting to watch them slip away into some dark hole. After today, she'd go back to being Kelsy Williams, the woman who ran a coffee shop and talked about someday opening her own catering business. The woman who'd impulsively had a thousand business cards printed before she'd ever purchased a matching set of stainless-steel serving trays.

In a last vestige of hope, she glanced at Tate. He was painfully restrained. One ankle rested across his knee, on which he impatiently drummed his fingers. Kelsy suspected he was ready to bolt.

She waited breathlessly, suspense stringing her nerves taut like wires. Rather than fidget in the straight-backed chair, she held herself erect, unmoving.

"We just got a look at this morning's test." Gene thumped the erasered end of a pencil on the desk, raising his brows and thoughtfully pursing his lips. "What we saw was, well, it was pretty darned intriguing."

"That's not what you said to me, Theis," Tate cut in. "It was incredible. It blew us both away. Of course," he obviously revised for her benefit, "that doesn't mean we still don't have our reservations. The thought of an opportunity like this going to an amateur is unheard of."

Kelsy should have been thrilled the screen test was a success. But the doubts Tate expressed negated it. Gene ignored them.

"Incredible's the right word, Kelsy. You walked right off that screen and into the role of the Redheads Only girl. I've got no qualms about saying that if you want the job, and if you can fulfill our expectations, it's yours."

After all the anxiety of teetering on the brink of stardom and back again, Kelsy was speechless. A fullness spread throughout her shoulders, making her wonder if she was sprouting wings for the takeoff into a new, unknown destination. Her life would change, she was sure of it. There'd be no more worries about meeting Devon's tuition. This job could give her the seed money for the catering business she envisioned, too. After all, she wasn't foolish enough to believe this thing with Redheads Only would be anything more than short-lived.

"I wouldn't be here if I didn't want the job, Mr. Theis." In the recesses of her tumbling thoughts, she had sense enough to be aware that her response carried conviction. "I'll do my best to live up to your expectations as the Redheads Only model."

"Wash that thinking. You're no model, girl. You're more than that. Why, every nuance of your looks, your personality, even your temperament, will depict the Redheads Only integrity. Because of that, I aim to find out more intimate facts about you this afternoon than your last boyfriend ever dreamed of."

Kelsy flushed at Gene's blunt statement. Her last serious romance had gone up in flames when her boyfriend confided that, even after two years, he felt as if he really didn't know her. Kelsy had countered by saying if he'd taken his nose out of the sports section long enough, he'd have discovered she did have a life before and after coed softball.

"What would you like to know? I've no family skeletons, if that's what you're concerned about."

"Oh, we've got a contract to address family secrets. But it would be better for all of us if we didn't have to deal with that, especially after we plan to invest a small fortune in launching you as the Redheads Only girl."

"As far as I know, my background's flawless. And probably a little boring. My dad was a postal worker and my mom worked in a dress shop for most of her life. I did have a crazy aunt who once climbed a neighbor's tree and took shots at some sparrows with a BB gun."

"No kidding?"

"Well, they'd made a mess on her patio. It took three cops, one warrant, and two hours to get her down. I think it made the local news. But she never did anything like that again. My grandma was horrified. She even quit her bridge club because she was too embarrassed to face them again."

Gene squashed a smile, but his eyes crinkled.

43

Tate coughed; Kelsy saw he was trying to cover his own amusement.

"Are your folks retired?"

"Daddy died when I was fourteen; he had a heart condition. My Mom died three years ago— she was hit by a car that ran a stop sign. She was hospitalized but, well—" the light went out of Kelsy's eyes as she shrugged "—she never really recovered."

"I'm sorry." Gene's dogged attack on her past immediately let up, making Kelsy realize he was not only a hardheaded businessman, but a soft-hearted overgrown teddy bear. "Siblings? Brothers, sisters? Married? Single?"

"Only one. Devon. She's a year older than me, twenty-eight. She's single, and doing graduate work. Together we've been running a coffee shop at a business complex in Mount Hope. We bought it with the insurance settlement. Unfortunately it hasn't been a big money-maker. Do you know how many cups of coffee you've got to sell to turn a profit?" Gene's eyebrows lifted, yet he said nothing. "But it pays the bills, and most of Devon's tuition. See, she quit her job just before Mom died and thought she'd live at home and take courses full-time. She'd worked for the mayor's office and decided she wanted to get into city management. But it took a while to straighten out the estate, and well, we just kind of agreed to combine our efforts to get her through school first and then I'll get the coffee shop. It's kind of like my payoff."

"But you?" No higher education?"

"No. I started out in hotel management after high school, but I took a job with a local restaurant and got into the catering end of it. I liked it so much I left college. I was with them full-time for about six months before they folded."

"No other jobs?"

"I bounced around at a few other things, sales-clerk, receptionist—I even did telephone sales for a while. But there was something about catering. I just liked being in the middle of a family or friends during the happy times in their life. All that euphoria and good cheer seemed to rub off."

Gene smiled a little too indulgently, as if he knew every party couldn't be that much fun, that an occasional wedding gave birth to a miserly father-in-law or a shrewish grandmother, and that birthday parties were as easily rent by whining brats and petty jealousies.

"So," she went on, "when the deal with the coffee shop came up, I jumped at it. It's a congenial sort of job and I like it. But considering the profit margin's so slim, I don't think I'll be opening up a chain in industrial parks. Devon hates it, but she helps out, knowing it pays the tuition."

"Tell me what you did growing up, Kelsy."

She did. She told him everything. About playing on a city softball league, getting the lead in a high school production of *My Fair Lady*, how she'd taken voice lessons for four years, and that her grades, all through school, hovered near a

45

B+. Before her dad died, she said, he surprised his family with a trip to the Wisconsin Dells; before her mother died, she'd taken Kelsy to Lake Okoboji, Iowa.

She gave him her views on God, family, and the state of the world. She even told him how it felt to be teased about having red hair.

Then they put the contract in front of her and briefly explained it. If she signed, the terms were renewable, as well as renegotiable. It wasn't hard to guess that meant more money, more perks. Visions of a sports car danced through her head. She thought about taking winter trips to Florida and buying new furniture for her bedroom.

They'd set the contract up with ironclad clauses, some of which overwhelmed her. Modeling in ads for other hair-care or grooming items was strictly prohibited. Endorsements, without Elsethe Industries approval, on anything from consumer products to social issues, could nullify it. Her attendance at social functions was expected. All invitations to appear, or correspondence on her behalf, would be strictly handled by the company.

Filming in Hawaii, doing still shoots in New York, and frequent promotional tours throughout the country were part of the deal. All the clothes she wore on tour and in commercials became her personal property.

There was a built-in incentive program: the harder she worked, the more she earned. The initial figure they named as a salary astounded her.

46

The idea of setting money aside for Devon's schooling fell apart; Devon could manage the coffee shop, hire someone to run it, and enroll in college full-time.

Life couldn't get much better.

"So take this home and look it over." Gene pushed the contract at her and leaned back in his chair. "It's worded as simply as we can possibly make it. But if you're unsure, talk it over with a lawyer. Now—" he sighed, lacing his fingers together over his plump middle "—you've told me all about yourself, so let me tell you about Elsethe Industries. I founded the company eighteen years ago with a half-baked idea and a lot of gumption. Tate joined me six years later as a chemical engineer, one who added a little more flair to my rather staid approach."

"What he's trying to say," Tate interrupted, "is that he used to refer to me as 'that hippie in the lab coat,' until I made him realize today's woman prefers blow dryers to the old bonnet-style dryers."

Gene grinned. "Okay, so he's more progressive than I am. The Redheads Only shampoo illustrates that. It was his idea and his baby. He's a partner in the company and this project is his—he'll be responsible for it, and for you. But, here's the rub—as president, I get final veto power over the direction of the campaign and over advertising. We work as a team, but we each know our responsibilities."

Kelsy stared at the contract, knowing that

when the last *i* was dotted, she'd sign away her life. Once under contract, she fully expected to live, eat, and breathe the Redheads Only campaign for the next twelve months.

"We'll put an initial ten-thousand-dollar cap on wardrobe," Gene added, his attention on Tate. "Providing Kelsy joins us, we'll leave for California in two weeks. How's that sound to you?"

"It sounds fine," he said, "but not a lot of time. Looks like we should've started on her wardrobe yesterday."

"How soon can you give us a decision, Kelsy?"

"I can let you know tomorrow."

"Fine. I'll pick you up at nine sharp the following day," Tate said, automatically assuming her answer would be yes. Unfolding his legs, the demeanor of taking over his part of the program ruled his no-nonsense behavior. "Wear something comfortable and—" his gaze skimmed over her "—easy to slip in and out of. This will truly be a shop till you drop excursion. If you have any other plans for the day, cancel them."

"I understand." Eager to comply, Kelsy knew she'd close the coffee shop if she had to. "But—" she hesitated "—if you make all the final decisions on wardrobe, what if something doesn't fit, or . . . ?"

"It's my job to see that it does. I expect to see that everything is a perfect fit." Everything. Right down to your underwear, he silently vowed, determining that nothing, not even a shred of silk, would jeopardize this campaign.

His decree had an ominous effect. One that made Kelsy carry the contract out of the office as if she were handling plutonium. The thought struck her that accepting the job could have the same explosive effect.

Once home, she fidgeted, twisting her hair, and anxiously rocking back and forth on the heels of her shoes while Devon studied the contract. But true to form, Devon kept her mouth shut, reading it with a supercilious air. When she was finally ready to talk about it, Kelsy was a wreck.

"In my opinion," Devon said, pulling off her reading glasses and setting them aside, "you'd be an absolute fool not to sign."

Chapter Three

If Kelsy hadn't been so concerned about her clothes and what she was wearing, she would have jerked Devon back from the front window of the home they shared. As it was, she was debating between her loafers, which looked as if they'd been pulled from a Salvation Army dumpster, or her skimmers, which pinched her feet.

"Devon? What do you think?" She held up both pairs.

Barely looking over her shoulder, Devon made a snap decision. "The loafers. If he sees you actually wear those, he might take pity on you and up the clothing allowance."

"Devon!" Kelsy put them on anyway, tossing the skimmers behind the living-room recliner. "So how do I look?" she asked, stretching the pullover down over her jeans.

"You aren't wearing a sweater, are you? You'll be pulling it off and on so many times your hair'll frizz."

Kelsy looked horrified and darted back into the bedroom, emerging a moment later with a green velour top. "What about this?" she asked frantically.

"Forget that. It's hopelessly out of style. Didn't you paint your bedroom in that?"

"So?"

"Relax, Kels. Wear what you've got on. I was just kidding about the frizz."

Kelsy's shoulders slumped and she dumped the top behind the recliner, along with the shoes. "What about my hair? Does it look okay?"

Devon shrugged, bending deeper at the waist to see farther down the street. "It looks just like usual."

"Like usual? It has to look better than usual. That's what they bought — they bought my hair."

Devon snickered. "And they paid scalper's prices, too."

"Not funny."

For Kelsy, there remained only tense silence. Devon finally gave up shouldering back the draperies and lapped them over the back of the couch. Her dark hair was cut into a sleek bob, one that emphasized her clever brown eyes and her intent to succeed as a professional. Her features were always animated, as if she had a perpetual question on the tip of her tongue — and a ready argument for any answer she received.

"What kind of car does he drive?"

"I don't know."

"I'll bet it's expensive. What if he picks you up in a limo?"

"Don't be ridiculous."

"I still can't believe you're going shopping with a man you barely know."

A shudder ran down Kelsy's spine. "I don't have to know him. He's my boss. It's a job."

"What a job, you lucky stiff. New clothes, a huge salary, a trip to California, promotional tours."

"Look at it as a working vacation."

"Right."

"There is one thing . . ."

"What?"

"The best part about it is we can afford to have Cass work the coffee shop this morning. So nice you could stay home and harass me as I trot off for my first day's work."

Devon flashed her a big grin. "You're welcome," she said magnanimously. "But afford it? Why, you haven't even gotten your first paycheck yet." They exchanged glances, the kind sisters save for one another, the kind of understanding that threads through their lives, lacing them together. "And you call it work? Trying on clothes is your strong suit."

"Yeah. But at least now I can buy them."

"And I only want one thing for all this sibling support I'm offering up."

"And that is?"

"Your castoffs. I figure if you're going to be next season's fashion plate, in a few months I won't be looking half-bad in graduate school. After all, they won't want you to be seen that many times in the same outfit."

"That's not supporting. It's self-serving."

"Don't forget I look best in soft colors. Blue would be good."

Kelsy reached for her purse. "Did you want me to take your color chart, too?" she asked dryly.

Devon didn't answer. Instead, she stared out the window. "Is this him? Omigod, he's beautiful — and he's driving a Fiat."

Kelsy joined her at the window, pushing down the drapes, anxiously hoping they'd fall into place before Tate saw the movement of fabric. But she'd paused long enough to glimpse the sports car. It was new, red, and, from the width of the back tires, looked as if it carried a lot of power beneath the hood. Not unlike the driver, she thought.

"Why didn't you tell me he's so good-looking? Or so young?"

"Because . . ."

She wanted to tell her sister that beneath Tate's well-honed exterior, she sensed a brooding quality, one she secretly feared working beside. He was kind, yes. But he was also critical, demandingly so. How would she perform beneath his assessing eye? Would they be friends or adversaries?

"Because he isn't what you expect. Not at all. He's head over heels in love with his product, and I'm only the vehicle to promote it. There's something about him that's kind of forbidding. I don't think I'll ever really get to know him."

Devon shook her head sadly. "I don't know, I'd sure as heck give it a try."

On the way to the mall, Tate amused her with the myriad buttons and dials on the dashboard of his car. Kelsy didn't understand a whit of it, but she was content to hear him talk. He didn't abuse the speed limit — by much. Just enough to keep from getting a ticket, and just enough to keep him in the left-hand lane.

"We'll buy off the rack," he said when they stopped at a red light near the mall. "We want you to look good, expensively so. But in classic good taste, the kind of thing any woman would want to go out and duplicate, and the kind of thing any woman *could* duplicate. And don't forget — ever — that the focus is on your hair." Pulling his gaze from the intersection, he studied her hair, his eyes narrowing.

"You looked like you were giving me a haircut in your mind," Kelsy said, grabbing the armrest as the car sped around the corner and into the parking lot.

"I was," he said, easing into the first available

space. Switching off the engine, he reached out to touch her hair.

It was a fluid motion, one that surprised Kelsy. Hearing the squeak of his leather coat and then feeling his fingers twine through a lock of her hair made her shiver. He tested the weight of it as if it were a length of red silk.

"Thoughts of what we could do with this kept me up half the night," he said huskily. "There are so many ways it would look good."

"Oh? How?"

"In my mind's eye, I see it swept up turban-style at the beach — or wet and streaming down your back. I imagine it flying behind you from the back of a motorcycle. Or spiraling against your neck." Loose over the shoulders of a nightgown, he added to himself. Trickling over the edge of a pillow.

Kelsy paused. She'd expected him to say blunt-cut or layered, bobbed or permed. But he hadn't, and that in itself jolted her. It was as if he'd left something unsaid between them, something she could only speculate about. The thought made her realize they were too close, too aware. The shell of the sports car became a protective capsule, one that shielded them from view, removing their dreams from the mainstream.

For Tate, it was a vision of seeing his dreams realized. Kelsy made a conscious effort to remind herself of that.

"There's endless possibilities, Kelsy."

"But will I always be comfortable about what you choose to do? Or how it makes me feel?"

"If you trust me." His hand dropped away, brushing over her coat sleeve and leaving a warm path in its wake. "And you will. I promise I'll only do what's best for both of us."

He got out of the car and, before she had time to gather her purse and put her sunglasses away, he opened her door. Kelsy stepped out feeling like a princess, the golden highlights from the Redheads Only shampoo her tiara.

Overnight, the air had grown bitingly cold, dipping to near zero and making Kelsy snuggle into her jacket. When the skiff of snow beneath her loafers made her slip, Tate automatically reached for her elbow, claiming it until they were safely inside.

"It's your job to keep me from breaking a leg, huh?"

"It's my job to see that you, our investment, breaks a leg only for the camera and an adoring audience." Unbuttoning his coat, he slid it back on his shoulders, giving his size even more formidable bulk.

Kelsy peered past the hefty width of his shoulders and started walking, her face brightening with hopeful expectancy. "Oh, I saw the cutest outfit in that little shop. We should—"

"Uh-uh."

She stopped as he walked on. "Why not?"

"Because," he explained, glancing back over his shoulder while he slowed for her to catch up, "if I see it on you, I might like it. And we're looking for something classic, natural. Something subtle. Absolutely nothing trendy."

"Who said it was trendy?"

A firm smile pursed his lips and he looked straight ahead. "Call it my intuition and your body language."

"Oh, c'mon," she laughed, half whirling in front of him.

"Nope. I'd liken it to mixing pills and alcohol." He turned her toward him the way a lover would, ignoring the few people milling in the mall. Trailing his gaze over her, the same critical assessment she'd come to expect rested on her hair. "Mixing the two could be deadly."

She felt confused. "I don't know what you mean."

The seconds ticked away as he made no hurry to answer her, his expression emotionless.

"You see, Kelsy, we don't want to take it to the edge," he said softly at last. "Our company wants to be safe, secure, dependable. Nothing with too much flair. Certainly nothing flamboyant. It's an advertising problem. We want something distinctive, but with good taste. Just like the color in your hair, we only want the hint of something special. That uniqueness that sets you apart."

Kelsy stared at him, refusing to accept the

comparison as a compliment. "So, I guess that means you don't trust my judgment in clothes."

"Not at all, lady, not at all. It's just that I'm not taking any chances." Grinning, he guided her into the largest, most expensive department store.

They wandered through the racks for an hour, holding up colors, debating styles, and studying price tags.

"Try this." Tate held up a dress in periwinkle blue.

Kelsy eyed the round neckline. "It's kind of plain."

"That's the idea. We don't want anything detracting from your hair."

The dress fit. So did the russet one. The camel-colored silk-blend blazer was hip-length, coming together with three fashionably mismatched buttons; Tate insisted on the co-ordinated pants and skirt.

After that, she tried on a couple of dozen sweaters and blouses.

Too busy.

Too drab.

Too many ruffles.

Too many buttons.

Her hair, which had begun to go limp, gained body only through static electricity. Wryly, Kelsy thought about Devon's prediction of frizz. When Tate came to meet her with another load of clothes, her hair met him first, reaching out with spontaneous lift.

"Hmmm," he observed, "the way your hair's aching to go into a topknot, I think it's time to try on some evening clothes."

He brought her long dresses and short chiffons. Tea lengths and knee lengths. Strapless and backless, two split up the side, three split up the back.

"I hate this." Kelsy stood before him in the latest gown he'd given her to try, a sour expression puckering her face.

"Nice color."

"For a flower garden."

She rearranged the six petallike blooms of fabric mushrooming over her hips. In lemon yellow and white she felt like a daisy waiting to be plucked.

Tate leaned a shoulder against a pillar, reaching to poke a finger against the stiff fabric jetting out from her waist. "Can you sit down in that thing?"

"If I want to look like the wilted garden variety."

He curiously lifted a petal, tweaking the fabric before peering between the folds to her knees. "Hmmm. She loves me, she loves me not."

"Ha. You want a guessing game?" Kelsy spontaneously challenged. "Try this one. I'll wear it, I'll wear it not."

"You shouldn't be so hasty, Kelsy. It could make a great reception-line dress or something for one of those standing-room-only concerts."

"Great. The only thing I'd look like would be a wallflower."

"Well, I guess we can't have that," he admitted, a slight smile turning his lips. "We are, after all, creating a hybrid."

After that, they turned their attention to coats. The salesclerk was unabashedly pleased, and obviously calculating her commission. Finally, Kelsy slipped into a buff wool. Simple in construction, it hit her mid-calf. Once she glanced into the mirror and into Tate's pleased eyes, she knew. The coat was the cement that held all their other purchases together.

Later, after the coat had been boxed at the cash register, and Tate was studying a lengthy receipt, Kelsy joined him.

"Most men don't like shopping," the clerk commented to Tate while she slipped the last of the sweaters into an oversize bag. "But it's fun if it's with the right woman, isn't it? My husband, he always gets the biggest kick out of me modeling my purchases for him."

Kelsy tried not to be embarrassed and she tried not to laugh; Tate simply signed his name with a flourish.

"Now you be sure and ask for me when you stop in again. I remember my customers and I know what they like. We've got some new jackets coming in next week. They'd be just the thing for a weekend trip, or—"

Tate shook his head. "I don't think so. The lady's practically broken my bank account now."

"But it's worth it, you know." The salesclerk offered Tate a knowing wink, making Kelsy turn away and smooth her hair. Obviously the clerk thought theirs was something other than a working relationship. "Looks like your hair's rebelling over this shopping trip," the woman observed. "Mine does the same thing. If you're ever looking for a good hairdresser, I've got the greatest, and he's located right here in the mall."

The opportunity was too great to pass up and Kelsy darted an amused look at Tate. He remained impassive. "Really?" she said. "I'll have to remember that." Then she impishly confided, "A good man's so hard to find. But the truth is, I've always been a little shy about a man working on my hair—why, sometimes they get the strangest ideas. The last one said it looked like I'd had my hair cut with nail clippers. Now, is that a comment made to win your confidence?"

"Oh, I know what you mean." The woman nodded. "You've got to ease into a relationship like that. If you want his card—"

"Not necessary," Tate said, scooping several packages under his arm before sweeping up the two shopping bags. "I think it's time we ease on out of here."

"What's the matter?" Kelsy asked when they were back in the mall. "Didn't you want to defend yourself in there?"

"I shouldn't have to. Just remember, no matter how you cut it, you're still at my mercy — and Bruce's scissors — for the next year."

"How you cut it?" Kelsy emphasized, stopping to gaze into a shoe-store window. "Your puns are as bad as my sister's."

"Unintentional."

"I doubt it. Your subconscious was probably working overtime." Smiling up at him, she pointed to black satin pumps. "What do you think? Would they go with that black evening gown?"

"Beautifully."

After that, they concentrated on the ordeal of finding shoes. But, with her narrow feet, Kelsy was hard to fit. Eventually their salesclerk, a young college-age kid, looked like he was fighting for his life beneath a barrage of scattered boxes. At one point, Tate, thoroughly exasperated, paced the floor and insisted it was a losing battle.

But Kelsy, worried her uncooperative feet would nullify her contract, forged ahead and found four pairs of shoes and two purses. Later, they loitered over a counter in a jewelry store.

"Gold earrings," Tate decreed, nudging aside her hair with the back of his hand. He wedged a plastic earring holder against her lobe. "You should always wear them."

Double loops of burnished and rubbed gold swayed seductively against her jaw, luring him into the purchase. Kelsy was hooked—until she saw the price.

"Too expensive," she whispered when the clerk had her back turned.

Tate simply smiled. "We'll take these," he said loudly.

"Great. I was just bringing the matching gold chain. Perhaps the lady—"

He started to hold the eighteen-inch chain up, not just for Kelsy's inspection, but to the back of her neck and against her sweater.

"No."

Rocking back, Kelsy looked at Tate in surprise.

"Nothing to detract from her hair."

"But it would look perfect with that cream-colored sweater. And it would work with the suit, too."

"Nothing to draw attention from your hair," he repeated severely, drawing forth his billfold to settle the matter.

The clerk, taken aback by Tate's intensity and unwilling to let one good sale slip away, obediently hung the chain back on the rack, but not without first making a brief, apologetic show of sympathy for Kelsy's crestfallen face.

Tate, tapping the credit card against the glass-topped counter, hesitated. He stared at her hands.

"Do you ever wear rings?"

"I've got an emerald. It's a little small, and it needs to be re-sized, but—"

He turned to the clerk. "What do you have in cocktail rings?"

Kelsy nearly fell over when a glittering tray of gold and diamonds popped up in front of her. Tate drew her back, his arm snugly, possessively, around her waist as if he were making a conscious effort to draw her back into the fun of the occasion. He picked first, a cluster of diamonds nestled in a thick band of gold. Kelsy chose a smaller stone, but it was framed by a dozen eye-catching baguettes. The triangular symmetry of the ring was enticing, unusual yet simple.

Once on her finger, Tate lifted her hand, studying the refracted highlights and the blue-white brilliance. His thumb trailed down to the tips of her fingers to her short, unpolished nails.

She ignored the tremors he was causing, guessing he was judging she was badly in need of a manicure, and probably could use a set of acrylic nails glued to the ends of each of her fingers. When he slowly turned her hand over and traced the line of calluses on her palm, Kelsy felt heat pummel her cheeks.

"It's the ice machine," she explained lamely.

"You have to lift these buckets, and—"

"You're not lifting buckets anymore. Start rubbing these with a pumice stone every night, and I've got some lotion . . ." Absently rubbing the slightly discolored line of flesh, Tate looked up, seemingly surprised the clerk still patiently waited. "Oh, and we'll take the ring, too."

Self-consciously extracting her hand, Kelsy started to work the ring back over her joint. "I think this puts you over budget."

"Not by much." Between two fingers, Tate extended the credit card. "Just bag the box. She'll wear it."

"It's so beautiful." Stunned, Kelsy rolled the ring beneath the lights, watching it sparkle. "I can't really believe this. Is this really mine?"

Tate grinned. "After your contract expires it is. Until then it's part of the package that works for Redheads Only."

When they left the store, Kelsy was particularly aware of the unbalanced weight on the third finger of her right hand. Yet she'd never been so exuberant, so excited. Her heart thrummed with anticipation each time Tate stopped to eye a purchase or lift a garment for her inspection. The best was when he paused, chuckling at the antics of the puppies at the pet store. Vaguely she wondered what kind of a dog a model would have. Something sleek and exotic? Or fluffy and cute?

"This is like Christmas," she finally breathed,

"with Santa driving a tandem trailer instead of an ordinary sleigh."

Tate grinned, picking up on the comparison. "Hmmm. You must've been very good this year. Just don't forget we've got to get all your presents into a sports car."

Without warning, he held up a silk nightgown, the apricot paisley slithering over the sleeve of her jacket, antique lace catching against her collar. "I wonder if they have a matching robe for this?"

Kelsy stared at the plunging neckline. "You don't think I'm modeling this for you?"

A wicked expression stole into his eyes, and when his mouth crimped, she wasn't sure whether he was serious or not. "I told you. Santa Claus needs to make sure everything fits."

"Now wait a minute. That's nothing I'll be wearing in any reception line or promotional tour."

"Probably not. But if you plan to order off the room-service menu, you'd better not show up at the door in a tattered robe and worn-out nightgown."

"Room service?" she squeaked, temporarily dazed. "Why, there's nothing I like better than to be waited on." Lifting the hanger out of his hand and pulling a matching robe off the opposite side of the rack, she headed for the dressing room, adding over her shoulder, "I'll let you know how it fits."

Kelsy had no compunction about making Tate wait in the lingerie department while she twirled in front of the mirror in the dressing room. The nightgown was exquisite, making her feel as if she'd just stepped onto a pedestal reserved for the very wealthy. The cream-colored lace lapped against her throat and the silk rippled over her skin.

She was tired, but happily, agreeably, so.

Again, Tate paid for the purchase, amicably taking her word on the perfect fit. But Kelsy cringed when he stuffed the gown and robe in with all the other packages. Did silk wrinkle?

"After waiting in a place like this," he vehemently declared, heading for the door, "I'm decreeing a moratorium on shopping while we find a restaurant."

"I'll tell you what. After watching you blow the company's money all morning, I figure it's only fair if I show you how to stretch your food dollar. Come on," Kelsy urged, tugging on his leather cuff. "I know just the place."

In five minutes they were seated in a cozy restaurant that featured tiffany lamps and an endless buffet and salad bar. The waitress pushed huge tumblers of iced tea in front of them along with platters. Kelsy made a green salad, reserving one side of her plate for small portions of everything else. Tate loaded up with chicken wings, potato skins, and a horrendous mound of black olives.

Beneath the tiffany lamp, the cocktail ring glittered on her finger. Kelsy studied the changing lights, subtly tilting her finger so the blue fire winked at her. "This is probably the most exciting day of my life," she said softly, not daring to look at Tate. For some reason she feared giving too much of herself away, wary of his reaction to the things she longed to share. Yet she knew they were things that needed to be said. "Whoever starts a job with a dream shopping trip? One that includes gemstones and evening dresses?"

He said nothing, but unfolded his napkin and picked up his fork to poise above the steaming potato skins. He stared at her, and she realized she was twirling a finger through her hair again.

"Don't do that. You'll break the ends of your hair, and make Bruce very unhappy."

"Sorry. It's a habit. I always do it when I'm a little nervous." She hesitated, putting her hands in her lap and expecting a response. Tate gave her none. "I guess what I'm trying to say is that this job means a lot to me, Tate. It means I can pay for Devon's tuition, and it means I can do a lot of the things I've always dreamed about. Travel. Meet new people." Taking a moment to rearrange her tea on her paper place mat, she gazed at the double ring she'd unwittingly created. "I just want you to know I'll do my best for Redheads Only and I'm happy you think I'm qualified to do the job."

Tate laid down his fork; he hadn't taken a single bite. "Kelsy, you should know I expect you to do your best. And if today's shopping spree is any indication of what you're capable of, you may do exceptionally well. Better than any of us could have imagined."

An uneasy prickling began on her neck. She sensed there was a big *but* coming.

"Don't misunderstand me, but I think there's something you should know about me and about how I feel. I like your smile, and I'll be the first to admit you've got an infectious personality. It'll definitely be an asset to the campaign." He paused. "But the truth is, Kelsy, I figure I've got some justifiable concerns about your being the Redheads Only model."

Chapter Four

Kelsy pushed her plate aside, and her fingernail began tracing the scalloped edge of the cheap paper place mat. "And what, exactly, are they?"

"You're a very nice girl, Kelsy. But that doesn't always cut it in this business."

"You don't think I can do this?"

"Hold on. I didn't say that. But you're inexperienced, like a fish out of water. And, let me warn you, there're a lot of sharks out there just waiting to take a great big bite."

"You don't think I can hold my own with the professionals?"

"I think we should've held out for someone who has more qualifications in the media."

"Then why didn't you?"

"Because Gene didn't agree with me—and he's the boss."

"Thanks a heap."

"Look, it's just that everything's going to be so new for you. Everything's going to be that much more difficult the first time round. It's going to add extra stress, and—" He quirked a brow—"honestly?"

"Yes."

"I don't know enough about you to even venture a guess as to how you're going to handle that. The fact is, I'm worried about it."

Kelsy flashed him a wide, very contrived, smile. "Good nature is my middle name."

But he didn't accept that and he didn't back down, his features as grim and set as his prediction. "We fly to California in less than two weeks. Once there, we'll ready a film crew and you'll be paired with the actor we've already chosen—just to see if the chemistry's right. After that, it's on to Hawaii for half a dozen commercials. In between there's grueling photo sessions, public appearances, and public relations work. The Redheads Only campaign will be very stressful."

"So I'll handle it."

He coughed up a laugh, one that made the dimples in his cheeks ripple. "I hope so. But once the money starts rolling in, and everyone's at your beck and call, and there's a rose on your breakfast tray every morning, it gets pretty easy to be a little demanding. Or, I believe the word is—" he paused, stabbing two black olives with his fork "—temperamental." Arching one brow, he wagged the olives at her before popping them into his mouth.

"That's ridiculous," Kelsy muttered, flapping

open her napkin and spreading it neatly over her lap, thinking she'd like to set him straight in precisely the same manner. "You don't know one thing about me. Not one thing."

"Maybe that's part of the problem, Kelsy. I like your exterior. But I really don't want to know what lies beneath."

"Why?"

"Because I don't want to be around when you throw the bud vase on the wall because your eggs are a little runny. I don't want to have to smooth things over when you stomp out of a filming session because the makeup artist got a little heavy-handed with the eye shadow."

"You're putting me on, aren't you?"

He returned her incredulous stare with a straightforward one of his own. "No, I'm not. I've known a couple of models very well. I've picked up the broken pieces of vases. I've made excuses for them to film crews. I simply don't want to have to do that anymore. Maybe it's not fair to compare you—"

"You're right. It's not."

"Kelsy." He sighed. "I have a lot of bad memories, that's all. And a campaign like this, well, it's got a lot riding on it. There's a lot of artistic expression involved. Everyone's got an opinion, and you're the one who's supposed to carry it all off. No matter what happens, you're the one who's visible and you're the one under the gun."

She shook her head, unable to believe what he was saying. Didn't he know what this job meant to her? No matter what kind of emotional stress it put her under, she'd manage. "You do realize you're talking to someone who runs a coffee shop, don't you? I don't plan to get myself all out of joint because my eggs are runny."

"What I realize is that I'm talking to someone who has little or no experience. I'm sorry to say it, but the lead role in *My Fair Lady* nine years ago does not give you experience." Picking up his roll, he stuck both thumbs in the middle, breaking it in half. "Look, it's nothing against you. I just wish we'd held out for someone with a proven track record."

Kelsy picked up her fork and laid it down again, definitely disturbed. But she swore she'd refuse to show it. Carefully composing her face into a serene mask, one the camera would have loved, she put both elbows on the table, steepled her hands over her plate, and calmly met his gaze. "If you're laying the ground rules for the campaign," she said evenly, "I'm willing to listen. But if you're trying to discourage me, you'll have to try again. I'm rather looking forward to a lap tray and a single red rose, and I don't care how hard I have to work to get them."

* * *

Kelsy replayed the jarring scene in her head over and over again on the way home. Certain words jumped out at her, standing the red ends of her hair virtually on end and making her scalp tingle with indignation. Inexperienced, unproven, unqualified—all the words Tate had used to undermine her confidence. Gradually, almost inevitably, she became filled with misgivings. Maybe he was right. Maybe her lack of experience *would* be her undoing.

They maintained a cool, somewhat guarded, conversation on the drive home. Tate fiddled with the cassette player, and concentrated a little too heavily on beating everyone else through the intersections once the lights turned green. She guessed he was just anxious to get her home and out of his hair.

Ha! she soundly, silently berated herself. What a horrific and painfully appropriate pun!

As he pulled up curbside at her north Minneapolis home, she worked the seat belt, glad it automatically rolled back into place—she felt a little too trembly to tussle with it.

"Wait," he said, reaching across her to twist the buckle back into proper alignment above her head. "About this afternoon—"

"You don't need to say another word, Tate. You made your position quite clear." Staring straight ahead at the overgrown privet hedge bordering the lot, she thought of how tangled life had become since her mother died. She refused to look at the small frame home she shared with Devon for fear her sister would be hanging her head out the window. She was quite capable of barging out and over to the car to ask what the hold up was. Kelsy couldn't hide anything from Devon, and the last thing she wanted to do was let Tate see her blubber.

"I made it clear I don't want to put up with temper tantrums and theatrics. But what I didn't say, and what I should've said, is that if you have a problem with something or if something doesn't feel right, I expect you to come to me. I want you to. If you've got an idea . . ."

"Given my inexperience, you'd probably laugh at it."

His lips formed a wry smile, and with his thumbnail he picked at a tiny gouge in the steering wheel, before soundly thumping it with his knuckles. "I probably deserved that."

"Probably."

"Look. I want to think we understand each other over this and that there's no hard feelings." He gave her a sideways glance, one that made her stomach pitch and roll.

"Right."

"And we'll do the best we can to accommodate each other."

It was her turn for a sideways glance, one that did little to conceal the incredulous glimmer in her eyes. She nodded as if her head were wired by remote, her enthusiasm as slow and reluctant as any mechanically programmed response. "Right."

Devon, sitting in a jumble of bags, boxes, and plastic garment bags, oohed and aahed over the ring, tried on the earrings, and squeezed her size-nine foot into the satin dress pumps, making her arch buckle like a warped two-by-four; Kelsy sat there and endured it.

Endured it, for crying out loud—she should have been as enthusiastic and as excited as Devon. More so. Instead she sat there feeling a little numb, looking a little glum, and asking herself, Could she do it? Could she pull it off? Could she convince the world, as well as herself, that she was indeed the Redheads Only girl?

Sure, she'd come home with thousands of dollars of purchases, all intended to add credence to the claim that she was, but suddenly, stricken with the thought she was a fraud, she could barely manage to face her own sister.

"What's the matter?" Devon goaded her, flexing the satin-covered pump beneath her downcast nose. "You're supposed to be enjoying this."

"I am."

"Huh." You look like your balloon has just burst and someone—was it Tate?—took the helium out of you."

76

"I'm just a little tired, that's all," Kelsy lied, refusing to admit, even to Devon, her misgivings and doubts.

"Don't tell me with all this star treatment, you're getting temperamental already?"

Kelsy stiffened, reminded of Tate's words. "Could you give me a break? Please?" Kelsy shoved the silk nightgown back into the bag before Devon asked to try that on, too. "I have all this stuff to put away yet tonight."

"I know, I know," Devon said sympathetically, prying the shoe from her foot and dropping it back in the box. "And you're worried about suffering from bulging-closet syndrome."

"Desperately. No, actually, it's because I'm just beginning to understand how much this job, these clothes, my schedule—and Tate—are going to change my life."

"No kidding. He really turned you inside out today, didn't he? I knew he would."

"Yeah," she said dully, gathering up an armload of packages. "He really turned me inside out."

But disappearing into her uncarpeted cubbyhole of a room, Kelsy silently vowed Devon would never know how far her imaginings were from the truth. Dropping the packages on her unmade bed, she promised herself she'd meet Tate the following morning for the makeup session with a smile on her lips and grim determination in her heart. She'd show him, she declared, pulling out the silky nightgown and rubbing its satiny texture between her fingers. Finally, she draped the shoulder straps across the worn one-eyed teddy bear her daddy had given her so many years ago. Patting Teddy on the tummy, she winked at the spot where his eye should have been.

She'd show Tate Alexander exactly what kind of a mindset lay beneath a hank of red hair!

Turning back to his desk in the swivel leather chair, the one Gene's interior decorator had chosen for him, Tate uncrossed his legs and pulled another folder off the stack. But he didn't look at it. Instead he stared at the three-hundred-dollar framed print he loathed and the decorator insisted on, and wondered what kind of coffee Kelsy served in her coffee shop. He could use a cup right now.

His sigh seemed to echo off the credenza and bounce back to the brass sculpture of his half-naked Boopsie—at least that's what he'd affectionately dubbed this artist's rendering of Lady Luck. Ignoring the fact she always seemed to be lurking over his shoulder, he ran his forefinger down the projected dates for the filming schedule and grimaced. They hadn't even started on the campaign and they were already behind.

But maybe with Lady Luck sitting at his shoulder, they'd turn Kelsy Williams into an advertising miracle—and in record time. Glancing at the day's schedule, he mentally clicked off the sequence of events that would put Kelsy through the paces. He jabbed the intercom button, impatience throbbing in his veins. "Carol?"

"Yes?"

"Let me know as soon as Miss Williams arrives, will you, please."

"She's waiting, sir. She arrived about twenty minutes ago. Shall I send her in?"

Tate's hesitation was brief, but decisive. "No. No, I'll come out to take her down to makeup." He leaned a little too far back in his chair, the angle just precarious enough to remind him that taking Kelsy on this modeling journey was as precarious. He didn't think he could handle a marketing disaster.

Slapping the folder shut, he tossed it on his desk and willed himself to remember Kelsy wasn't there to sabotage his efforts. She was there to help.

She was waiting in the reception area in her own clothes, the pair of designer jeans he'd first seen her in and a peach-colored top. For a moment, he wondered if she'd come in to quit. She stood up when she saw him, pulling the top down over her jeans and rocking a little nervously on the balls of her feet. At least she wasn't twisting her hair.

A stubborn streak made him refuse to acknowledge her presence. Maybe it was because he was as nervous as she was and didn't dare show it. "Carol, the next time Miss Williams arrives early, let me know immediately. We can always put her to work. There's no point having her sit here and twiddle her thumbs. We're far enough behind as it is."

"Yes, sir."

He didn't turn to Kelsy, he wheeled on her. God knows what prompted that. Maybe he was trying to steel himself against the magnetic smile she usually offered. Maybe it was because he realized there was something so appealing about Kelsy Williams he'd need to maintain a keen professional edge if he wanted to work with her. "I see you wore your old clothes."

She straightened, her jaw sliding slightly off center as if she were silently debating whether to offer an excuse. "I didn't know what you wanted me to wear, so I brought some things along instead." She nodded to the garment bag hanging behind him on the coat tree. "I can change if you want."

"No. No, that's fine," Tate answered, ushering her into the hall, torn between feeling guilty over his rudeness and thwarted by her foresight. "I'll take you down to makeup. We're going to do something with that hair first thing."

Briskly walking through the maze of halls and offices, he was conscious of the subtle change in her demeanor. Saying nothing, she was quiet, attentive . . . and almost obedient. Too damn obedient, as if she was tiptoeing around his all-business, no-nonsense approach.

In the salon, Bruce was sweeping up the remnants of someone's trim. Seeing them, he pushed the dark fuzz into a pile, angled the broom over it and propped the handle against a wall. "You're early," he said, twirling the chair for Kelsy to sit. "Know how you want to do this yet?"

"Something classic, a little sophisticated. With as much versatility as possible." It was clear Tate had decided what he wanted.

Bruce stretched taut a lock of her hair. It fell two inches below her shoulder. "Let's start with length . . ."

"Off the shoulders."

"To her ear?"

Kelsy shuddered as a vision of a hothouse tomato, plumped up and ripe, settled above her neck and between her shoulders. Bruce could give her that and a career that went splat. Wasn't that part of the artistic expression Tate had warned her about?

"No, a little longer."

Bruce pulled her hair to the top of her head. "She's got the face for a short cut — it'd bring out her features."

"Don't get creative on me, Bruce. We're trying to bring out the hair, not the face."

"Yes, well, I have a feeling the cut you've got in mind is boring."

81

"So jazz it up. That's your specialty."

Bruce dropped her hair, his fingers scissoring off three inches of length near her jaw. "I hate that word versatile. Every time you use it, it makes me think my scissors should turn into a magic wand." He petulantly rolled his eyes, yet his smile was pleased, as if Tate's compliment had done the trick. "Okay. But I'm barely going to take it off the shoulder. We can always go shorter."

Relief threaded through Kelsy, unbidden thoughts striking her that this job could be annihilated with just one haphazard stroke of the scissors. Could Bruce possibly know how much of a stake she had in this?

Even more disconcerting was the way Tate wedged a hip against the vanity and waited, hawklike, anticipating Bruce's every move. While Bruce shampooed her hair, Kelsy concentrated on the ceiling, noting that it was a pockmarked collection of broken tiles and sagging metal framework. When Bruce dropped another towel over her forehead and paused to pick up a comb, Tate's unnerving features floated into her line of vision.

Standing over her, he allowed his expression to lose some of its critical edge. His eyes, a fragile shade of blue, traveled over her temple and down her chin to her lips, pausing there before meeting her look. Immediately, Kelsy felt vulnerable, as if all her flaws were being exposed to be scrutinized or condemned. She didn't feel beautiful, or graceful, or confident. Wondering what Tate saw when he looked at her, she realized it mattered to her how he perceived her as a woman. It mattered very, very much.

"Ready?" he asked, as Bruce's hand went to the chair latch to raise her up.

For what? she wanted to ask, something inside making her a little trembly and unsteady. Dropping her eyes, she saw that the hem of his suitcoat and the leg of his pants had been freckled with suds from her shampoo. It surprised her he hadn't moved back, yet the possessive gleam flickering in his eye told her why. "I guess," she finally said, her fingers curling around the armrests as if she were preparing herself for takeoff, "but you guys better do this right."

Tate indulged her with a smile; Bruce snorted.

She expected Bruce to take dramatic swipes, but instead he only whittled away at her hair spending a good deal of time and care. When her hair dried before he was finished, he misted it with a spray bottle, never apologizing when the water trickled down her chin.

Snatching up a towel, Tate blotted it away, dragging the terry cloth over her skin before turning the cloth to dab at the moisture on her cheek and below her eye. For someone who guaranteed her a grueling campaign, he was incredibly gentle in seeing to her comfort. Maybe the man did have a heart.

"Thanks," Kelsy said, her brows lifting.

"Don't move," Bruce ordered, silencing them both, his elbows poised to take another minuscule cut.

Tate quirked a lip as Kelsy sat, her gaze fixed, her body frozen as she submitted to Bruce's merciless perfection. She hadn't uttered a word of complaint, but seeing that Bruce had actually finished the cut twenty minutes ago, Tate was beginning to get restless. He shifted to his other hip. "Let's blow it dry and see what we've got," he suggested.

"The bangs aren't right. I'll have to use a curling iron for the stills."

"Fine."

Reluctantly, Bruce picked up the blow dryer and fingered through her hair. He never once used a comb, the pads of his fingers massaging her scalp as if he were raising every wisp of hair to his command. He pulled and tweaked, and rolled and turned, coaxing her hair into brilliance.

But he refused to let Kelsy look in the mirror, turning her to Tate like an offering. "What do you think?"

Tate's features were implacable, his eyes veiled, his mouth firm and hard. His lips were in a straight line, slightly turned down at the corners as if he was torn between approval or criticism. It was then she realized his nose was slightly crooked, as if he'd taken a bad tumble on a ski slope, subtly rearranging it.

"Marvelous."

The single word drew Kelsy from her reverie. Guessing it was a description Tate rarely chose, she strained to get a glimpse of her reflection in the mirror. The haircut wasn't at all what she'd expected. It was casual, windswept. It looked as pleasantly tossed as a snowfall at twilight with winter's first snowflakes still glimmering in the depths, hesitant to melt yet waiting to dazzle.

"That's it. That's the look." Tate raised his hand, reverently touching a wisp at her temple. "That's it. That's the look I've been waiting to see. Damn. This is cover-girl material."

Euphoria welled inside Kelsy, making her feel idolized, cherished, revered. But, sadly, she also realized it was not for herself. Tate's praise was for the image someone else had created.

The sheet was light blue, and as slick and shiny as a length of silk. When he first held it up, Kelsy could only stare at it, refusing to argue and refusing to take it.

"You've got to be kidding," she finally managed. "We bought thousands of dollars of clothes and you want me to wear this? It's a sheet."

"Don't argue. This photographer charges a thousand dollars a day."

Kelsy dubiously plucked up a corner of the drape. "And this is the best he can do?"

"He sees clothes as a distraction."

"Well," she said, just loud enough for Tate to hear as she pulled together the lapels of her robe and reached for material, "it's obvious he and I'd never understand each other." She drew the folded square of fabric over her breast. "Everything goes?"

"Well, no . . ." Tate cleared his throat a little too noisily. "You can leave your panties on."

"Oh, I get it," she quipped, with a sassy wink of her eye and trepidation in her limbs, "just like the doctor's office, huh?"

Seeing the wry twist of his lips, Kelsy flew to her dressing room and threw aside the shower curtain on what was little more than an large closet. Peeling away her robe, she gingerly stepped over the gritty tiled floor, firmly believing the cleaning woman intentionally avoided the makeup room. Kelsy wondered if her hard work this past week had put a chink in Tate's armor. She hoped so.

Everything was set up when she returned. But for one odd moment she wished the drape would simply swallow her up. As it was, she hunched her shoulders and twined her arms in the ends before crossing them over her chest. When she strode before the cameras, she was clutching it like an Egyptian mummy.

"What's this?" the photographer asked, instantly at her side, his fingers working to pry loose the folds of cloth. "We're looking for something soft, not entombed."

Before she knew what was happening, he'd settled her on a stool and discreetly pinned one of her hands and a fold of fabric to her breast. Then he'd thrown wide the drape, letting it trail down her shoulders and ripple down her back. To her amazement, she was more covered than she'd been for the swimsuit shots. He didn't even trifle with her hair, but started snapping pictures, luring out minuscule movement and sensual expression. She didn't have to look into the faces of Gene and Tate to know the pictures would be exquisite. Tate hovered as if transfixed; Gene wore a particularly expansive smile.

She worked another half an hour before Gene left, obviously satisfied. When the door opened at his exit, Kelsy brightened. Devon entered, unobtrusively taking his place against the wall.

The drape was lowered and raised as the photographer worked, his whims bringing her to the edge of wantonness and back again to near prudishness. She had one shoulder exposed and one thigh nearly so, and her heels locked on the stool rungs when she first saw Tate approach Devon. It only took one plaintive reply from Devon for the mood, as well as Kelsy's enthusiasm, to evaporate. Leaning back, the stool tottered as she strained to listen. That was when she lost her balance.

The seat beneath her rocked, making her legs flail within the tails of the sheet, her toes against the rungs. Struggling to right herself, she clutched the drape for modesty's sake. A fleeting vision of herself in a tumble, pooled in blue with only the bedraggled ends of her red hair sticking out, flashed through her head.

"Damn," the photographer swore, grabbing her elbow and settling her back on the seat. "You want to topple over on that thing, is that it?" He threw the sheet across her lap as if he, too, was suddenly interested in protecting her modesty.

"No, I—"

"Now what's going on?" Tate demanded from the back of the room. "We're supposed to be getting this thing wrapped."

"Wrapped? It's pretty difficult to wrap when your model's falling off the stool half-unwrapped," the photographer barked, protectively patting a bit more fabric back over her breast. "If you want to do business, maybe you should take it back to your office and quit disrupting her concentration."

"I'm trying to see to it her concentration isn't disrupted," Tate argued.

"Devon?"

"He's telling me I have to leave." Devon's indignant reply came from outside the circle of lights.

"This is a job, not a spectator event," Tate

imperiously decreed, his voice magnified by the cavernous room.

Kelsy slipped off the stool, her bare thigh making an undignified screech against varnished wood. Striding beyond the glare of lights, she left a baffled photographer and blue drape dragging in her wake. "At a thousand dollars a day, you're wasting a lot of hard-earned money," she said to Tate, one finger poking through the folds of her cover.

"Believe it or not, I'm trying to save it by not cluttering up the place with uninvited guests."

"Uninvited guests? That's where you're wrong. Dead wrong."

Tate stared at the finger that jabbed him between two buttons.

"Tate Alexander, meet my sister, Devon Williams. When I asked if I could give her a tour of Elsethe Industries, Gene suggèsted I invite her to come for part of the shoot this afternoon." Kelsy paused, relishing the fact she'd never actually seen Tate at a loss of words before. Somehow it made her relish the moment even more. "I think," she said calmly, "you've been upstaged."

Extending his hand, Tate said, "So nice to meet you, Miss Williams. Apparently I am the misinformed party. Please make yourself comfortable." But when he turned to Kelsy, brooding dissatisfaction clouded his eyes. "Kelsy, we need to talk." Motioning to the hall door, he looked over his shoulder and advised the photographer they'd take a short break.

Kelsy didn't follow Tate to her dressing room, she led the way. She wasn't exactly sure how she was going to handle the interrogation she expected of Tate; she only knew she was going to be honest about what she thought of the whole thing.

"Kelsy?" Tate closed the door behind them, his shoulder blades leaning into it, his hand still on the jamb. "No matter what Gene says, this can't be a habit."

"It won't be. After all, we're leaving next week." He didn't look convinced. "I just wanted Devon to see what we're doing. She'll be alone while I'm jetting off to California, and I thought that—"

"Elsethe Industries doesn't hold open house. While Gene may want us to be one big happy family, you have to understand we've dumped hundreds of thousands of dollars into this campaign. That's the priority. And it's my responsibility. I don't care whether we're talking about profit margins in the boardroom or your haircut with Bruce. If anything intrudes on this campaign, it's my job to take care of it."

"I know. I'm just concerned about Devon, that's all." Kelsy shrugged, unconsciously winding the corner of the sheet around her fingertip. "With our folks gone, we look out for each other."

They regarded each other, each digesting the other's intents and needs. Tate knew he wasn't working with a regular model, which both irritated and intrigued him. Kelsy knew Redheads Only was Tate's pet project, his culmination of years of work. She envied his ambition, detested his drive. The disquieting thing was that they each, secretly, admired the other. He admired her spontaneity; she admired his focus. It was a nonsensical thing, like a melody that didn't quite play out.

"Considering this is going to be a tough campaign, Kelsy, it might be wise to distinguish between commitment and involvement."

"You can't change the way I feel, Tate."

"Maybe not, but here's the problem . . ." his chin lifted as if he were challenging her loyalties. "I saw you change out there. Your sister walked into the room and the mood that big-bucks photographer worked so hard to create vanished." He snapped his fingers. "Just—like—that."

Kelsy was stunned, her defenses dropping the moment she understood his logic. This was what he'd been talking about days ago. The professionalism he was worried about. If anyone was costing them money, it was her own inexperience. She should have known better. "Tate, I'm sorry, I didn't realize—"

"I never expected you to," he answered, brushing aside her apology as his hand slipped off the doorknob and came to rest on her elbow. "Look, Kelsy, you've done a great job this week. But a few minutes ago I saw this dreamy expression on your face, and then I saw it change and . . ."

He didn't realize he'd increased the pressure on her arm until he felt her muscles twitch. Relaxing his hold, his thumb circled the spot. "This campaign is the biggest thing in my life. You have to understand that no matter what, I curtail any involvement that interferes with my work."

"And you think I should, too?"

"I *know* you should. Whether it's family or friends." His gaze held her fast, his hand reluctantly falling from her elbow.

She guessed they were both conscious of the mounting electricity between them. It surrounded them, pulling them together. But the focus had subtly changed. It was no longer on the campaign, it was on themselves.

"Kelsy?"

"Yes?"

"There's one other thing."

She stayed silent, waiting.

"I'm speaking from experience about keeping your personal and professional life separate." She still said nothing, expecting him to give her an explanation. Sighing, he complied. "I guess you're going to hear about it anyway. There's not a camera crew going that knows when to keep its mouth shut. The thing is, I had a pretty sour experience with a model once, and I refuse to let it happen again."

"That shouldn't have anything to do with me, Tate."

"Maybe not. She certainly wasn't like you. But she wasn't happy unless she was the center of attention and manipulating things to her advantage. I got weary of the little white lies and petty annoyances. We were a twosome for longer than I care to remember. But occasionally, seeing you work in front of the cameras—"

"Don't, Tate. I understand." She didn't, but she said it anyway.

"So that's why, from here on out, everything is strictly on a professional level."

"You call the shots, Tate, that was the original game plan." Kelsy wondered if he heard the quaver in her nonchalant answer. "But you have to know, too, that for me this job is everything. I wouldn't do anything to jeopardize it.

"Good. I'm glad to hear it."

"I wouldn't want you to do anything to jeopardize it either," she went on. "Not even when you're waging war against your own private memories."

He hesitated, refusing to acknowledge she'd touched a nerve. "Just as long as we understand each other, Kelsy. I'll see to it your sister's made to feel welcome for the rest of the day; you see to it the shoot goes as we anticipated."

When he turned the doorknob, indicating she should precede him, Kelsy had the uncanny vision the door swung free in much the same way the lid opened on Pandora's box.

Chapter Five

"So whatcha need?" Gene tucked his tie into the waistband of his pants before collapsing into the broken-down chair behind his desk.

"About half an hour of your time," Tate said.

"Since when have you started asking? Usually you just take it anyway."

"I need to talk to you about the campaign."

"What else?" Gene sank back, hooking his thumbs in his belt. "The last stills with the drape were really something, weren't they?"

"Yeah. Really something."

"I saw a couple of shots that'd make a helluva poster to distribute to salons, beauty shops, that sort of thing. I swear there's one that's absolutely fascinating. It'd generate talk, and I figure word of mouth through the shops over this product wouldn't hurt one bit."

"Gene. About this campaign . . ." Jamming his hand into his pocket, Tate strolled to the window, silently wishing the cool blue water of the small lake four floors below could reach up and soothe his disjointed feelings. "I'm beginning to think maybe we should have someone else manage the business end of it. From here on out we're looking at a high-stakes advertising game. I can fool around in the lab and come up with products, I can even lay the groundwork for a campaign, but I'm having second thoughts about directing this one."

"Gimme a break." With his thumbs still hooking in his belt, Gene propped his elbows on the armrests of his chair. "You know this thing inside and out. You laid out the game plan, we both knew the risks. We've test marketed, we've experimented. Hell, we're ready. You're the one to spearhead this campaign, and you're not backing out on me now."

"There's more involved than I'd originally—"

Gene cackled. It was something he did rarely, only when he was delighted to find the joke on someone else. "Damned right there is. And her name's Kelsy Williams. You always did have a thing for models, but the real drawback is this one's no regular clotheshorse. This one's got a life outside the business, and that's what's making you quake in your boots, isn't it, boy?"

Tate turned from the window, his stance as feisty as a seasoned debater. "You're drawing a pretty simple conclusion, one that isn't even accurate."

"But it's a damned pretty picture, isn't it? Just like that redheaded beauty walked out of your dreams and into your life. Or—" Gene chuckled, pleased with himself "—out of your lab and into your bedroom."

"Oh, Lord. Just because you maintain a fairy-tale marriage, don't go pigeonholing the rest of us into the same blissful state." Tate thumped one fist on Gene's desk before he realized they were nearly nose to nose.

"Marriage? Whoa! You're really ahead of me, boy. I was just speculating about your weakness for models is all. You don't need to go that far."

"Theis . . ." Tate drew back, his expression sagging in the face of Gene's amusement.

"Now the way I see it, there's no possible way to hand over this project to someone else. Why, Redheads Only is your baby, and considering the circumstances, you jolly well better start figuring Kelsy Williams is your baby, too. At least until her contract expires."

The Minneapolis-St. Paul airport was a controlled hubbub of activity. Kelsy was overwhelmed. The sporadic calls of flight numbers made her anxious, instilling a fear she might miss her flight. When a man in a business suit ran past, she wondered if she should follow him. Obviously he knew where he was going and how to get there. All she'd managed to do was to stare, immobilized, at the overhead monitors and the concourse metal detectors.

"Kelsy. Here you are. I thought you might meet us over at the counter." Tate started to pick up one of her bags, then stopped, blanching at the litter of her mismatched suitcases.

"Devon dropped me off, but she had to get back. Cass wasn't able to work late this morning."

"You could've called. I'd have picked you up."

"No, that's okay. I had a lot of stuff, and—" she trailed her hand over the hodge-podge at her feet "—I didn't think it'd all fit in your car."

"We could've called the limo."

Kelsy's eyes nearly popped out of her head.

"No, no," he clarified, "the airport limo." The first suitcase he picked up looked like World War I vintage, the handle held with rusty screws, the stitching over the vinyl trim broken and snagged. He figured one lap around the luggage carousel should just about demolish the priceless antiquity of it. The makeup case Kelsy picked up was a fifties relic. He could've sworn he saw Connie Stevens carry the same thing in an old movie he rented not long ago. He'd have to spring for a new set of luggage, or the wardrobe they'd invested in would be flying the friendly skies from here to Hawaii in pieces.

"Tate?"

"Mmm-hmm?" He picked up the plastic garment bag, throwing it over his arm and wondering if he'd offend her by going out and buying

98

her a set of matched Samsonite.

"I have to tell you something."

"Shoot."

"I've never been in a plane before. I've never—" she lifted her palm into a slow, ridiculously painful ascent "—left the ground."

"There's nothing to it. It's just like sitting in a chair in your living room. Smack in front of a big screen showing last year's movie, with a TV dinner on your lap."

"When I was nine I threw up the whole way to the Wisconsin Dells." She swallowed when he set the suitcase back down.

"Motion sickness?"

She nodded, either nervousness or embarrassment making her look a bit peaked. "The thing is, my sister gave me a going-away present and I don't know if I'm going to need it or not." Dipping into her coat pocket, she extended her hand, stiffly unfurling her fingers to reveal a packet of Dramamine. "Is there a water fountain around here?"

"We'll find one," he assured, snapping up the suitcase and praying the whole mess would hang together until they hit California. "Take one before we leave and don't sit next to Bruce."

Kelsy likened the waiting area at Gate Five to a holding pen, where bored people read magazines or enthusiastic ones stood by the windows and rattled off aeronautical trivia. She tried to look unconcerned, despite her frequent visits to the water fountain to moisten her dry mouth.

"Excuse me," the grandmotherly woman in the waiting-room seat next to her said. "I've been noticing your hair, and I just have to tell you it's beautiful, absolutely beautiful."

"Why, thank you."

"I have a redheaded daughter, you see."

"You do?"

"Oh, yes. But she's a lot older than you, nearly fifty now, so there's a little gray mixing in it."

"Uh, does she do anything special for it?"

"Color it? My, no. Doesn't have time."

"Well, here's something she might have the time for," Kelsy said, drawing her purse on her lap and reaching inside. "Redheads Only shampoo. Here, take a couple of packets for her. I recommend it because I use it. I'm spokesperson for the product, too. I swear it's the best thing that's ever happened for redheads." Tate, sitting on her other side, had stopped writing in the margins of his paperwork to listen.

"Why, isn't that nice. This must be new."

"It is. It was developed especially for redheads. It's been on the shelves in targeted areas across the country. But it'll soon be available everywhere. You should even be able to ask for it at your salon. You'll have to watch for our commercials."

"Well, isn't this wonderful," the woman said,

rising as their flight was called. "Thank you, dear. My, you redheads are so lucky."

"Thank you. We like to think so," she said, smiling.

Both she and Tate got to their feet. Tate pulled the strap of his leather garment bag over his shoulder and laid a hand on her wrist. "That was neatly, and very impressively, done," he whispered.

She shrugged, unable to stall the surge of confidence she felt. "That's what I'm being paid for, isn't it? To solicit customers and brag about a product I believe in."

When he shook his head, obviously mystified by her casual attitude, she decided against telling him Gene had suggested she carry a few samples with her. After all, she reasoned, glowing with self-assurance and stepping with new poise, it wouldn't hurt him to believe she possessed a few talents other than a set of genes that had given her a head of red hair.

In the aircraft Bruce was several rows ahead of them in an aisle seat, and although Tate had some misgivings, he'd chosen a window seat for Kelsy. Anyone on their first flight, he declared, deserved to see mid-America's crazy-quilt beauty from thirty-five thousand feet in the air.

The meal, as Tate had promised, was so-so, but Kelsy hardly noticed, taking in instead the glorious symmetry of the landscape below. After takeoff her fear dissipated almost entirely, and she ignored the pilot's warnings about a storm front moving in over Denver. Nothing, she believed, could blot out the dazzling sunshine or the brilliant panorama below.

But somewhere over Nebraska the intensity of winter sun faded to a dull blue, and at the edge of Colorado it changed to a drab gray. Almost immediately, the swirling effect of moisture-laden clouds danced past her window. Kelsy was mesmerized.

Tate threw his pen into his briefcase and dropped the lid. "We'll have a two-hour wait for our connecting flight. I hope we get out of here before this thing hits."

Bucking the turbulent air and diving as if it had lead in its belly, the plane pitched right, making Tate grab for his coffee cup. Kelsy offered him her napkin. While the pilot apologized for the air turbulence, switched on the seat-belt sign, and confirmed that the runway was clear, Tate checked Kelsy's seat belt and pulled out a paper bag from the pocket in front of her seat.

"I'm fine," she said and meant it, thrusting the bag back in the pocket. "Actually this is kind of fun."

"You amaze me," he said. "Every time I least expect you to be cooperative, you sail right through the problem."

She raised both hands, palms upward. "So what can you do about a snowstorm?"

102

"Hope to heck we get out of it," Tate answered as they started their descent.

They didn't talk on the way down. Kelsy strained to see out the frosted windows, hoping for even the slightest glimpse of Denver. But she saw nothing, and when the airplane kept pitching she clung to the armrests. Tate covered her hand with his own, offering a comforting squeeze each time the wings shuddered and the engines roared.

Kelsy supposed she should have told him she wasn't frightened. But it was really too nice to be shoulder to shoulder with him, his lean fingers patting her polished nails. Occasionally he paused to test the length of each ovaled tip or stroke the delicate joints of her fingers, all the while resting the weight of his palm atop her wrist. Even the erratic motion of the plane didn't dispel the dizzying sensation he aroused with his fingers.

Considering that, she didn't think there was anything wrong in letting him believe he was playing the role of protector. Besides, in the unlikely event the plane should crash, she couldn't imagine any other man on the face of the earth she'd rather be holding hands with.

The descent was rough. Sidling a glance at Tate, Kelsy saw he'd closed his eyes, his head resting against the seat. When the landing gear dropped, his eyes narrowed to drowsy slits, ones that focused on their coupled hands. Because he didn't know she was watching him, it became all the more intriguing. He picked up her hand as if he saw something else and thoughtfully rolled it within his grasp.

She longed to know what ideas flitted through his mind. Was he simply protecting his investment, or was he considering a different manicurist for her? Did he wish her hands belonged to a professional model, or had her efforts these past two weeks satisfied him? There were moments she'd have sworn he was grateful her hand came with calluses across the palm, and there were moments she thought he would have liked her ambition to be self-serving to the point of selfishness. Would he ever understand that she saw the Redheads Only job as a vehicle to establishing her life, that her role in the public eye was, to her, just a temporary fling? No one would take her role in it seriously, certainly not her. She'd simply work as hard as she could, and maybe later, this stint would lead to another opportunity.

Realizing she'd been studying him for some minutes, she dropped her gaze before he caught her watching him.

"You okay?" he asked, smoothing her hand palm side down over the armrest.

"I am now. This first airplane ride has been kind of like experiencing the beauty and the beast."

He chuckled. "You're going to feel the same

way about Redheads Only and your next year as a model."

She guessed his next gesture was pure impulse. He pulled her fingers off the armrest, drawing them to his lips for a kiss. His mouth was firm, yet velvety. Intent, yet pliable.

"For luck," he whispered.

"For luck," she whispered back, a feeling of total calm spreading from her fingers through her shoulders and down into her middle.

Neither of them realized when they skidded over the ground, though the passengers around them breathed a collective sigh of relief. Tate merely released her hand; Kelsy merely tucked it back in her lap. The moment was over. As they taxied to the terminal, he became a businessman again, and she became a spokesperson. They both straightened their clothes and gathered their belongings, each refusing to acknowledge that what had transpired between them was as intimate as an evening alone.

Inside the airport, the mood was harried. At the confirmation desk, they were immediately told their connecting flight had been canceled. With splotches of color mottling his neck, a frustrated Tate looked at Kelsy, obviously expecting her to be equally frustrated. But finding her annoyingly composed, he turned his attention to Bruce. "We've got at least a six-hour wait," he said. "They're predicting this is just a squall."

"Great. I'm going to go hang my elbow on

the nearest bar." Bruce picked up his travel bag and slung it over his shoulder. "Is Redheads Only picking up the bar bill? I figure they owe me a good stiff one for that hellish landing."

"Forget it."

"Never hurts to ask, Tate." Bruce smiled wanly before toddling off in search of the bar.

"And you? What do you figure Redheads Only owes you?" Tate asked, making no effort to hide his grumpiness as he pocketed the new boarding passes inside his suit coat.

"Not a thing. Actually, I figure this snowstorm is a bonus. I might not get to see Denver, but it looks like I'll get to know the airport inside and out."

"Just what we need—for you to have intimate knowledge of the airport. I was hoping we'd get settled in our hotel and you'd get some intimate knowledge of what's going to be involved in the commercials. Even this six-hour delay is pushing back our plans."

"How about—" Kelsy cocked her head at him as if wondering whether he'd take her up on her challenge "—you explaining the commercials to me while we take a walking tour of the airport?"

"I guess, after we ditch these bags. But later I've got to sit down with some paperwork." Stowing their carryons in a nearby locker, they slipped into a small shop to browse.

"We have an agency on the coast that's putting together a film crew for us," Tate explained, skimming through the sports magazines as Kelsy twirled the paperback book racks and listened. "We hope to leave in ten days' time for Hawaii, providing the test shoot you do with the actor we chose a month ago goes as we hope. If we don't see the right kind of chemistry there might be another delay."

"How could you choose an actor before knowing who the actress was going to be?"

"We'd tentatively made a match. But I always had the feeling Gene wasn't quite satisfied with the woman—he kept stalling. Then, just as we were pulling the film crew together, she up and quit, backed right out of the contract."

"Really?" Kelsy picked a Broncos T-shirt off the rack, pretending to study the price tag, but silently calculating how this had affected their decision to hire her, a virtual unknown. "So I was second choice. You must've been desperate to have someone. Why, you'd have taken any redhead, wouldn't you?"

The pages of the magazine Tate held rippled beneath his thumb before he slapped it shut and thunked it back on the shelf. "No. That's the reason organizing the campaign was so difficult. We weren't ready to settle for less than the best. We were ready to postpone introducing Redheads Only for another six months, even longer, until we found what we wanted."

She felt slightly embarrassed for putting him

on the spot. Her fingers were stiff when he took the hanger out of her hands and briefly studied the T-shirt before holding it up beneath her chin. Soft unwashed cotton brushed her jaw, the Broncos logo fell over her breast, the hem snagged on her hips.

"But then," he said softly, "we found you."

"Tate, I wasn't trying to—"

"I know." He peeled the shirt away from her front, seemingly intent on scrutinizing the quality. "You think this is a good price?"

"I suppose. I—"

"Fine. Let's get it. It might look good as a cover-up for the beach. Kind of simple, everyday. Fun. Who knows, maybe we could use it in one of the commercials."

"Tate. You don't need to—"

"I know. But look at it this way, Kelsy. Maybe the shirt's sort of symbolic, too. A peace offering that says we know where we're going, we know where we've been." He bunched up the shirt front, emphasizing the kicking hooves and twisting back of the bucking pony. "We've been through a rough ride, both with our feet on the ground and at thirty-five thousand feet in the air. But somehow we've managed to hang on."

"No matter who's got hold of the reins?"

"No matter." As if to settle it, he tossed the shirt across the counter to pay for it. " 'Cause we're both going for the full ride."

Kelsy derived a crazy thrill when he handed

the bag to her. Sure, she was tickled by the impulsive nature of it all. If she wanted a shirt, shoes, or jewelry, he pulled out his billfold and paid for them. It wasn't that the item was new, that it was cute, or clever, or fun. Certainly that had been part of the appeal in the past. But this time, it was that Tate was doing it for her. Like indulging a whim, one that made the heart smile.

"Does this come under business expense?" she said, thanking him.

"Not this time." He paused, tucking his wallet away before ushering her out onto the mezzanine. "Personal expense. The stuff like toiletries, postcards, stamps, and amusement."

The flashing lights of a pinball machine caught Kelsy's eye, the lure of the dark recesses of a video haunt pulling her to the entrance. "Amusement?"

"Uh-huh."

"Then I owe you one," she said, drawing him by the wrist as if it were the most natural thing in the world. "C'mon. Let me treat you to a game of Elvira's Revenge."

If Tate hung back, Kelsy ignored his uncertainty by plopping the bag by the pinball machine and inserting three quarters. "You first," she offered, as a dozen silver balls rolled into place.

"Me? I don't know anything about pinball."

"You should. This Elvira gal has more than

enough hair for you to work with. Imagine you're taking a couple of shots at that."

He laughed, then assumed a dogged stance in front of the machine. "Anything I need to know?"

"Just that I plan to beat your score by five thousand."

"That shouldn't be difficult. But let me warn you," he said, flipping out the first ball, "that I have very good reflexes."

"Now, that," she smiled, watching the ball sink into the first trap, "is a very good thing for a girl to know. But just remember, Tate, there's a big difference between good and fast."

The second ball disappeared into another trap as he paused to look at her. If she was offering an innuendo, her innocent features didn't admit to it. If she wasn't, it was a helluva thing to speculate about. Maybe that was what knocked off his game. She trounced him soundly.

"You know what the problem is?" he asked.

"What?"

"Elvira's not a redhead."

"Hah. How about I treat you to an ice cream to help you forget your misery?"

The ice-cream shop was next door. Without asking, Kelsy ordered him a double French Vanilla.

"How'd you know what I'd order?" he asked, watching the attendant give him two humongous scoops.

"Vanilla's solid, forthright. Like you. The French is for flair."

He grinned, but a wicked light shot through his eyes as he leaned across the counter to take the cone. "No ice cream for you. From here on out you've got to watch your weight for those cameras."

She just laughed, as if that were the most outrageous thing in the world. "A double French Silk," she instructed the waiting attendant and, sliding a contrary eye to Tate, added, "in a waffle cone with whipped cream and a cherry on top."

Chapter Six

To Kelsy, who had always taken all four seasons both in stride and routine order, flying out of six inches of snow and landing in sunny climes among ocean-whipped palm trees was unbelievable. The first thing she did when reaching her hotel room was walk right past the fruit basket, flowers, and bottle of wine, and throw open the drapes.

She was mesmerized. If this was what a glamorous job was all about, she had no regrets. The fruit basket scented the room, the flowers—a gorgeous blend of daisies, mums, and baby's breath—added color, and the wine, a local vintage, promised a special flavor.

Tate saw to it that the bellboy deposited her battered luggage inside the door, then handed her the room-service menu. He told her to order anything she'd like and get a good night's sleep. They were expected at the studio by six the next morning. But he neglected to tell her they were going to be picked up in a limo—probably because he wanted to see her reaction when the chauffeur ushered her into the luxury car.

When the moment came, she felt like royalty. But that was on the inside; on the outside, her expression was that of an awed commoner. She couldn't resist trailing her hand over the rich velour upholstery.

Bruce was like a kid. He played with the phone, turned on the television, flipped through the channels, helped himself to soft drinks, and then looked bored. Wearing a 'what can I do now?' expression, he stared out the side window while Tate poured her a glass of orange juice.

Kelsy didn't have time to be nervous about meeting her counterpart for the commercials because Tate was too busy pointing out landmarks and outlining the day's game plan. It wasn't until she reached the studio that she heard his name.

Daniel Marston.

It seemed a solid name, one that spoke of frontiersman, banker, and sportscaster. But when she met him, anxiety settled with a kerplunk in the bottom of her stomach.

He didn't look approachable; with his broad shoulders and slim hips, he looked like an inverted triangle, ready to tip over and pin any unsuspecting female with his rugged machismo. His sunstreaked hair was greased back, exposing a forehead she considered too flat and wide. His jaw, when clenched, was as formidable as a junkyard dog's, and its stubble of blond beard was like coarse sandpaper.

"Hello, Kelsy, so nice to meet you." He offered his hand, and his face broke into a smile that softened the planes to inviting angles. His voice was resonanced, as if he had resilience, as if he'd successfully weathered a few storms.

As he pumped her hand, Kelsy watched his muscles flex and felt as overpowered as a dewdrop in a rain barrel. From his astonishing musculature to the tips of his blunt fingers, Daniel Marston overwhelmed her. He was poised, a man who wore his professionalism like a mask, and his clothes, the slim jeans and ribbed knit sweater with the sleeves pushed above his elbows, like a walking clothes hanger. He looked like a man who knew exactly what he was doing.

"So nice to meet you, too, Daniel," she said, sensing immediately that something more than her redundant rejoinder was off between them. Was this what Tate meant by chemistry? What if the shoot they did together was a disaster? Then what?

Kelsy dubiously studied the script she'd been handed, stealing a glance at Marston. He was already scanning his lines, no doubt memorizing the highlights, making mental notes of necessary inflection, expression.

"All right, folks, let's get going here," the director said, herding them together. "I don't need to remind you that time is money. We'll do a rundown starting on the third page and going to the stage directions on page five. A read-through once and then we'll put it on tape. No flubs. Got it?"

Around her everyone started flipping through the scripts. Kelsy did the same, though she was far more conscious of Tate at her elbow and wondered if he, too, was worried about how the scene was going to work. When the director pointed them to the stage, she hesitated, half-expecting Tate to give her last-minute instructions. When he didn't, she flicked at a piece of imaginary lint on her skirt, held her head up, and went to join Daniel as if she did this every day of her life. She'd be darned if anyone was going to know she was quaking inside. Besides, she only had a couple of lines to Daniel's four. Why should she worry?

She still had the sense that something was not quite right between Daniel and her, something not quite genuine between them. The camera was bound to pick it up. That meant either she or Daniel would have to cover it with a superb acting job. Could they?

If they couldn't, the campaign would be postponed indefinitely. Kelsy had only a glimmer of what that could mean to Elsethe Industries, but she knew how it would ultimately affect her. It would change the filming dates, it would change the market response to the product. It would change the perks from her contract, maybe even the salary. It could even be detrimental to her relationship with Tate. She realized it was this last that troubled her most.

She'd have to put her all into the scene. If it meant looking at Daniel Marston with lovesick eyes, she'd bat her lashes. If it meant using a sexy voice, she'd match Lauren Bacall. If it meant kissing him, she'd concoct a smacker that'd reach right down to his toes, curling them back as effectively as Bruce's white-hot curling iron.

It was almost a disappointment the script wasn't particularly imaginative. It didn't have a thing to say about shampoo or hair color or split ends. But there was an aura about the words, as if they were just waiting to be puffed up by some magic voice and sculpted by creative expression.

Rather than wince when Daniel towered over her, Kelsy pretended she was narrowing her gaze to admire his Arnold Schwarzenegger body. If she held herself away, she imagined it was because she was gauging the man-woman response with timidity, cautiousness. Let the camera have a heyday with that, she silently challenged, reading her lines with a mechanical eye but infusing them with emotion dredged from her heart's past.

Before they finished the first read-through, Kelsy realized what a competent actor Marston

116

was. He never tried to upstage her; he let her have the good camera angles. He worked with her inflection, his own response honing it even finer. It was like a tennis game, serving and returning, adding a bit of unexpected bounce or sending a line high into flight only to be knocked down by a quick, insistent rejoinder.

People around them were smiling, amused, and at first Kelsy didn't know why. Vaguely she wondered if the read was so bad it was laughable. Then she looked at Tate and knew it was not. He stared as if seeing something beyond their performance, something far into the future. Others were openly grinning; Tate was solemn as a line judge at Wimbledon. Then, when Marston bumped the tip of her chin with his knuckles, he looked a trifle annoyed.

This was weird, Kelsy thought. During the past few minutes, she hadn't come to feel any differently toward Daniel Marston. Yet something was happening, something was making it easy for her to work with him, easy to appreciate his flexibility, his casual nature. In fact she *liked* working with him. He gave her a sense of stability, a sense of purpose and goal. And when the director whistled low and appreciatively, she positively glowed.

"Pretty damn good, huh, Cobb?" Marston asked the director. "Where'd you find this girl, Tate? I want to work with her every damn day."

"Looks like you're going to get the chance,

Marston. At least for the next few months."
Tate didn't look enthusiastic when he said it,
but Kelsy guessed his reaction was sincere.
"When Gene okays the tape, I figure he's going
to hand you a pen and a contract."

Marston looked down at Kelsy as if together
they'd just moved the mountain. Then he
winked, one blue eye momentarily disappearing
beneath a lazy fold of skin. "This is gonna be
great," he promised.

The first take was even better than the first
read-through. Tate felt his insides react like a
taut coil. The chemistry Kelsy and Marston projected was powerful. He'd never guessed she was
that accomplished an actress. Or, he chided
himself, was she? Really?

Perhaps the camera lens had magnified, dis-
torted, their emotional play—at least that's what
the aching reminder in his gut longed to believe.
Sure, maybe he could dismiss his response as
nerves. He could just say he was anticipating
audience feedback, but even that feeble excuse
left a disquieting ripple in his middle.

The hell of it was he'd never have guessed
Marston was her type. They'd chosen him because of his look. His portfolio showed that he
looked as good wading in from the ocean, kicking up sand from his heels and wedging a surfboard over his shoulder, as he did standing in

the middle of a rumpled bedroom wearing a pair of silk boxer-shorts.

But instead of taking two typecast actors and coaching them, the director was taking them to new heights of exploration — heights Tate wasn't sure he wanted explored. All he wanted was a simple thirty-second commercial, one that captured an audience and sold shampoo.

With one foot propped on a chair seat, he stared at the unfolding scene and fumed. His fingers drummed on the card table in front of him. When Cobb shot him an annoyed look, he jammed, his hand in his pocket, debating whether to tell Cobb to speed things up, thus risking alienating him, or just keep his mouth shut and suffer in silence. But reminded of Gene's fervent ravings about how lucky they were to have Cobb as the director, he opted to keep his mouth shut.

"Why . . . Tate? Is it you?"

A chill feeling danced through him. "Zadora?" He knew before asking, but he wouldn't give her the satisfaction of that.

"What on earth are you doing here? It's so good to see you!" She threw her arms around his shoulders as if she were genuinely glad to see him. Only Tate knew better.

"The Redheads Only campaign. What else?" he asked, pulling back to untangle himself and look at her. She'd changed little, but the look she trailed over him was shot full of memories. Intimate ones.

"So you're still wrapped up in that little project."

"Still."

"I thought by now that . . . well, you know, that you'd have moved on."

"Sorry. My life moves more slowly than yours does."

"Sorry? No need to apologize." She took a deep breath, stretching as if she'd just come from an aerobics class.

"I don't know if Cobb—"

"Oh, he won't mind if I watch. He and I get along famously. Actually, he's the man I came to see."

"Suit yourself."

"Thanks, I think I will. So how's the model working out?"

He shrugged. "She's new. Fresh. I think she can make something happen."

"God, you remember how much I wanted that part? Remember?" She tossed her short shock of red hair and laughed. As she lifted her head to point a finger at him, the bangles on her arm clacked together like the drawer of a jewelry chest dumped on end. Those were her trademark. Always the bracelets.

"You wouldn't have had time. You got so busy working for that new designer."

She grimaced. "Oh, that. Definitely not a

good career move. Not enough exposure. He flopped, I fizzled."

In spite of himself, Tate grinned, remembering what high expectations she'd had. "The same thing could happen to Redheads Only."

Zadora laughed right out loud, ignoring Cobb's "Quiet on the set." She looked at Tate and said, "Yes, well, a lot better to fizzle on national television than on center stage at a fashion show in a shopping mall."

Cobb demanded quiet again, insisting that this take was going to blow Elsethe Industries out of the calm and propel it into megabucks distribution.

Living up to his expectations, both Kelsy and Marston rendered a performance that was solid for Tate, riveting for the onlookers. Kelsy positively glowed when she finished, and Marston playfully looped a towel around her neck, holding it beneath her chin as if she'd come out the victor in a professional boxing match.

"And the winner is . . ." Marston joked, raising her wrist.

"Redheads Only shampoo!" she finished, spontaneously picking up his cue.

When they laughed, Zadora seemed a bit vexed, her waxed brows curling together like a misshapen pretzel. Tate could only guess what it was like for her to meet the competition head on. Modeling was a tough game, a harsh profession for those determined to maintain a foothold.

"That's a wrap, Tate," Cobb said, coming by to whack him on the shoulder. "I promise you it won't get much better than that. They're both spontaneous, impulsive actors. I'm afraid if we do too many takes it's going to get mechanical."

"No problem. Looked good to me."

Cobb chuckled, poking a thumb underneath a belt loop to hitch up his pants. Then he leaned closer in confidence. "Look, kid. I don't know if you realize it or not, but you got a real gold mine here. These two work well together. I swear, you better start bottling cases of that shampoo because they're going to snare you one hell of an audience. I don't know where you found her, but that Kelsy Williams is going to make a name for herself."

Tate grunted, as if reluctant to agree to Cobb's appraisal. "Just don't tell her that, will you?"

"Yeah, I know, you're just afraid she'll start screaming salary, and then you'll be after my hide."

Tate chuckled.

"Come on, Zee," Cobb said to Zadora, tipping his head toward an open doorway. "Let's hit my office and take a look at that project."

"Give me a minute?" she pleaded. "I want to say hello to this Kelsy Williams, Tate's new protege."

Cobb ambled to his office without her.

Kelsy was at Tate's side in seconds. "So what'd you think?"

"When you're working with Daniel," Zadora answered, "define your space in front of him. Otherwise, given his size, he's getting the greater portion of the shot. Girls like us can't have that." Zadora winked good-naturedly, extending her hand for an introduction.

"Thanks for the tip." Kelsy clasped her hand, obviously eager for the camaraderie.

"Zadora Kane. I'm a friend of Tate's who's been in this industry a long time."

"Kelsy Williams."

Though she seemed pleasant enough, Zadora appeared ultra-sophisticated. Kelsy reckoned it was all part of the image. Her makeup was heavy, particularly her eyes, but that meant nothing in this business. She could be coming from a job, or preparing for one. Kelsy had already learned that first impressions meant nothing, in fact were most often deceiving.

"So Tate tells me you're the new Redheads Only girl," Zadora said, adjusting the strap of her shoulder bag before withdrawing a vial of perfume attached to a key ring. Pulling the stopper, she doused both sides of her neck with the scent. "It seems you're one lucky gal. You've stumbled onto quite the opportunity here. Elsethe is known to go all out on its promotions."

"Thanks. I'm excited about it, and I want to do my best for them. It seems there's so much to learn."

Zadora smiled while she stuffed the key ring and vial back in her purse. "Well, you might want to talk with Cobb about getting a voice coach. You know, one who'll help you develop something more distinctive. Every little bit helps."

"I'd never thought of it." Kelsy looked to Tate to see if it was an option she should seriously consider.

He didn't respond.

"Grab your bag," he said instead. "We'll have lunch, and then I'll see you back to the hotel before my afternoon meeting."

Kelsy was safely inside her dressing room before Zadora offered up her opinion to Tate. "Well, this is an interesting twist of events. I'd always imagined you wanted a big name to sell your creation. You're taking quite a chance, aren't you? After all you've put into it?"

"You know Gene. Once he finds what he likes . . ." He shrugged.

"Come on, Tate. This is a high-stakes game. You know what the odds are of the product going belly-up on the market."

He grimaced, barely managing to turn it into an unconcerned grin. "You didn't have to remind me, did you?"

"Somebody should."

He paused, sliding a nearby chair back against the wall. "We think she can handle it. Every time I think I'm second-guessing myself I see her on that screen test. You should've seen it."

"I'd probably have been jealous."

"Probably."

"What if she's a flash in the pan?"

"Don't think so." He shook his head, convinced Kelsy's career could be everything she chose to make it. "She's an attention-getter because of something deeper. Call it wholesome, natural. Call it all-American. Whatever you want to call it, it doesn't matter. It's going to sell."

"Can I call it corny?"

He lifted a sardonic brow. "You would."

"We both know images are made, not in-bred. It's an illusion, all of it."

Some defense mechanism was triggered in Tate's head, one he rarely succumbed to. All the painful memories were resurrected, but he wouldn't give Zadora the pleasure of knowing that. After all, it didn't do any good to look over his shoulder. Hindsight wasn't the issue; foresight was. "Not this time, Zee," he said softly. "Not this time."

Chapter Seven

Kelsy saw little of Tate the following ten days. While he worked grueling hours to get everything set, she spent most of her time playing. She went sight-seeing and shopping, craning her neck at landmarks and gasping at price tags. On two afternoons she and Daniel Marston posed for stills, and on another they experimented with voice-overs. It took one whole afternoon to get her acrylic nails just right.

Through it all Tate seemed distracted, removed. But that wasn't surprising. He was busy—up to his ears making arrangements for the film crew to leave for Hawaii. During the hours Kelsy spent without Tate, she began to realize how much she'd learned about him during their flight from Minneapolis; she also more thoroughly understood his involvement with Elsethe Industries. The long hours he worked without complaint told Kelsy more about his ambition than a thousand-word character sketch.

She knew it would be best for both of them

if she simply concentrated on her performance as spokesperson and maintained a comfortable professional distance from him. That was all he'd ever asked of her. She'd be confusing the issue to give more.

At the airport, Kelsy glanced over her set of matched luggage to the entourage Tate had assembled. The group was formidable in size, mismatched in intellect, and diverse in taste. Yet they meshed together like old friends. Those who were new were welcomed. Those who were acquaintances found passing friendships became the basis of a new foundation—like the pilings in the shifting sands of filming.

The flight accommodations were drastically different from the ones on the flight from Minneapolis. This was an ordinary tourist-laden flight, and their bodies would be sandwiched together, nine to a row, with their knees to their noses, as flight attendants stood in the aisles distributing cold lunches and half-filled tumblers of free drinks. The film crew hung together, jabbing each other, ribbing each other, and watching like undisciplined kids for the excitement to unfold between them.

That was it. Excitement.

Kelsy found it building within her. It burgeoned and bloomed, reminding her she'd never seen the ocean, never drunk a Mai Tai, and never lounged on dazzling white beaches. That same excitement heightened her impatience, making her smile broader, more expansive. Her eyes shone like emeralds — emeralds shot with diamond bright sparkles. She was thrilled when Daniel Marston patted the seat beside him.

"Here, Kelsy, sit next to me."

Happily, she crawled over him and plunked into the spot next to the window. With his long legs, he'd chosen the aisle.

"This'll give us a chance to talk," he said, grinning down at her. "I always like to know my leading lady."

"Maybe you shouldn't get to know her too well. Your disappointment might show on film."

"Ha! I like your self-deprecating humor. Shows a healthy — and interesting — self-regard."

She was a little surprised by his use of big words and even bigger ideas. The propensity seemed at odds with his persona.

Tate had come along just then and, seeing the seating arrangement, suggested Bruce take an inside seat so he could sit across the aisle from Daniel. Bruce didn't look happy, but obligingly moved over, kicking his carryon under the next seat and out of Tate's way.

By the time they were airborne, Tate had struck up a conversation with Marston, leaving Kelsy to stare out the window at the shimmering surface of the Pacific.

"I've never seen so much blue," she breathed at one point, pulling back from the window long enough to pick at her dry sandwich. "Between the sky and the ocean it's nearly blinding."

Tate and Marston exchanged amused glances.

"I can't believe you've never seen the ocean before," Marston said. "What with you being native to Minnesota, though, you can swim, can't you?"

"Like a fish. A rainbow trout to be exact, not a porpoise. I'm not exactly sure how salt water will agree with me."

"I guarantee it's not going to agree with your hair," Tate said, throwing his napkin over his uneaten tray of food.

Marston laughed. "Is he always that protective of that head of hair?"

"Yes. If it wasn't out of vogue, I swear he'd wear it on his belt. Not as a trophy, of course. Just to keep track of it."

Tate didn't argue, but a faint smile did firm his lips, and his eyes slid over her hair as if he'd gratefully accept responsibility for it.

"Tell you what, Kelsy," said Marston. "We get to Hawaii, I'll show you what the ocean's really like. Not with just a quick dip. But a real personalized tour. And soon as we get settled, we'll do some surfing."

"Really?"

"On my honor. Hawaii's great for it." He half-turned to Tate. "You ever surf, Tate?"

Tate reached between his legs to draw out the leather portfolio that was his constant companion these days. "Hardly." He pulled out some paperwork as if he wanted to avoid Marston's invitation.

"Ah, you'll have to take some time out and join us. It's great for stress. I figure it's something Kelsy's really going to pick up on. She's got the moves for it." He shifted back to her. "You are going to let me teach you how to surf, aren't you? As long as you're in Hawaii, you don't want to miss the waves."

"Surfing? You think I could actually learn during the time we're there? Why, that'd be wonderful! Devon would never believe it." Kelsy, casting a look out the window at the white rifts of foam, missed Tate's scowl. "Surfing?" she repeated. "And they call this a job?"

"One of the perks of the job is being near the ocean, Kelsy, not risking your neck experimenting with some silly sport," Tate advised, looking up from a sheet of cost runs at her.

"Hey, Tate, not to worry. Let it be known, I make a solemn promise not to get her hair tangled up in seaweed and make a redheaded mermaid out of your little girl."

"The Redheads Only girl," Tate clarified, returning his gaze pointedly to the sheet of figures beneath his nose.

"Ah, yes, the fair-skinned ˙Redheads Only beauty," Marston echoed, critically picking up her hand and noting flesh so clear, so porcelain, the veins beneath looked like delicate ribbons.

"You are going to burn, baby, burn. We'll have to be sure you get a good rubdown with sunscreen. Stop by my room at the hotel when we arrive. I always carry some."

Hearing that, Tate pitched his pen onto his food tray and stared at it.

They landed in Honolulu and arrived at their Waikiki hotel on schedule. But the filming had been arranged for the following day, on a remote private beach. Kelsy could hardly wait.

The next morning, when they left the towering high-rise hotels behind, she was impressed by the lushness of everything about her. It was nearly a forty-minute drive to the shooting location, but worth every pleasurable minute.

The beach was beyond her imaginings. Stretching endlessly, it reminded Kelsy of a constantly changing line, one that separated rushing blue water from the banded trunks of sheltering palms. In that first moment of arrival, she felt insignificant. Dwarfed by the vastness of sea and sky, her gut reaction telling her that any performance she gave could not possibly match the incredible surroundings Tate had personally chosen.

But a strange thing happened when she was struggling with her confidence. She realized she didn't need to loom as large as the ocean or as bright as the sky; she only needed to meet their beauty with realism. She only needed to provide a vicarious existence for an audience.

Maybe all she was doing was selling shampoo, but from the moment her feet sank into the sand and fine grains oozed between her toes, she knew she had an experience to share, something to offer an audience who, like herself in her life before Redheads Only, would never have the opportunity to vacation in Hawaii or cruise the Caribbean.

Instinctively she knew there was an audience out there who was waiting to trust her, who *wanted* to trust her honesty, her credibility, her endorsement of a product she believed in. They wanted to feel the warmth of a tropical sun on their shoulders. They wanted the same kind of confidence in love and life she was hired to exude for the camera. Purchasing Redheads Only enhanced a woman, the way the backdrop of sand and sea did Kelsy. She'd discovered it; she wanted others to discover it too.

Redheads Only couldn't guarantee a woman that she'd find herself on a beach with a handsome man, but it could make her feel better about herself — whether it was sloshing coffee in front of a cheap tipper or being punctual for a filming session.

Granted, a filming session with Daniel Marston was delightful, and a lot easier than she'd anticipated. She had to admit that, in spite of the strange vibrations between them, she'd grown to like him. He'd never have been her first choice, but she appreciated his sincere effort to make her feel good about the work and at ease with him.

When Tate shot him dark appraising glances, she couldn't understand why. Why, Marston had overextended himself to make sure everything would go right, that they developed a strong rapport. Was she attracted to him? Like the illusion they created for the camera?

Not in the least.

Marston happily trotted off to do the first shots, while Jean, the makeup artist worked on Kelsy. After she'd been patted and dried, plucked and sponged, brushed and outlined, Kelsy felt as if she'd offered up her face for renovations. When Jean finally stood back to admire her handiwork, she declared Kelsy a natural beauty. The irony thoroughly amused them both.

When Bruce soaked her hair until it was dripping, wound a towel about her head, and announced she was ready, Kelsy was floored. "A turban!" she half-shrieked, staring at herself in the mirror. "I'm supposed to be selling my hair and you can't even see it?"

By this time Cobb was at her side, and Gene, who had flown in the night before, was with him. The reflective glass covering Cobb's eyes wasn't able to conceal the crinkled creases at their corners. His pudgy rosebud mouth blossomed into a smile. "Cheer up, Kelsy. This is a take-it-all-off commercial. An audience teaser. You'll see. You're gonna be all the more beautiful for it, darlin'. Give us that sterling performance, Kelsy. We're counting on it."

With their note of encouragement and a tad of pressure, Kelsy readied herself for a last run-through of spoken lines and stage directions. Together, she and Cobb stepped to the filming area.

The props for the filming seemed simple enough. Marston's surfboard, Kelsy's towel, and a red convertible. Kelsy realized the convertible had garnered as much attention as her hair. It had been washed, dried, dusted, and polished. Beneath the midday sun, it gleamed.

Dropping the cover-up they'd given her to wear, Kelsy wasn't sure who, but someone, probably an extra, picked it up before it hit the ground. She adjusted the spaghetti straps of her swimsuit and pulled at the elastic about her thighs.

Tate had had the suit made for her. It was cream and copper, the long shots of swirling color jetting about her torso like the metallic paint from an artist's brush. It made her look especially slim, her belly flat as an aerobic instructor's, her legs long and shapely. She preferred not to think about the cleft between her breasts and how the neckline dipped just low enough to tease the imagination.

Before stepping into the convertible, Kelsy scanned the sidelines looking for Tate. They'd both been busy, and she'd seen him only briefly this morning, and then from a distance. Now she felt as if she needed his nod of encouragement. He'd brought her this far, and she wanted to share the moment with him, see if he, too, was ready to take it to the next step—a strip of celluloid that would bring national exposure.

When she shaded her eyes he came into focus. As usual, he was standing behind the cameras, looking as if the sunshine was made to burnish highlights into his hair, the breeze to whip the wildly colorful Hawaiian shirt against his body. He looked like an enigma at that moment, one she'd like to duplicate, one she was glad she could not.

As Marston walked past the hood of the car, he rapped it with his knuckles and said, "This is it, baby. Give me your best."

Kelsy grinned and sank into the supple, sticky-warm leather seats. She didn't know why, she wouldn't need it, but maybe nervousness made her adjust the rearview as Cobb leaned over the door frame.

"Okay, Kelsy. You know the punch line. When you hit it, I want you to take that towel down slow and provocative-like. Just peel it away and let it fall." He paused, pulling his sunglasses down to the tip of his nose so he could look her squarely in the eye. "Let it fall like the drape over a million-dollar sculpture. And then run your fingers through your hair as if you're offering Marston more than just a come-on glance. Why, you're offering him mental telepathy, you're offering him an opportunity. And let me tell you, don't you know it . . ."

Cobb laughed as if the illusion were too good to be true, then he poked his glasses back into place with his middle finger and pushed himself away from the car. "We both know he'd be a damned fool to turn that down. If nothing else, we want that audience rooting for you, we want them incensed, intrigued. We want them curious enough to be asking what gives between the two of you at the end of this thirty-second commercial and, by God, we want them wanting more."

She turned the key in the ignition, and the car hummed to life beneath her, the engine vibrating an assurance that from here on out things were going to be better, that if she worked hard she could set enough aside to change her life, to have all she ever dreamed of.

She wasn't aware of it, but the camera started rolling the moment Cobb stepped away. Putting the car in drive, she lifted her chin and pushed her shoulder blades against the bucket seat as she nudged the gas pedal. The car barely moved, just a slow roll.

When she slammed on the brake, her timing was instinctive. The car lurched, sending her forward and making the turban wobble uncertainly on her head. Before her, near the left front fender, Daniel Marston had stopped short, his legs apart, and the flat gray shade of asphalt showing within the inverted vee. He wore neon green swim trunks, and against the blue expanse of water, he was built like a powerhouse. His chest was puffed to twice its normal size, the surfboard on his shoulder a mere trinket. Like a special effect, the breeze ruffled his hair just as he offered a lazy, calculating smile.

"So?" he asked, "how's the water?"

Kelsy wasn't even aware another camera was on her; she just played out the scene. She lifted a brow, her forehead wrinkling against the terry cloth to return the once-over he'd given her. Her expression changed, from perceptive to demure, the tip of her tongue barely skimming her lips.

"Wet," she said, forcing unspoken innuendo to flicker through her eyes. "Very, very wet. Shamefully, shamefully wet." Spreading her fingers, she swept the towel from her head. As she threaded her fingers through her hair, she knew her hands had never looked better, knowing they were the uncallused hands a lover wanted to feel on his back in the middle of a long, intimate night.

Sensuously, she finger-combed her hair and stared at Daniel Marston. Water droplets scattered, randomly quivering on her shoulders like quicksilver, the red of her hair tumbling to a deep, dripping shade of russet that stuck to untanned, ivory flesh. Her eyes locked with Daniel's and a slow, appreciative smile turned her lips, giving her the appearance of a saint who was wrestling with the appeal of some particularly disturbing — and very mortal — thoughts.

The surfboard slipped to the asphalt as Kelsy let the car inch nearer Marston.

"Hey — " he leaned closer, as if he needed to stop her, as if he were afraid she'd drive away " — you come here often?"

Kelsy propped one elbow over the door and another against the steering wheel to look up at him, raking her fingers through her hair one last time. "Every chance I get."

"Then I'll see you again?"

Her response was automatic, but she thought of Tate when she did it. She twisted a length of red hair through her fingers, twining it like a strawberry licorice whip. She drew it across her cheek, touching it against her lips, the feathered end barely touching the tip of her tongue. Her voice took on a sultry quality, holding the provocative note Cobb had asked for. "Of course. After all," she said, letting her hair unwind and drop back to her shoulder, "no one misses a redhead."

Euphoria was an emotion Kelsy was beginning to accept as part of the modeling business. Whenever she finished a project, adrenaline flooded her system, making her feel invincible, making her feel as successful as someone who repeatedly topped the list of multimillion-dollar investors. Every scene was fun, every accomplishment a thrill.

They'd worked the entire day, reshooting the scene and perfecting camera angles. Between takes, Kelsy was carefully secluded in a cabana Tate had set up especially for her. He'd stopped by late in the afternoon.

"You aren't burning, are you?"

She dropped the magazine she was reading over the arm of the chaise. Watching his eyes trail over her arms and legs, she felt a wave as big as any in the Pacific wash through her middle. "Nope. My body's had such a workout with sunscreen today, I figure it's been permanently embalmed to resist such things as the elements and aging."

His lips squashed a smile. "I hope not. I hear older is better."

Kelsy grinned, hoping to lure his smile out into the open and squarely onto his face. "I know, I know. You just want a model you can take into her forties."

"Not a half-bad idea for you." He dropped to the end of the chaise, not nudging aside her feet but putting his hand around one and running his thumb down the sensitive inner sole. "But sometimes I just want a model I can stand." Before she could take him seriously, he flicked at a skiff of sand clinging to her arch and tweaked her big toe. "Sorry. A bad habit I have. One you're going to make me control."

"Thanks," she said dryly, laying her head back. "I'm glad you think I can do it."

He smiled, apparently unaware he was stroking her foot. But Kelsy was wildly aware of it. Forcing herself not to move, she refused to acknowledge the sensual strugglings and suggestions her body suffered.

"This commercial's a wrap. We've got some close-ups we want to do tomorrow, but otherwise Cobb's satisfied. I am, too. Of course, Gene's ecstatic. No one expected it to be so easy. Everyone's ready to party tonight—they all want to celebrate."

"Celebrate? Tonight? Isn't that a little premature? We've got a long road ahead of us." She thought of Tate's projections for the campaign. There would be five more commercials all sequentially designed to follow the subtle romance of Kelsy and Marston. They were plotted like a time-release capsule, one that would pique viewers' interest and eventually make Redheads Only a household name.

"Yeah. But we're going to push for immediate release. Elsethe Industries has enough other products that we prepurchased all our commercial air time, figuring we could slot in the Redheads commercials as they became available. The music and the information segment and the still shots are ready. It's just a matter of splicing and—"

"Dicing?" She wiggled her toes, not knowing where in the world that had come from. Tate stared at her red-painted toenails as if he were baffled as to why her feet were still in his hands.

"Right." Standing up, he awkwardly patted her ankle, a gesture quite foreign to Tate Alexander's self-assured, take-charge manner. Then he shifted from one foot to the other and finally just kicked at a bit of sand before backing out of the cabana. "Well . . . thanks for the great job today. I just wanted to stop by and tell you that. The reservations are for seven at the hotel. I suppose I'll see you there."

Chapter Eight

The hotel had set up a table for a dozen. Nearly everyone was there when Kelsy arrived, and all were sprawled in the bamboo chairs, nursing drinks and showing off their latest Hawaiian prints. Jean, the makeup artist was twirling between her fingers the little paper umbrella she'd gotten in her drink; Bruce was picking his teeth with his.

Cobb and Marston were in deep conversation at the far end of the table with Gene, making Kelsy suspect they were already blocking the next commercial. Just then, Tate came in and sat down next to Cobb. Kelsy wondered where she would sit. There was a vacant chair next to Bruce and another, inviting one next to Tate. She hated to think of enduring an evening next to Bruce while he flopped in his chair, insulting people with his scathing insights.

Surprisingly, it was Bruce who settled the matter. "Take the chair next to Tate, Kelsy," he suggested. "Tommy just spilled a Mai Tai all over this one. Right now, he's holding his crotch under the hand dryer in the men's room."

Kelsy needed no more urging and sat down beside Tate. Though he hadn't heard what Bruce had said, Tate smiled at her as if he'd expected her to join him all along. "Hello. I ordered you a drink."

"You did?"

"Mmm-hmm. I wanted to be the first person to buy you a drink on your first working vacation."

"So, this is a night of firsts."

"I guess so."

The speculation made Kelsy quiver. But then, just being next to Tate made her do that. He always had this magnetic charm that made her want to absorb it, then linger in the aftereffects. "An exotic drink shared on a remote, but very—" she cast a glance over the crowd of people surrounding them "—inhabited island."

"And a Blue Hawaiian for the lady," a sarong-clad waitress said over her shoulder, placing a tall frosted glass on the coaster before her.

Kelsy stared at the frothy blue drink. It was filled with crushed ice, a pineapple wedge and red cherry balanced against the rim, skewered with a plastic sword. "Thank you."

The black-haired beauty grinned, her dark almond eyes winking as she dropped the subservient role. "Watch out, honey. He said to keep 'em coming."

Kelsy laughed; Tate immediately defended himself.

"For no other purpose than to keep my leading lady happy."

While they ate, the crew exchanged banter and Kelsy found herself the center of some good-natured teasing.

"Yeah, did you see that look she gave Marston?" the cameraman asked.

"Did I see it?" the sound man countered. "I thought the lens was gonna steam right over or bust right out. And you should've heard that breathy quality on the headphones—I swear the viewers ain't going to know whether it's the heat or the waves, or a red-hot mama ready for action."

Kelsy had spent enough time behind a counter to know how to take the teasing in stride and meet it with retorts of her own. They loved it, and she unwittingly won their approval. Unfortunately, as they joked, she was unaware of how often a Blue Hawaiian, sweet and smooth and deceivingly harmless, was placed beside her elbow.

"I'd better call it a night," she finally said, pushing back from the table and rising, a little unsteadily, to her feet. Tate grabbed her elbow when she leaned down to grab the shoulder strap of her purse and nearly fell. "Mmm, I'm going to need some rest," she said woozily, still bent over and clinging to his chair back as she momentarily wedged a hand over her eyes.

"Let me walk you back," he offered, swooping down for her purse. Still claiming her elbow, he ignored the catcalls and raucous laughter.

"Hey, Alexander, what's this? The opportunity run?"

"Don'tcha like his line—'The drinks are on me'?"

"Yeah, his timing's as great as Marston's."

"I bet if you asked him, he'd say he was only looking out for his investment."

"Wouldn't you?"

"Damned right."

"Look, you guys," Tate told the snickering crew as he ushered Kelsy toward the door, "I'm just walking the lady to her room."

"Yeah," Kelsy agreed, holding her head high and unaware she was slurring her words, "and I'm just sober enough to let him do it."

Around them, the table collapsed with laughter. But Tate and Kelsy didn't look back. They concentrated on linking arms and threading their way through the lobby. When an elderly blue-haired woman toddled toward them, her ample girth swaying inside a hot-pink muumuu, Kelsy watched her hands flutter over the lei riding atop her jiggling bosom.

"I wonder what it would be like to come here as a tourist?" she said dreamily after the woman passed. Vaguely, she realized her shoulder was leaning against Tate's. But she didn't really think about it until she looked up at him and saw the puzzled expression in his eyes. Then she straightened, unlocking her arm from his to swipe at her cotton-knit top and pull the rumpled hem over her slacks. "But it doesn't matter. I suppose all flowers wilt the same way, whether you're a tourist or a working girl."

Tate hesitated, then steered her away from the elevators. "I think, instead of rest, you need a breath of fresh air." He led her to the wide doors opening onto the beach. "How about a walk?"

She sighed and nodded, closing her eyes and concentrating on the sound of the surf thrumming in her ears, storing it as a memory to take it home with her. She wished she could share it with Devon. She'd like to remember it in the middle of a Minneapolis winter when she was shoveling snow from the sidewalk or shivering in her winter coat. Maybe she'd make enough money from Redheads Only to come back to Hawaii every year. Wouldn't that be a kick?

"The trouble with coming to Hawaii to work," Tate commented idly, "is that you miss some of the best things Hawaii has to offer."

"Such as?" Her eyes barely flickered open before closing again.

"An escorted sight-seeing tour."

"You've told me all I need to know."

"A luau, where you get a roast-pig dinner."

She chuckled, her eyes still closed, imagining. "You'd tell me it was fattening."

"A lei."

"A what?" Kelsy's eyes popped open, and she steadied herself on his arm.

Tate withheld the trace of amusement he must have felt, deftly moving Kelsy to the counter next

146

to them. "That one," he said to the clerk, pulling out his billfold.

The aging clerk smiled knowingly, and darted a curious look at Kelsy. Then he reached into the glass case to hand Tate his choice. Lifting the weighty length of flowers, Tate looped them gently over her head.

"Aloha, Kelsy. Welcome to Hawaii." Crooking a finger, he withdrew a strand of her hair, gently twirling it about his forefinger and leaving her nearly breathless. "I get to do what you did today on camera, huh?"

Embarrassed, she drew the lei to her nose, letting the heavy scent of orchids anesthetize her senses and cover the flush that was creeping over her cheeks.

"Do I have to keep reminding you you're going to break the ends of your hair doing that? It's not very professional, either."

She lifted one shoulder, still cradling the lei in her hands. "I know. But it looked so convincing, didn't it?" she wheedled. "Just like the real me."

"Mmm-hmm . . ." Loosening his finger, he slowly drew away, allowing the ringlet to trail over the flowers. As if it were an afterthought, he pushed the string of flowers closer to her neck, making their velvety petals tickle her chin. "How about if we play tourist for the next few minutes? Ready for a walk on the beach?"

"But—" she lifted the flowers, debating "—it's windy out. It'll damage my lei, and it won't last as long."

"It won't last long, anyway, you know. Whether you're a tourist or not. Either way, the whole thing's only temporary."

She traced an orchid petal, savoring the texture as the nighttime breeze swooped inside the open doorway to warm and unleash the scent of the flowers. It's only temporary, he said. Maybe she read more into the phrase than she should have. But it nagged at her, and she didn't want to turn away from the opportunity he offered. She knew better than to fantasize about Tate Alexander, but saw nothing wrong in taking advantage of an opportunity.

"So I'm going to enjoy it while I can," she said gently, as though she were settling an argument in her head. "Thank you. But you didn't need to do this. You don't need to be so good to me. I don't think it's considered part of your job."

"Tonight it is." With his hand on her back, he ushered her through the door, guiding her to the expanse of sand. The moon was like a golden coin suspended high in the heavens, and Tate's fine features were gently carved in its light. He smiled down at her, reaching for her elbow. "Take your shoes off. Tonight is a night for carrying them in your hand."

"Does that mean I can get my tootsies wet?"

"Absolutely."

"Funny, isn't it? Here I spent the whole day at the ocean and never even went in. Everybody was either worried about my hair, or my swimsuit, or the fact I might burn."

"Prudently worried." Tate carelessly kicked off his loafers. They slapped the sand, making Kelsy wonder if they'd ever find them again. But it didn't seem to matter—to either of them.

Bending to slip the skimmers from her feet, she was conscious of the way the wind whipped Tate's pants against his legs, outlining them enticingly. When she straightened, he led her across the sand to the edge of the bubbling surf. The water was as warm as the first splash of bathwater, nibbling at her toes and luring away the sand surrounding them. When her feet started to sink, she hitched up her pants.

"Wonderful," she breathed, anchoring herself against his arm and tipping her head back to savor the wild pull of the wind in her hair. Laughing, he looped his arm around her, making the sensations more heady, more impulsively intimate. She wanted to swing as she had when she was a child, swinging against another eager body as she had when she'd played motorboat, or red rover. Need spiraled within her just as surely as the sea spiraled at her feet, carrying away all logic and worry and reservations. With the changing tide her emotions were shaved away, honed into an honest, innocent response. Childlike, she swayed, her body in motion with his. "I love this. It's unbelievable. It carries all your troubles away."

"What's really wonderful is when you can be all in it. To have the ocean pull at your legs and tug at your arms. It's like it's begging you to swim, begging you to come and play."

"Why, Tate Alexander," she said softly, turning within the circle of his arms and spontaneously pushing back an errant wisp of his perfect hair, "you're a poet. And you think the same things I do. I'd never have thought it."

"I imagine there're many things you'd never have thought," he huskily admitted, pulling her so close she forgot the hems of her pants had fallen and were dragging in the surf. She felt the gentle tug, but was aware only of how close they were, so close she was unable to discern whether it was the ocean breeze or his breath caressing her cheek. Her breasts pressed against his chest and she felt the slight, uncomfortable crush of fresh flowers. The skimmers in her hand bumped beneath his arm and against his thigh. His belt buckle poked her middle.

They were wonderful sensations. Excruciatingly sweet, all of them.

His lips whisked lower, closer, and she met him full on, aware she wanted this moment more than she wanted a day at the beach. More than she wanted a couple of those incentives in her contract.

"Another good reason for you not to get burned," he whispered, his hands massaging her back before settling on the scant bit of flesh above her hips. His touch nagged at her, coaxing her with pleasure. "We couldn't be nearly this close if you had."

"Ahh. So the cabana was to keep me in good working order?"

"Absolutely."

"That's one thing about you—you're all business. You don't even know you're having fun when you're having it."

"Oh?"

"Oh," she answered, as if that settled it.

"I wouldn't make such a hasty claim—I'm having fun now." He continued to stroke her, roaming her spine and jetting back down to the hollows above her buttocks. Eventually he worked his way back up, tarrying here and there, before settling at her neck and gently working the tension from her shoulders.

Studying her briefly, he made it seem as if he was calculating the moment before his lips claimed hers. Then he explored her mouth and body as slowly and carefully as if he'd discovered her drifting toward him in the tide . . . with her hair to her waist, and wearing little more than a skimpy swimsuit.

But she believed the vision because his nuzzling kiss sent her into a dizzying world of discovery. She thrilled to the stubble of his beard against the corner of her mouth, ached when his tongue intruded behind the privacy of her lips. When he probed deeper, she wondered if he tasted the pineapple reminder of too many Blue Hawaiians.

A hundred thoughts catapulted through her mind as his lips wandered from her mouth and found the sensitive spot beneath her earlobe. She

151

thought of the first time she met him, his cool demeanor, his impeccable clothes. She thought of the time he'd lingered over her hand in the jewelry shop, tracing her calluses with his finger, wishing them away and soothing her anxiety with straightforward instructions. Best, she thought of him enjoying an ice-cream cone in the Denver airport and neglecting his paperwork. The memories were all Tate, and all equally endearing.

But the moment was shattered by the gleeful shouts of a handful of young people who ran, splashing past them, sending drops of saltwater airborne to spatter their clothes. Tate stepped back, holding her at arm's length, seemingly appalled at what he'd been doing. His touch was stiff, brittle.

"Kelsy, I—" he shook his head, seeming to mentally berate himself "—didn't mean to so overdo this romantic tourist thing. it's not that way. I'm sorry, I shouldn't have—"

"No." She straightened, her hand splaying across his chest. "Don't."

In the moon's half-light, he looked as bewildered as she felt. He'd shaken her emotions, toppling them like a mischievous monkey might shake a coconut loose from a palm tree. But he'd never know how much he'd shaken her resolve; she'd refuse to show him that. She'd be level-headed and cool. The only thing she'd ever acknowledge was how much the Redheads Only job meant to her. Because before this was all over and done, he'd learn she was capable, self-sufficient, and determined. She'd show him, she vowed. She'd show him. After all, no one ever kissed her like that and drew back to apologize.

Maybe that was the real underlying problem, she chided herself. No one had ever kissed her like that.

Deliberately she touched his jaw, her forefinger riding the length of it as the tip of her pinky stole across his lips. She doubted he could feel her trembling inside, but if he could he'd never know whether it was anger or thwarted passion.

"Just don't apologize," she explained, pulling gently back from his embrace. "Just leave the moment as it is — a beautiful night, with two people on the eve of a fairy-tale dream. Your product's going to make you successful; this job's going to do the same for me. Don't apologize by saying we shouldn't confuse the two. You don't have to. We both know the difference."

He didn't argue with her, but his hands fell away from her waist, leaving a cold spot where recently there had been warmth. They walked silently for a few minutes. But it seemed pointless; both were ready to head back to their solitary rooms, to their solitary thoughts.

At her door, the moment was awkward. Kelsy deemed it unnecessary to linger, her fingers straying to the fragile lei about her neck as they hesitated.

"Kelsy . . . about the beach . . ."

She drew a deep breath, impatiently wondering what else he could say. Nothing could change it.

Nothing could erase the myriad emotions she'd experienced.

"I do understand what you meant out there," Tate said. "I guess I'm glad—no, maybe relieved—that you aren't taking that moment too seriously. After all, it could hamper the rest of the filming. Neither of us wants that."

She said nothing. But her eyes were glassy and her expression remained fixed.

"I guess the crew sort of gave me a few ideas of their expectations. And you're right," he went on, oblivious to the disappointment she was fighting, "it'd be better for both of us if I didn't try to live up to them."

The next time Kelsy saw Marston he wasn't using his surfboard for a prop in a camera shot; he was riding in a wave like some jovial sea god mounted on a dolphin. Given his size and strength, he made the whole thing look effortless. While the camera crew set up for the shoot, Kelsy cheered him on. When he slid onto the sand only feet from her, she wheedled, "And when do I get that surfboarding lesson you promised me?"

He shook his head like a dog, flinging water over her cover-up before giving her a reckless grin. "You ready?"

"Of course."

"What's Tate going to say? He probably won't want your hair messed up for the next shot. He'll give me some kind of guff about responsible behavior."

Having Tate's name come up was like probing a sore spot. If nothing else, it prompted her to insist. She rolled her eyes, dryly adding, "Like it matters. The last time they didn't even do my hair. Come on. Besides, Cobb says we're not filming till after lunch."

"You know you're strong-arming me, Kelsy." He winked at her. "Promise not to get a sunburn? Tate'd really have my hide over that one."

She extended her arms as if inviting his inspection. Suntan lotion smeared the length of her, leaving a telltale trail of white goo. "I'm slathered in waterproof sunscreen."

"Sold." Marston grinned as if he'd been duped, and stepped on the end of his surfboard, catching the other end as it rocked up to his waiting hand. "Come on, darlin', we'll make 'em all wish they were playing in the water today."

It was a beautiful day to do just that. The temperature was perfect, a balmy eighty degrees. Marston took her fifty feet from shore, explaining all the details she didn't really understand about tides and currents. Then he helped her up on the surfboard, letting her get her sea legs. Of course, she failed miserably. But in time she got the knack of it, and simply splashing in the water, as she tumbled from the back of the surfboard, was glorious.

Later they wandered nearer to shore and a water fight ensued, one that culminated in shrieking and ribald challenges. But they were a match for each other, Kelsy palming the water in a straight

155

line that always caught Marston full in the face. He'd come up spluttering, threatening to dunk her. From the sidelines the crew egged him on.

"Bah," he finally said, pushing the surfboard back out to the ocean, "dunking's too good for you. You're going to ride this thing in and show 'em all what a good teacher I really am."

Kelsy paddled after him, thrilled by the encouragement, relaxed by the waves. To her astonishment, when they were far enough out, she caught the first wave and, at Marston's nod, clambered to her feet, the feel of it reminding her of walking the hotel lobby under the influence of too many Blue Hawaiians.

But she mastered it!

She rode that surfboard within twenty-five feet of the shore to the applause of a cheering crew. When it slipped out from under her, her bottom pulled her backward as if someone had a firm clutch on the seat of her suit. She came up spluttering, and offering a victory wave.

Tate was the only one on the beach who didn't look pleased. He said something to Cobb, and Cobb immediately called them both in.

When Marston and Kelsy trudged back onto the beach they looked a little like reprimanded schoolchildren; the rest of the crew had fled. Cobb busied himself with the sound man.

"I think, Kelsy," Tate began, looking over her head and to the pounding surf, "that you need to be aware the saltwater can damage your hair."

"I really wasn't out there very long."

"And Jean was worried you'd snap a nail. We don't have time to repair it for close-ups, not if we want to use the light effectively."

"I—" Kelsy rolled her hands over, drawing an apologetic breath "—guess I didn't think about that."

"Blame me, Tate," Marston offered, hooking an elbow over the top of his surfboard. "I couldn't resist the good time. And I did promise her a lesson. Sorry."

"Don't apologize. It isn't necessary. If you want, you two can take up where you left off after the next two commercials are wrapped, okay?" He shot Kelsy a strange look, and she detected an undercurrent in his magnanimous manner. Only this time she wasn't sure if it was goaded by personal or professional reasons. His crack about not having to apologize was oddly reminiscent of their own previous encounter. She assumed he was really trying to comply with the ground rules they'd laid out the night before about their working relationship.

"We were going to take a break after the third commercial anyway, so that would be a good time," he amended, offering Marston a forced smile.

Chapter Nine

The next two commercials were ridiculously easy to film. Kelsy marveled at how easily she adapted to the demands made of her. She smiled at Marston as if she really meant it, as if he made her heart flutter and her mind pit-a-pat. Or was it the other way around? No matter, Cobb assured her the camera recorded a very convincing performance.

The second commercial was a riot. Kelsy had so much fun she nearly forgot the cameras were rolling. The biggest fear of Cobb and Tate's, however, was that she'd burn because it was scheduled around a beach volleyball game during the hottest, brightest time of day. During the days they filmed, she received a liberal and thorough coating of sunscreen. It had to be carefully applied so no marks were visible. Oil was out, Tate decreed. He didn't want the ends of her hair brushing against it and looking greasy.

Every day they filmed they played volleyball with the extras for at least an hour, just to get in the mood. Marston was as good a mood-setter as anyone. He typically issued challenges, then turned around and spiked the ball effortlessly. Kelsy could see where he could be a betting man, or at least a hustler with a stacked deck or loaded dice. The rapport he developed was astounding.

Compared to the second commercial, where Marston caught an out-of-bounds ball and sent her signals more electrifying than the follow-up pitch for the shampoo, the third, at least to Kelsy, was painfully boring. Stretched out on her stomach on a beach towel, she spent most of her time fumbling through a canvas bag for suntan lotion. The trick was to make the bottle of Redheads Only spill out. They shot a dozen takes before it landed just as Cobb wanted. And when it finally did, Marston, who was to scoop it up and study the label, dropped it. Everyone groaned. The next take went off without a hitch.

In the following days, the makeup artists ground a paste of sand and water into her legs and upper arms — for a natural look and her line, "Mmm . . . I'm doing a slow burn. Do you do backs?" But she found the scene difficult, because every time she rolled onto her back to say her line, Tate seemed to be leaning over the cameraman's shoulder, studying her every move. He seemed as intent as Cobb, his eyes narrowed and his hands busy with a clipboard and paper. Sensing Tate was a distraction, Cobb eventually pulled rank and removed him from her line of vision.

After that, she delivered her line flawlessly. They shot the scene a number of times, but none was as compelling, nor as sexually potent, as the first good run. Even though they were simply delivering lines of a script, Kelsy could feel the magical building of tension, could see where an audience would enjoy their subtle play of words and expression. More than that, she hoped they'd be hooked. Enough to make Redheads Only a success, enough for her to carve her niche in the company. She knew she was giving unforgettable performances, and that left her with a strange sense of power, one that was gratifying, yet unsettling.

Everyone on the crew agreed they were having an exceptional run of filming luck. Bad things were supposed to happen occasionally; the extras might have been uncooperative, or Marston temperamental, or a can of film ruined. But nothing happened — and that in itself was extraordinary. Maybe that's why everyone was so jubilant, everyone so intent on a good cleansing party. They reveled in the anticipation of one that would clear their systems and ease them into the second half of the commercials.

And what was more appropriate than a beach party?

After Gene announced the first commercial had already aired and was scheduled for further national exposure, he endorsed the plans for a party.

Tate had it catered, with coolers of soft drinks and platters of finger foods. Kelsy knew his ulterior motive was to keep everyone in a good working mood, but it didn't change things in the least. The camaraderie continued, the commitment grew stronger.

"Hey, Kelsy," Marston hollered, up to his knees in rushing blue water and one hand on his bobbing surfboard, "you ready for that second lesson?"

Kelsy popped the cracker spread with crab dip into her mouth and set her tumbler of diet cola on the table. "You have to ask?" Flitting across the sand as if she had been raised on it, she splashed through the surf and wended her way past Jean, who was floating on an air mattress in ankle-deep water.

"The surf's coming in just right for a good ride. Come on," he invited. "I want you to show off for the crew."

"Show off? Me?"

"Of course." He grinned. "Just like any good actress would. You know, the way you've been on film."

Kelsy trailed after him. "You make it sound like I'm trying to upstage you."

Marston looked over his shoulder, and when he did, he had a thoughtful, almost vulnerable look on his face, one that was definitely at odds with his intimidating physique. He pushed at the surfboard, forcing a laugh as he did so. "Let's just say you're making me play this role to the fullest of my potential."

"You're doing the same for me. I don't think Tate would ever have guessed it was going to turn out like this." They were chest deep in water and still slogging through it, talking as if surfboarding were the furthest thing from their minds.

Marston turned, putting the surfboard between them and propping his elbows on it. Kelsy held on with her fingertips, bobbing in the water with every crest and swell. "Tate's an ambitious man. I figure there's not too many people who realize what he's got riding on this product."

"What do you mean?"

"He's smart. But the market's fickle. Unpredictable. He had a product fail about six years ago. It was a disaster. They were ready to launch a line of men's shampoos. It was great stuff, all of it. But the public wasn't ready for it, and the packaging wasn't classy enough to be in a big-bucks barbershop. This time I get the feeling he has to make it a success, if for nothing more than to salvage his pride. A man like Tate—" Marston chuckled, shooting a glance to the shore where Tate was standing next to Cobb watching them "—has got a helluva big ego. Good thing there was a man like Gene to neutralize his fall back then."

Kelsy followed his gaze to Tate. "How do you know all this?"

"Because Gene had me do some of the stills for the ads. We never used them, though. The whole campaign was aborted before it ever started. They got out by the skin of their teeth and dumped enough of the product to break even."

"Tate never told me."

Marston snorted. "He wouldn't. He's trying to forget it ever happened." As if the subject were closed, he pushed the surfboard into an oncoming wave and swam after it. Kelsy followed.

They didn't go much farther before Marston started issuing instructions, coaching her on how to take the best course in to shore. Kelsy was game, even eager, but her mind was still on Tate and his near calamity. She kept asking herself if that was why he seemed so driven, so intent on the success of Redheads Only. It made sense, all of it. He wanted to give the product the best possible chance of success — anyone in his position would — but now it looked like he had another motive, equally strong. To prove himself.

The wave Kelsy chose to ride crashed and spun beneath the surfboard. It was a ripsnorter, far more so than she guessed she could have mastered.

And that was the problem. She couldn't.

Her balance was fine. But the board kept lurching, testing her as if it had a mind of its own, as if it ached to whirl out of control. When she realized how high over the edge of the water she was, a shudder needled through her shoulders. That was her undoing.

Pitching over the front of the board, she somersaulted like a novice in a gymnastics class, making the result just as unwieldy, just as awkward. As she plunged headfirst into the ocean, the roar of the water was deafening, the once-soothing sensation a torment. The waves clawed at her flailing limbs as if ridiculing her efforts.

When she surfaced, she was disoriented and groggy, her mind riddled with confusion as swells enveloped her. Her head hurt like the devil and her arms barely had the strength to keep her afloat. Instead of treading water, she felt as if she were clambering in slush. When it all became too much, she went down, succumbing to the pull of the ocean depths as if she'd intended to take an underwater swim.

She bobbed to the surface once. She swiped at the tangled length of hair plastered over her face and gazed, bleary-eyed, when her hand came up watery red.

She wanted to be horrified, but she was too stunned. Before she could react, another wave crashed over her and she submitted to it, letting it carry her farther to shore. Then she floundered, aware only that Marston was cutting the water behind her, catching up with her using the strength that weights and body building had rewarded him with.

She was limp when he reached her and just conscious enough to hear him swear under his breath. He used a dazzling variety of four-letter words, none of them particularly flattering to his otherwise extensive vocabulary.

"Not good for you Redheads Only image," she chided, her voice a ragged whisper as he swept her up.

He grunted and towed her to shore. She glided along, pulled like a fish on a string. Her view of the sky was spectacular, save for the cloudy pink stains that kept interfering. She knew the moment his feet hit the ocean floor, because he grabbed her under her arms and pulled her upright just as a swell knocked her against his muscular body.

In front of her there was considerable splashing. It took a moment before she realized the crew was clustering about them, everyone jockeying for a spot.

"Here. Use this." Someone slapped a beach towel against Marston; Kelsy didn't have the foggiest notion why.

Wadding an end of it, he used it like a blotter against her forehead. Wincing, she retreated and pushed it away. "What the—"

"Hold still."

"I'm fine."

"You're not." Tate's vehement reply sliced through any indecision in her head. If she wasn't fine, then she guessed the only alternative was to be worse.

That was probably why she simply surrendered to the rolling shades of darkness and collapsed.

Tate lost all his good-looking charm when he was pale. His tan looked like the complimentary mistake of the local tanning parlor. Either that, or he was trying to cover up some mysterious ailment. When he clutched the steering wheel and his knuckles whitened, it made the situation look even more desperate. Kelsy kept trying to reassure him it wasn't.

"Lean back," he ordered when she sat up to help him find the emergency entrance to the hospital.

"Watch your driving," she countered. "After all, this is not a life-threatening loss of blood." She held up the end of the towel for him to see. "It's just a little cut."

He grimaced and stared straight ahead. "We'll let the doctor decide that, thank you." Swinging into the first available parking spot, he switched off the ignition of the rental car, cursing when it continued to idle before pulsing to a slow death. "Stay there. I'll get the door."

He was at the door before she could find the handle. "Really, Tate, I'm fine," she said as he solicitously helped her to her feet.

"Fine? You scared the wits out of me. You fainted, looking like the limp contents of some godforsaken shipwreck. I thought for sure—"

"Tate. It was just a bump on the head. That happens sometimes. The doctor will dab a little peroxide on it and send me home. You'll see. Don't be upset—the filming schedule won't have to change."

He stopped and a slow dawning stole over his face. It did, at least, put a little color back into his stricken features. "The filming? Hell, I never even thought about the filming."

"Well, that's what this is all about, isn't it?" she demanded, dropping the towel and bunching it into a bundle near her waist.

He stared at the gash over her eye, looking confused. Blood had smeared into her hairline, trickling over her temple. "Oh, hell. Don't ask me. I don't even know anymore." An attendant came out of the emergency door and Tate straightened as if the presence of a professional had righted his thinking. "Well, of course it is. Of course I'm concerned about the filming. We could be put days behind schedule." He shook a finger at her. "You should have thought of that."

"Me?"

"Do you need a wheelchair, sir?"

"No," Tate snapped. "It's just a little cut." But

when he looked back at her, he didn't look convinced. He looked as if he'd rather chop off his right arm than have to face the jagged gash over her eye. "Yes, right away," he revised, taking a rasping breath. "It's a head injury."

"What?" Kelsy looked dumbly at them both. "Don't be ridiculous. I can walk twenty more steps under my own power."

"It could be a concussion," Tate said to the attendant.

The tender way Tate snagged her waist, did, in fact, make Kelsy want to swoon a second time. But when the attendant went to fetch the wheelchair, Kelsy followed him. He looked a little disgruntled at her offering the admittance clerk information at the same time he was offering her a chair. She waved it away. "I'll walk."

As Kelsy predicted, the doctor swabbed the area with disinfectant and offered them an option. Stitches or butterfly bandages. The bandages, he believed, would prevent scarring.

Tate's eyes drifted closed, as if he were the one being treated. Either that, or he was visualizing the battered remains of his carefully constructed campaign.

"Butterfly bandages," Kelsy decided. The doctor, anticipating her response, had already ripped open the first package. He put a sponge over the gash, kneading the flesh together like bread dough. When he pinched it shut, she winced.

"Hurt?" he asked.

"Not much."

"Maybe you should prescribe some pain pills

167

just in case," Tate put in, hovering near Kelsy's shoulder. "I'll see that she takes it easy, but we'll want her to get her rest, and—"

"She'll be fine," the doctor reassured him. "It's a pretty superficial cut. But a facial wound can really bleed. I imagine it scared you more than anything. It's normal to feel that way with people you care about."

Tate straightened and turned toward the window at the end of the examining table. Leaning on the windowsill, he jammed a hand into his pocket. From the corner of her eye, Kelsy could see he was upset. It was easy to guess he didn't want any more stress on her body, that he wanted her in top shape for the next commercial.

"Don't worry. I'll take it easy. This was just a minor hitch in our plans," she reaffirmed. "From here on out, things are going to just keep getting better."

When Tate turned to look at her, it was as if he couldn't comprehend what she was saying.

Gene, on the other hand, had no such difficulty.

Where Tate was a seesaw of emotion over the incident, Gene dropped his usual boisterous self and called Kelsy and Marston both to task. They sat in his hotel room, on his bed, looking guilty as sin and just as remorseful.

"God, Gene, I'm sorry. I thought she could handle it."

"The girl's a flyweight, for cryin' out loud. She's never even been on a surfboard and you've got her ridin' a wave only a pro would tackle."

Marston swallowed. "It wasn't quite that big."

"Damn near. But no matter. This little escapade

is not only going to delay filming, it's going to cost us thousands of dollars. The first commercial's already been released. We're ready to pounce and the timing couldn't be worse. We can't be tripped up by this. I won't allow it," he said imperiously, raising a finger as if to challenge the gods.

"But everything's gone so well until now . . ." Kelsy's meek voice evaporated when Gene glared at her. "I just meant—"

"And what if you scar?" he demanded, wagging that same finger her way.

Kelsy flushed, acknowledging that was a matter over which she had no control. She reached up to finger the bandages, but a warning look from Tate squelched that. She reached for her hair, thinking one good twist would really relieve a world of tension. But sneaking a second glance at him, changed her mind about that, too.

Gene sighed like a distraught father. "Look, Kelsy, we've got a great opportunity here. You have a part in it," he said, sinking into the chair next to the table and clapping one hand on his knee and running the other over the top of his head. "I'm concerned about you, not just the Redheads Only campaign. You have a responsibility to do your best, and if that means suspending future horseplay until you're out of contract, then you've got to do it."

Kelsy nodded.

"We can't afford to take any chances. Surely you understand that?"

Biting her lip, Kelsy twisted her hands in her lap. Gene had an uncanny way of making her feel guilty, as if the entire scenario had been her fault, as if she were guilty of more than just falling off a surfboard, as if she were to blame for tides and undercurrents and the gravitational pull of the Pacific Ocean.

"Why, this afternoon could have turned into a disaster. You do know that?"

"I know," she said miserably. "And I'm sorry. I guess I've just been taking this whole thing too lightly. It was just so much fun and . . ." She spread her hands helplessly.

"We want you to have fun," Gene said. "That's what this product and the campaign designed for it is all about. But we want you—both of you—" he included Marston in his pointed stare "—to use some common sense. I don't think that's too much to ask, is it?"

There was dead silence in the room as everyone, including Tate, fidgeted beneath Gene's scrutiny.

"We'll suspend shooting for ten days. That'll give Kelsy time to heal and Cobb plenty of time to work on reblocking the next commercial. I've already talked to him about it, and he's thinking he can get around a few of the problems with some creative filming." He sniffed and scratched his forehead. "I hope so. Now—" he pulled himself to his feet, tucking his shirt back into the waistband of his pants "—as long as we've got a self-imposed vacation, let's make the most of it. Kelsy, you're instructed to do some sight-seeing. Marston, I expect you to find yourself a good time without your surfboard. Tate, you've got instructions to relax. If I need something I'll let you know."

"What about you?" Tate asked. "What are you going to do?"

A pleased grin split Gene's face. He looked as happy as a clam and as irrepressible as whale. "Me? I'm going to fly my family over for a real vacation. What the heck. I figure we may as well make the most of a bad situation. The kiddies'll love the beach."

Chapter Ten

Kelsy followed Gene's advice to make the most of her vacation. The first morning she went shopping and didn't even flinch at a single price tag. She bought what she wanted, paying for it all out of her earnings. At noon she called Devon and derived real satisfaction in not worrying about the phone bill. Everything was fine at home. The coffee shop was making a small profit, she'd given Cass longer hours and hired an extra employee, school was fine, Minneapolis had had eight inches of snow that closed down the airport — something unheard of — and the heater on Devon's old car had broken and was going to cost a couple of hundred dollars to fix. Was it worth it, or should she consider getting another car? Kelsy, slathered in sunscreen and stretched out in her swimsuit on the balcony of her room, generously volunteered to send her the money for repairs or the first payment on a new car, whichever Devon decided was best.

The following day she went shelling, but couldn't really work up a lot of enthusiasm for it. She picked up enough shells, though, each one intriguing, and each one begging to go back to the sea. She obliged, working her pitching arm in earnest. The physical release put her in the right frame of mind for a drink.

Spying Jean on the beach, she offered to buy her a Piña Colada. It was idyllic, the two of them sipping an exotic drink beneath the Redheads Only cabana.

"You're a natural in front of that camera," Jean said, leaning over the end of her lounge chair to pat a little sand about the bottom of her glass. "Marston's nearly green with envy that it's coming so easily for you."

"You're kidding?"

"Nope."

"I can't believe that. He's the one making it all so easy. It's his performance I'm trying to match."

"He's a likable guy, isn't he? I think he felt just terrible about your accident." Jean rolled her head over on her forearm, squinting at Kelsy's bandage. "Hurt much?"

"No. Not now. It was pretty stupid of me, actually."

"What'd Tate say?"

Kelsy thoughtfully picked up a handful of sand, letting it sift through her fingers. "He was a little concerned about the filming schedule. He really should've been madder at me—I gave him enough cause."

"You mean he didn't rant and rave and fall on his back, kicking his feet?"

"No. But maybe he's doing that now." Picking up

another handful of sand, Kelsy poured it into the barrel of her hand. "It's been two days and I haven't heard from him since."

Pulling her glass from the sand, Jean wiped a speck of sand from the rim. "He isn't known for his patience with models."

"Well, it wasn't that he was short-tempered."

"Still. After that deal with Zadora Kane, he changed."

"Zadora?"

"Yeah, she was a model he was involved with."

The wheels inside Kelsy's head began to turn as she remembered her meeting with Zadora and how she'd thought the woman was trying to be helpful. Now, she was irked to learn Tate had had a relationship with her. "Are you sure? With Zadora? I met her at the studio in California. It never occurred to me that the two of them—"

"Am I sure?" Jean cackled, plopping her drink back in the sand. "Let me tell you, they were hot. Really hot. Of course, it was all at Zadora's orchestration. She fixed him up with some good connections. She took him to the best parties, introduced him to the right people. But why wouldn't she? He looked good on her arm. What woman in her right mind wouldn't do the same? God, he's a hunk."

The definition pinched. Kelsy remembered her first meeting with Tate—she'd used the same description. A hunk. But the picture of Zadora and Tate together truly disturbed her. "The two of them together? She seems so . . . so ultrasophisticated, and he's, well, it just doesn't click."

"Click? Honey, it was like the tick-tock of the

atom bomb when they parted ways. She used him and she used him good. Nobody knows all the details, but he hasn't had a nice word to say about anybody in the modeling industry since."

He must still be hurting . . . That was the only thought that popped into Kelsy's head. It made her feel a little sad, even a little sorry for him. Tate was a good guy. But it settled one thing in her mind — Zadora Kane was the reason he wouldn't allow himself to be attracted to her. Suddenly she wanted to know all the reasons. She wanted explanations. Thinking of his crack about runny eggs and a broken budvase, she wondered if it was Zadora who . . . Surely not.

Without knowing it, Jean had confirmed that the kiss Kelsy shared on the beach with Tate was just what he'd claimed it was — a spontaneous mistake.

And, damn, that realization hurt.

The booking agent was trying to persuade her to go to the Polynesian Cultural Center, but she didn't really feel like getting culture and kept wrinkling her nose the whole time the agent talked. It didn't matter; the woman never looked up from her paperwork to notice. Finally, Kelsy interrupted her by saying, "I don't think so."

"How about a day trip to Maui?"

"Isn't that expensive for just one day?" The words were out before Kelsy could recall them. The agent, obviously appalled she would even ask, looked up.

"It's a nominal fare," she said smoothly, her eyes lighting on Kelsy's expensive clothes, her ring, and perfect haircut. "A guided tour to the top of Haleakala is always a pleasant experience. It's a dormant volcano, and you travel to the peak and look for miles across the crater. The view is not only spectacular, but a wide variety of plants and minerals, unknown to the lower elevations, abound." She pushed a brochure in front of Kelsy, making her wonder if the woman's canned speech wasn't part of the copy. "Of course, Maui also offers miles of good beaches, great shopping, and a number of fine restaurants. Other tours are available, too. You may study this brochure if you'd like, and I'll be happy to book your reservations for early tomorrow morning."

The minute Kelsy opened the flyer she felt someone slip into the seat next to her. She concentrated on the brochure, debating whether to give up the agent's attention to another tourist or hang in there and book something fast.

"Decide yet?" a masculine voice prodded her. "Maui is a good choice."

Kelsy looked over and saw Tate.

"I'm glad to see you're taking Gene's advice." His gaze wandered up over her eye. "How's the bump?"

"Fine. It's looking better, too." He nodded. "I've met Gene's family. But I—" she hesitated, debating whether she should let him know she'd noticed his absence "—haven't seen you around."

"I just wanted to get away. Get a breather. Take a few days to think a few things through. You know."

"Yeah. That's why—" she tilted the brochure to him "—I thought it'd give me a different perspective."

176

"A different perspective, huh? That's not a bad idea for either of us." As he slipped the brochure from her fingers, his glance offered dual meaning. "You don't really like to travel alone, do you?" he said, appearing to read the copy. "I always find it sort of—" he shrugged, as if searching for the right word "—empty."

"Jean made plans to look up an old friend tomorrow or I'd go with her."

"Pity." He tapped a finger on a picturesque shot of Lahaina. "I'm free tomorrow."

"Do you want me to ask?"

"Nah, I'm not proud. I'll just invite myself along." Grinning, he arched an eyebrow as if challenging her to argue with him. When she didn't, he turned to the agent. "Book two for a morning flight." He shot an appraising glance at Kelsy as if waiting her approval. "We'll play it by ear and pick up a tour or something once we get there."

They had to meet the hotel limo at 6 a.m. to make their inter-island flight. The morning was still cool, the air pungent with the scent of foliage. Tate had thrown a sweater over his shoulder and was lounging against a column in the hotel lobby when she came down from her room. She'd worn one of the outfits they'd chosen together in Minneapolis because it had a matching sweater top, but also because it was reminiscent of another good time together.

"Ah, my favorite outfit," Tate approved. "You remember to bring a swimsuit?"

"Right here." She patted the small carryall, which contained not only a swimsuit, but a towel, the contents of her purse, and packets of Redheads Only shampoo.

Tate probably would have laughed if he'd seen that. But she didn't go anywhere without them. She'd already offered them to the hotel maid, the desk clerk, the bartender, fellow tourists, and anyone else who looked like a candidate. Even though Gene had declared a moratorium on work, she kept finding ways to make the Redheads Only name known.

Their inter-island flight from Honolulu to Maui left at seven. But when she saw the puddle jumper they were supposed to fly in, she had second thoughts. Tate seemed to sense her apprehension.

"These have the propellers they start with rubber bands."

"No." She gazed through the window to the ground crew who were pushing a steel ramp into place near the cabin door. "I may be naive, but—"

"Excuse me," a short stocky woman said, crowding up beside her. Kelsy moved over, thinking the woman wanted room for her daughter at the window. "Excuse me, but aren't you the girl in that commercial? The one about the shampoo?"

Kelsy stiffened in surprise. Throwing her shoulders back, she became the girl in the commercial. "For Redheads Only."

"Yeah. That's it."

"Why, I'm pleased you remembered our product." Already Kelsy was digging in her carryall.

"My daughter has a little red in her hair." The

woman pushed her small, pudgy daughter forward, plucking proudly at the crown of the little girl's head.

"So I see. Here." She gave the packets to the girl rather than her mother, knowing that would win her far more points in the long run. "Try these. This will make your hair really pretty."

The child's gap-toothed smile was her thanks.

"Do you have a boyfriend?" Kelsy asked, giving her a broad wink.

The child nodded. "But when I grow up," she said, "I want to be just like you. I want to have a convertible like yours and have a boyfriend just like yours."

That made Kelsy laugh out loud. If the girl only knew the convertible was a rental and how hard she and Marston had had to work on making their romance come alive for the camera.

"Look, could I have your autograph?" the woman asked, shoving a scrap of paper and pen at her. "That commercial's just fantastic. We only got to see it a couple of times before we left California, but it really caught our attention."

A pleased smile eased onto Kelsy's face and she tried to catch the woman's eye—the last thing she wanted her to see was how her hands were shaking when she gave her first autograph. She tried to sign with a flourish, something prodding her to have a distinctive signature. "Why, thank you, we're so happy you like it. I think you'll like the product, too."

Beyond the woman's shoulder, Kelsy saw more interested faces crop up. Soon she was swimming in a mob scene of unexpected proportions.

"So you're the one on that commercial."

"I told you she was. You can tell by her eyes."

"Can I have your autograph?"

"Me, too."

"Well, I haven't seen it. I don't know why I'm standing in line."

"Be quiet, Herb. We might miss our opportunity to meet a real celebrity."

"I looked for it in the store — for my brother-in-law, you know. But I couldn't find it."

"Oh? Can men use it, too? In that case . . ."

Overwhelmed, Kelsy worked hard to satisfy all the demands made of her. There was a moment she felt frazzled, wondering what in the world she'd gotten herself into. But reminding herself everything had a price and noting Tate's narrowed gaze, she worked diligently not only to be a lady, but to have the kind of grace and good taste Redheads Only wanted to project. Finally, she resorted to passing out packets of shampoo to the same line of people the airline attendant accepted boarding passes from.

Her stint as a celebrity had been confirmed. In ten minutes, in an airport that catered to tourists and international travelers, she'd been recognized and thoroughly indoctrinated into the pressures of fame.

She and Tate were the last ones to board the plane. The smiling faces that greeted them would always be imprinted in her memory. People turned around in their seats for a second glimpse, nodding as if she were a family friend. Unfortunately, a few men leered, obviously recollecting how she filled out that copper-and-cream-colored swimsuit.

Tate said nothing during the entire episode; at least from his reaction she figured that was how he must have viewed it. He stared out the side window as the ground crew pushed the ramp away, frowning and biting his lower lip.

"What? The rubber bands aren't working?" she asked, stretching across his lap to see. Her elbow barely bit into his thigh, but she could feel the brittle tenseness in the muscle. With a sad smile, he pensively snagged a length of her hair and rubbed it between his fingers. Obviously his mind was on other things, none of which included their imminent flight.

Finally he spoke, his voice barely audible over the throbbing engines. "You know this job's going to change you?"

"I know," she said smugly. "It's going to give me that kind of classy self-confidence that goes with being in the public eye. The kind that Redheads Only would approve of."

"That wasn't what I meant."

"Oh? Were you thinking more along the lines of conceited, egotistical, spoiled, vain, and temperamental?"

"Nice description. Good choice of words."

"Won't happen," she vehemently asserted, patting his knee. "I'm firmly grounded. Well—" she hesitated, skimming a glance at the vibrating floor of the plane "—not right now, but—"

"I understand." He released her hair, pushing the tendril back into place. "Right now, you're floating on public adoration." Leaning back in his seat, his fingers curled around the armrests, he looked a little confounded. "The thing is," he added, "I should be, too."

The day trip to Maui was enchanting. Both Tate and Kelsy dropped their respective roles and discovered more things about each other than they did about the island. Tate rented a car for the day, and they hopped into it like excited tourists, driving to the top of Haleakala in record time. They didn't learn much about plants and minerals, but Kelsy learned that Tate had a mother and sister living in Wisconsin, that he was known as Uncle Tatum to his sister's three kids, and that he'd started a fire in the family home at age ten, experimenting with chemical reactions. Tate learned that Kelsy had spent every summer since she was twelve baby-sitting for the same family, that she started baton lessons at five, tap dance at eight, and that the only subject she'd ever failed was high-school physics.

By the time they drove back down and were almost at sea level, they were ready to shed their high-altitude chill for a heated sand beach. Stopping at a public beach, they quickly changed and spread out two small towels, staring at the rhythmic waves and confessing that neither one was particularly keen on Chinese food, modern art, or class reunions. They both loved tacos, tortillas, and burritos, leather bomber jackets, and restored vintage cars.

That afternoon they fed the sea gulls from a deck at a fishermen's bar and filled up on fresh fruits and seafood. Later, they picked up a cruise that was supposed to take them out to the whales' mating grounds with the hopeful promise of seeing a spouting, maybe jumping, whale. They saw nothing but the glassy reflection of clear water, and, hanging over the ship's rail, elbow to elbow, they enjoyed every second of it.

It was dusk when they finally boarded the plane back to Oahu, loaded down with puka beads, scrimshaw, Hawaiian prints, straw hats, two pairs of flip-flops, a grass skirt, two cans of macadamia nuts, a packaged sample of sugarcane, bamboo coasters, and a set of monkey-pod dishes, guaranteed to warp. They'd shuffled off the plane, exhausted but fulfilled. They'd piled back into the hotel limo like rag dolls amongst the tourist tokens.

Tate walked her to her room, the shopping bags stuffed beneath his arms and his carryon slung over his shoulder. She dumped her own packages on the floor and rummaged in her purse for her key.

"Thanks for the day," Tate said, sliding a shoulder into the wall next to her door. "Next time we'll skip the whaling thing."

"Next time?"

"Sure. Why not?"

"I just thought, with the campaign speeding up . . ." She shrugged, leaving it unsaid.

He left it that way, too. His gaze slipped from her limp hair to her rumpled outfit. Without the delicate trace of eye makeup her eyes looked heavier, sleepier, and the moisturizer she'd applied at the beach made her cheeks look supple, moist . . . kissable. She smiled with both lips together, her lashes dipping down as her mouth lifted, as if she was ready to say a congenial, amicable "Let's be friends" good night.

She'd never looked better.

And he was dead tired, and it didn't seem right that the evening was about to end. It seemed, the back of his mind goaded him, that there was some unfinished business here. But he'd have to drop his packages to do it.

His fingers loosened about the handles of the shopping bag and it slipped down over his knee. The tissue paper wrapping the monkey-pod dishes made a huge crinkling sound, one that was magnified in the empty hall. "I think our purchases are all mixed up." Lifting his hand, he wiggled the bag, realizing that a mixup could be more effective, and certainly less obvious, than helping with the key to her room. "Want to sort them out?"

"It's okay. We can do it tomorrow."

Deflated, he dropped the bag back against his leg. "Sure?" He knew without pressing that her reaction was his fault; he'd called the shots on the beach the night he'd given her the lei and kissed her. How could he expect her to respond any differently?

"Yeah, it's late." She moved as if someone else were pulling the strings to her limbs, making them move with caution, reserve, as if the spontaneous day before them had been wiped as clean as a slate. "We both better keep decent hours — we're scheduled to start filming again in a few days."

"Yeah. Well . . . good night." But he didn't move. He studied the way her top creased between her breasts, the way it clung, outlining them like plump little pillows. She'd taken out her earrings and he wondered if she'd indulge herself and get a nice pair of pearl studs before they went back to the mainland. Probably not.

"Good night." The softly spoken words were blurred when she bent to fumble with her packages and slide the key into the lock. The door swung open, and Tate watched Kelsy slip away into a private room that didn't include him. "How about if I come by for breakfast? The hotel's got a great buffet."

"Sounds good. But call first, will you? I'll probably sleep in."

The thought filled Tate with a delectable vision, one he chased away, one he felt a little guilty about — especially after they'd parted on such a difficult note only days before. He wondered what it would take for her to invite him in. What it would take to extend the parameters of their relationship. But when she shouldered against the door and inched it closed, he knew it wouldn't happen. "Sure thing. That's a promise."

It turned out to be a promise he couldn't keep.

Because the next morning he was pounding on her door at eight o'clock, a newspaper in one hand and Gene beside him. Cobb was coming down the hall from one direction, Marston from the other. When she came to the door, all bedraggled and still pulling on the sexy silk robe they'd picked out in Minneapolis, he barely noticed. "Get dressed," he ordered. "We've got a mess on our hands."

Chapter Eleven

The bellboy delivered a tray of pastries and two carafes of coffee, and Gene had been conspicuously silent since their arrival. Tate shredded his frosted doughnut, occasionally eating a morsel; but Gene worked a pat of butter into his cinnamon roll and poked huge chunks of it into his mouth, mashing it between his molars. He polished off three cinnamon rolls, listening while others around him complained and worried and stewed. Then he grabbed his napkin off his lap, wadded it into a tight ball, and tossed it over the leftover crumbs.

"I'd say it's libelous," Cobb said, dropping his cup into the saucer so hard the coffee sloshed over the edge. "People have been taking them on lately, and they've been winning. Maybe that's what we should think about."

"Damn, this could ruin our careers," Marston added, staring dejectedly into the bottom of his emptied coffee cup. "Instead of a turning point, this could be a suicide run."

Gene sighed, bending to retrieve a folder of paperwork. He flipped through some photocopies before pulling a paperclip from some faxed sheets. "I hadn't intended to show you this," he said. "Not yet. But I guess it's time. Here's a sample of the news clippings my secretary faxed me." He threw them down as if he was pitching aces from a stacked deck. "We're going to strike back and strike back hard. We're riding one of the biggest waves in commercial advertising today."

Kelsy, feeling outnumbered by the four good-sized men clustering the table in her room, picked up a clipping and scanned it. Everyone else did the same.

"Basically they all say the same thing," Gene said. "Redheads Only is generating interest, but the bulk of it is coming from the commercial that's being aired. Everyone's clamoring for more. No one's seen Kelsy before. Everyone wants to know where she's been. People in the industry are saying she's going to be a flash in the pan—though I don't think so. Men are calling in to television stations asking for her name, and the media are begging for a bio. Because of it, Elsethe Industries is being swamped with requests for shampoo from markets we never thought we'd get."

Kelsy gaped, shooting an apprehensive look at Marston and wondering if he'd be jealous.

"The teenagers," Gene went on, "have set up a hullabaloo for more of Marston. They're begging for posters. There's all kind of speculation about the two of you. We've stumbled onto something bigger than any of us realized. And we're not going to lose it because some tabloid—appropriately named *The Noisemaker,* no less—decides to get on the bandwagon and sell a few newspapers by printing a pack of lies."

Tate threw down the article he'd skimmed. "We were mobbed at the airport yesterday."

"That's just the beginning," Gene predicted.

"What if we get pigeonholed?" Marston speculated. "I can't afford name recognition with a single product."

"You can if we all stick together and play our cards right." Gene dumped a few more fax sheets in the middle of the table, narrowly missing the remnants of the pastry. "I'd wanted to wait until the end of the filming to lay out the game plan, but this tabloid article's forced my hand."

Kelsy seethed, staring at the front-page headlines and wrinkling her nose. "I can't believe they say I'm not a redhead. The way it reads, it makes it all sound like a scam."

"It sells papers, Kelsy. And right now you're a hot item, one that's getting her fair share of media attention. They can't afford to be left out."

Glumly, Tate fingered through the corner of the copy. "What if we just ignore it?"

"Nope. I won't do it. Because it's already planted a seed of doubt in consumers' minds." Gene leaned forward, propping both elbows on the table and steepling his hands. Now, here's how I see it. We've got to take a break anyway because of the surfing accident. It's a perfect time to get

Kelsy out into the public. Let her shake a few hands, get a little word of mouth going. We had a tentative schedule set up for a promotional tour on the mainland—we'll simply move it ahead. It'll be a whirlwind trip, but we'll keep her in the public eye. I'll see to the legal end of it, and I'll see to it that we get the press releases out."

"You want me out in the public with a gash over my eye?"

Gene offered a low sympathetic whistle. "My, my, it's a sad little attention-getter, isn't it? I imagine the press will eat it up. But the bandage is off and the worst of it can be covered with makeup." He paused, thoughtfully rubbing his forehead. "Now were you, or weren't you, rehearsing one of your own stunts for a future commercial? That part's a little unclear to me. But one thing I can recognize a mile off is a chance for public sympathy."

All the men around the table grinned; Kelsy squirmed, not quite as convinced. It seemed so manipulative, not at all like the Redheads Only she was trying to represent.

"What about the film crew?" Cobb asked, pulling a cigar from his pocket. Kelsy knew he'd never light it; he'd only chew on the end till it was a spongy wad of black mush. "It's going to cost money to get everybody back together."

"We're going to stay here. We're going to keep working."

"What?"

"We need background shots. How about having

189

Marston dub over some work for later release? He's got a distinctive voice, one the teenagers of America are clamoring for. Let's use it and splice in a little of the throwaway stuff from the first shoot."

"Throwaway stuff?" Cobb stuffed the cigar between his teeth. "That's why it ended up on the cutting-room floor."

Tate raised an eyebrow, shooting an appraising glance at Kelsy. "But a glimpse just brief enough to dazzle . . ."

"Something about 'My girl uses Redheads Only because . . . ,'" Marston added, getting into the spontaneous brainstorming session.

"You got it!" Gene boomed, slamming a fist on the table and making the lid on the carafe bounce. "We're gonna spin heads."

"And not just redheads," Kelsy added, suddenly admiring Gene's drive and ambition.

"I'll be on the phone this afternoon booking the tour," Tate announced. "It'll be just the two of us. The flight's already scheduled for late afternoon tomorrow."

"What about Bruce?" Kelsy asked.

Gene lapsed into silence; Tate shook his head.

"Bruce doesn't travel well," Tate finally explained, looking into her perplexed features.

"But my hair?"

"You did it before you had Bruce, didn't you?" Gene said. "You can do it now. Besides, we want things to go as smoothly as possible. I'm considering having him do special promo work with some

190

of the salons in Honolulu. It'll be a real ego trip for him."

"It doesn't bother me. Really. I can do my own hair." Kelsy ran a hand through her hair, recalling how carefully Bruce had nurtured every layered end. "I just want to look my best for Redheads, that's all."

"You will," Tate confirmed. "We can count on it. And if you handle yourself with the same kind of composure you used yesterday at the airport, this tour's going to be a smash success."

"That's what I feel like most of the time," Kelsy added dryly, shaking her head as if it were a little too much to comprehend. "A smashing success story."

The only thing that really disturbed Kelsy before she left the island of Oahu was that she hadn't time to return Devon's phone call. Tate, who'd been at her side as she was throwing things into a suitcase, had taken the call, learned everything was fine at home, and relayed the message that Kelsy would call her soon.

But Kelsy had never counted on the mind-boggling tour Tate could whip out of thin air. There were times she felt like she was in a pressurized advertising chamber, everything exclusively designed to wreak havoc with her cool demeanor. They caught late flights, they caught early ones, they rented so many cars Kelsy could fill out rental forms in her sleep.

191

They missed meals and ate stale dispenser candy bars in their hotel rooms, washing them down with fruit juice. Complimentary chocolates on a pillow looked like a full-course meal after working until the strip malls closed.

She saw the interiors of discount stores before they ever opened. She shook hands with employees and encouraged them to send their customers over to her specially arranged booth—which was usually nothing more than a card table and a basket of Redheads Only samples. Occasionally, if Tate could find a flower shop, he'd spring for a centerpiece of red carnations. If not, they'd artfully arrange the literature Elsethe Industries had prepared to introduce the product.

Kelsy signed autographs until her hand cramped. She answered questions about herself and about the product, her mind constantly working to cull a clever reply or induce a frugal spender into trying Redheads. Once in a while, she was forced to dodge personal questions, ones that could inadvertently put a dent in her Redheads reputation or tarnish her image. When that happened, she was always relieved to find Tate giving her an encouraging nod from the back row. It became routine for her to scoff at *The Noisemaker*'s claims she wasn't a natural redhead, frequently quipping, "When I was born, my hair was so red I was the only child in the nursery who didn't need an identification bracelet."

She not only increased sales at every store she visited, she improved customer relations. She returned three lost children, commiserated with four men about not having any hair at all, and directed dozens of people to the pharmaceutical aisle. It was, after all, the cold and flu season.

Ten days and dozens of stores later, they headed for their hotel in Omaha. It was a typical night, waiting too long at the luggage carousel, confirming the next day's plans at a phone booth in the airport, and hoping to snag a comfortable compact car at the rental agency. After she tried to reach Devon one last time, rather than the answering machine that unluckily seemed to field all her calls, she could kick off her heels and lie back, enjoying Tate's uncanny ability to drive them to their night's lodging.

But things were different in Omaha. Kelsy had just stuffed her swollen feet back into her pumps and was lugging her suitcase from the trunk, when Tate came out of the hotel lobby and into the biting wind, his face distraught.

"Leave it," he ordered. "We may be up a creek."

"Why?"

"The room reservation's been canceled and everything's booked. Come on in while we decide what to do."

Kelsy dropped the suitcase, not really caring that she put another scrape on the side. "So we're staying somewhere else?"

"Fat chance." He grimaced. "You ever wonder how fat chance and slim chance came to mean the same thing?"

Wearily, Kelsy dredged up a smile. She couldn't

remember ever being so tired. Her muscles ached, her shoulders felt like someone had danced a two-step across them, and her mind was as muddy as yesterday's coffee. Slamming the trunk, she trudged after him into the lobby.

"We've called all of the nearby hotels, sir," the receptionist informed Tate when they stepped back up to the desk. "Everything's booked solid. There's a livestock exhibit at Ak-Sar-Ben and we've got an insurance convention going on downtown. There may be something on the outskirts." She pushed a phone book at him. "You're welcome to call around if you like. We are sorry for the inconvenience."

If someone had smacked Kelsy with a two-by-four she wouldn't have been more surprised. Imagine not being able to find a single room in all of Omaha. For heaven's sake, March in Omaha was not the height of the tourist season. "I can't believe you can't come up with some kind of room. Not even a broom closet?"

"Well, our bridal suite's available."

Kelsy's pause was momentary. "Does it come with a rollaway?"

The receptionist smothered a smile. "I don't think so. Let me see if we can get one for you."

"Never mind. We'll take it," Kelsy automatically replied, before nailing Tate with a speculative eye. "I suppose this puts you over budget."

"Probably."

"Fine. I'll be happy to make up the difference. Heaven knows, you're paying me enough."

"I'm sorry, ma'am," the receptionist interrupted. "We're out of rollaways. There's a love seat in the room, though, if you'd like extra sheets . . ."

"Fine," they said in unison, then looked at each other and laughed.

The room was not what they'd expected. Sure, they expected a lot of room, a plush atmosphere, and a king-size bed, but nothing prepared them for the iced bottle of champagne, flowers, complimentary room-service dinner—or the heart-shaped hot tub and mirrored walls.

Tate ran a hand over the sleek red acrylic of the hot tub. "Just remember," he said, lifting a hand just long enough to wag a finger at her, "you asked for this. God, I can't believe they have something like this in Omaha, America's heartland."

Kelsy sagged onto the love seat, kicked off her shoes, and hooked her toes over the edge of the coffee table, staring at the suitcases the bellboy parked near the door. "Smart move on my part, huh? Under the circumstances, that hot tub's going to be a lot better than a vibrating bed."

"In this room? In the bridal suite?" Tate chuckled as he turned on the taps. "I doubt it."

Kelsy was too exhausted to be offended or even amused by the suggestion. Besides, she'd been in predicaments far worse than sharing a room and a hot tub with a man she admired. "You want the bathroom?" she asked.

"Go ahead. I'll call and order dinner for nine

o'clock."

"Fine."

"Kelsy?"

"Yes?"

"You do want to use the hot tub, don't you?"

"If I'm paying for the luxury, you bet I'm going to use it."

She didn't know why she took so long in the bathroom. First she thought she just wanted to tissue away the remnants of the day's makeup and slip into her swimsuit. Then she found herself brushing out her hair and dabbing on a light foundation and lipstick. That led to a touch of mascara and blush. Looking at her reflection in the mirror, she wondered if she'd gotten so used to looking good for the public that she couldn't face Tate without seeking the same kind of approval from him.

Looking good. Looking good on the outside. That was what it was all about. But it bothered her, wondering if Tate would ever look deeper, to the heart of her, to see what lay beneath.

Sighing, she blotted her lips on a square of toilet paper and flushed it away. She was too weary to be having these mental arguments with herself. Tate had clearly outlined their respective roles only a few weeks before. She certainly didn't have the energy or the guile to change it.

Snapping off the light switch, she opened the door, totally unprepared for what she saw.

Tate was head and shoulders above the swirling water of the hot tub, his rugged features carved in shadow and light. Both arms were resting atop the tub's edge as he absently traced the lip of a champagne glass with his forefinger. Beside it, a second untouched glass was filled, reflecting the only illumination in the room—the underwater light from the depths of the spa.

"I couldn't wait for you," he explained, sweeping up his glass to take a sip. "I hope you don't mind."

"Not at all. Uh . . ." Kelsy hesitated, skimming a glance to the rippling water and hoping he'd bothered to pull on a pair of swimming trunks. "Do you need a towel?"

"Right here." He lifted the corner of a stack of towels on the tile behind him. "They think of everything."

"If you want to just stretch out for a while, I can just—"

"Come on in, Kelsy. The water's fine."

The first few tentative steps to the water's edge were the worst, creating a panic in her midsection and trepidation in her heart. But before she had time to control the yammering in her middle, Tate rose, the water running down his chest and thighs. His bathing trunks clung to him, air bubbles puckering the fabric. Seemingly oblivious to her relief, he offered up a still-dripping hand. "It's a big step down."

"The big step," she said dryly, "is sharing a hot tub with my employer." Accepting his hand, her weight sank into the support, making his wrist wobble. Water rushed around her ankle, lapping up over the calf of her leg. She was in over her knees before she finally hit bottom. Tension whirled away from her limbs as her shoulders sank below the waterline, her hair floating on the surface. "This is decadent," she breathed, allowing her arms to be lifted by the surging water.

Tate reluctantly released her hand and raised his glass in a mock toast. "It may be decadent, but I imagine it's the first time the occupants of this suite ever bothered with swimsuits."

Kelsy laughed, dipping her head slightly so he couldn't see her blush of embarrassment. "Don't be so hasty. I'll bet there're others who've found themselves in the same fix we're in."

"A delightful fix to be in, too, isn't it?"

"Let's just say that tonight the timing was right."

They soaked for another half hour, unaware of how easily the water whipped from their bodies the tension of daily living, the strength of reserve. The constancy of it all lulled them into false comfort.

Before the steak and lobster arrived, Tate pulled on a terry-cloth robe; Kelsy slipped into the special nightwear Tate approved of during their first shopping trip. The silk slid over her skin and the apricot tones complemented the glow in her cheeks. They looked across a glass of champagne at one another in the cozy warmth of their room, and forgot about all that had happened between them.

"To the success of Redheads Only," Tate toasted,

clinking his glass against hers.

"To Redheads Only," she echoed, lifting the glass to her lips. But she didn't see the campaign, nor the product, and certainly not their roles associated with it when she looked into Tate's eyes. She saw only him, the man who played pinball in a Denver airport and the driver who took a rental car to the summit of Haleakala, the same man who grinned at her as he shook a grass skirt and coaxed her to model it.

He'd become so much more than Tate Alexander, boy wonder of Elsethe Industries. He'd become her friend, her confidant. She'd told him more about her family, her ambition, her life, than she'd told her best friend.

They sipped from their glasses at exactly the same time.

"Thank you, Tate. For everything."

"For what? Being stranded in Omaha without a room reservation?"

She shrugged, knowing that wasn't what she meant at all. But glancing over his shoulder, she saw the love seat. He'd thrown sheets over it and they'd landed haphazardly, making the thing look more like a makeshift bed he'd crawled out of rather than one he'd crawl into. She wondered how it would be to take to her own bed this night and listen to the even sound of his breathing. She knew how he slept. Occasionally he'd nodded off on a couple of their numerous flights. His chest moved with the even contented strokes of the rested, his hands furled like an infant's. His eyes would occasionally flicker as if his subconscious was reminding him of the thousand things that needed to be done for the campaign. He never looked more vulnerable than at those moments, and she never wanted to cradle him more.

"Like everything else, it worked out," she said.

"You worked out better than anyone could have guessed," he said softly, cutting into his steak. He forked a bite, then laid his knife aside. "Especially me."

"I just want to do you proud."

"You have. I never thought it would matter so much. I figured this would be just a routine campaign, with a lot of hard work and a lot of high hopes. But everything about it feels different—and I don't mean because we've suddenly found ourselves in the bridal suite surrounded by hearts and flowers." He turned the champagne goblet, making a small circular crease in the tablecloth.

"Hearts and flowers—some of the small, unexpected pleasures of life."

They ate, occasionally making small talk. They were both bone tired and famished, but the positive response they'd received throughout the country had infused them with adrenaline, making even the wearisome times feel sweet.

When they finished, Tate piled their plates on the tray and took it out to the hall. By the time he'd returned Kelsy had divided the last of the champagne between their glasses.

"You're sure you should do that?" he asked.

"It's a shame to waste it."

"But I remember what too many Blue Hawaiians did to you."

Her eyes fluttered closed, and with her glass in her hand she moved to the bed, sinking one knee on it. Pulling the glass to her lips, she finished the wine. "I know we should go to bed, but I'm not really tired enough for that."

"Oh?" His gaze traveled the length of her, settling on her lips and heavy-lidded eyes. Her hair was reminiscent of the first time he'd seen her, that full swing of a loose, layered cut, one unhindered by hairspray and curling irons. He guessed the humidity from the hot tub had relaxed the curl. But, still, it moved like an invitation. One he should be reminding himself to refuse. "Have you seen the view?"

Kelsy padded across the room to join him at the window. They were six floors up and could see the city unfolded into a symmetry of crisscrossed streets and winking lights. Leaning her forehead against the glass, she watched the cars pull up to the hotel, their occupants disappear into the lobby. It was the most natural thing in the world for him to loop his arm about her shoulder. She fit into the hollow perfectly.

He tipped his head close to hers, but he wasn't seeing anything but the arch of her brows or the fawn-colored sweep of her lashes framing her eyes. The smattering of freckles over her nose made him think the child in her was always lurking just below the surface.

Just tell her, Tate. For crying out loud, just tell

201

her. "There's something I've been regretting for a few weeks now."

She swiveled her head. They were mere inches apart, her dark gaze inviting, her lips full, immobile. She smelled like soap, the fragrance warm, lingering.

"That is?"

"That I cut our kiss on the beach a little too short. I guess it shocked me as much as it did you."

"Tate, you don't have to—"

"No, but I've been missing you, Kelsy. Every night I see you to your room and I go to mine, and I wonder what things would've been like if I hadn't—"

Kelsy stopped him by putting a hand on his chest. Then she did something she'd never done before. Leaning closer, she slid her arm beneath his, following the curve of the robe's lapel down to his waist to stop on the robe's thick belt. Offering up her lips, she silently beseeched the man towering over her to lose himself in her kisses, in her responses. She knew the moment he claimed her he hungered for her, for he parted her lips and drove his tongue to her depths.

Wheeling from the window, she was enfolded, his arms crushing her to his length. She felt the hardness of his muscles against her flesh as his chest rose and fell, his hands roving over her back before pausing at her waist. The robe he wore parted and his curling chest hair grazed her breasts. Against her, she discovered a man's passion; within her, she discovered a deep-seated need.

"Kelsy . . ." Her name was insistently guttural in his throat, and his fingers splayed over her hips as he drew her against his thighs. Her body shuddered, neither recoiling nor embracing. Pushing aside the strap on her gown, he allowed the silk to fall far over her shoulder, leaving it barely suspended on the peak of her breast. The provocative picture she presented made his blood pound, the suggestion of how soft, how pliable she was, charged him with anticipation. His muscles trilled as he ached to possess her, ached to be sated, with pleasure, with indulgence.

The hollow of her neck was thrumming, and his lips touched the pulse point. With his tongue, he drew tiny moist circles, absorbing the push-pull of pressure. He was smitten, knowing, secretly, that she'd dominated his every thought, his every aspiration. She'd come to him at night in his dreams, taunting, tempting, riding him with unshackled desire.

He'd fallen in love with another model once—something he'd vowed never again to do. Only this time it was different because it was the incomparable Kelsy Williams, the one with the trademark smile and halo of highlights in the swirl of her hair; the one who grinned and played peekaboo with a toddler, then winked at a doting mother and handed her a sample packet; the one who fainted on the shores of the Pacific, then helped him find the emergency entrance to the hospital.

How could he just walk away from this one? He was tied to her in thought, word, and contract, and he relished every bit of it. He saw her success in a throng of people, he saw their faces light with recognition, and he wanted to cheer, to rally around her growing success, to claim her.

Yet, inside, he felt like a tight coil when he drew her close. He ached to possess her sweetness, longed to nullify the contract that gave her to millions — he agonized because he wanted her exclusively to himself. Sharing her was already a torment, one that nagged at him constantly. The sexy smiles she offered Marston on camera drove him to distraction. Hell, he'd already lost three clipboards and two dozen pens just trying to make himself look busy while the two of them were mooning at each other.

Turning her head slightly, she guided him to the sensitive spot below her ear. His body responded, his hand dipping inside to cover her breast. His thumb reached up to whisk away the scrap of fabric from the thrusting tip of her nipple. Beneath his finger, the rosy flesh was firm. At his persuasive urging, it tautly knotted.

"Hold me," she whispered against his cheek, her legs spliced between his own. "Make me feel like I'm something more than a character in a thirty-second commercial. Sometimes it's all happening so fast, I need something to hold on to."

He chuckled huskily, raising his head against her hair. "What? You don't like all this stardom? There're a thousand men who'd give their arm to be in my shoes right now."

"But there's only one I want," she said, tracing the line of his jaw. The stubble grated her finger like a sanding block. "The man who created that image."

Tate's hand trembled, but the reminder of his role in her career made him nudge the ribbon of strap back up her arm and into place. He drew the silken material back over her breast, hating having to do it. He wanted her, but he was still too raw from another experience. Could he really be the only man in her life? Was he ready for that? He knew that's what it meant, especially with a woman like Kelsy. "You're making it hard for me to face that love seat tonight."

"Then don't." She ran her hands through the bristly ends of hair at his temple. "You created more than Redheads Only. Without knowing it, you created a woman who isn't afraid to go after what she wants. Tonight, Tate Alexander, I want you."

"Kelsy—"

"No, let me finish." Her hands framed his face, drawing him closer until they were nearly nose to nose. She saw the slight crook that gave him character; he saw the freckless Jean covered with makeup. "We've been playing this cat-and-mouse game for far too long. We find ourselves giving and then we draw back. We're not protecting ourselves, Tate, we're driving ourselves crazy. I'm offering up the other half of a king-size bed tonight. I'd be pleased if you'd take it."

205

She won him as surely as if she'd wantonly parted the overlapping front of his robe and seduced him with erotic kisses and sweet caresses. He chuckled, yielding to her plea. "I was kind of hoping we could both share the middle of it."

The laughter in her throat was little more than a happy gurgle, and that was finally drowned out when his lips covered hers. They didn't hurry to the waiting bed, but moved slowly toward it as if that were the natural progression of things.

Once there, they twined together, discovering, loving. She gave of herself, tempting him with heady, powerful strokes of her limbs. When she found herself astraddle his muscular frame, she peeled away the silken nightwear and thrilled to the touch of his inquisitive hands. Eventually he guided her atop himself, probing gently until he found the enveloping warmth that would nourish and sustain his love.

Gradually, without disturbing the committed link between them, he rolled over, his arms cradling her shoulders and his face nuzzling the hair from her neck as he cushioned himself against her belly. For the first moments he teased, lazily experimenting with half-thrusts and tender intrigue. But Kelsy would have none of it. Her body demanded—no, craved—a committed reply. Tate obliged, bringing her to the peak of ecstasy, mesmerized as he watched her surrender to its ultimate resolution.

Waves of pleasure racked her body, her palms flat against his chest when she arched, the joints of her fingers brushing over his nipples. The kittenish sounds she uttered incited him. As if to match her heady descent, his response was quick, hard, and aggressive, his spasms beginning as hers subsided.

For some minutes they lay entwined, awed, breathless. Then he slipped off his elbows and onto his side, massaging her upper arm and dropping to tickle the inside of her elbow. "You're very accomplished, some talents of which you neglected to report on your résumé."

She responded by running a finger over his collarbone. "Some things are better kept quiet—and under the covers."

He chuckled, hugging her quickly, tightly. "But it'll be nearly impossible to keep this quiet and try to act normal once we get back to Hawaii."

Her body spent, her eyes drifting closed, she merely smiled, lying languidly in his arms and asking herself why they would need to. The campaign? Her image? Falling into a fulfilled, but exhausted sleep, only this one thing troubled her. Why should they act as if life hadn't changed them?

Chapter Twelve

Landing in Hawaii was a relief. The temperatures soothed her weary body, and her mind ached for the same kind of freedom she'd experienced during the first days of filming. Everything was better now that Tate was securely at her side. She didn't hesitate to confide in him, knowing that together they could shoulder the demands of the campaign.

During the last leg of their tour, he was in her mind, the memories of their lovemaking always fresh, always beckoning. The stolen moments of night became the substance of daydreams—the kind that made her forget her aching feet and her frozen smile.

But the respite was brief. Almost immediately the jangling phone broke in on the solitude of her room, as well as her unpacking.

"Hello?"

"So, you're back."

"Devon! Yes, we just got in today."

"So nice you could trouble me with a call. Is

this a new method of communication between us? A few inquiries via the answering machine?"

"I'm sorry, but—"

"I see by the papers you managed to get hurt surfing, and that you took some kind of whirlwind tour through half the country. Let's see here. Chicago, St. Louis, Kansas City, Dallas. Ah, yes, you were in Omaha, too. But you never bothered to leave a single phone number where you could be reached."

Kelsy swallowed, not wanting the night in Omaha compared with the same hectic pace of the tour, and certainly not subjected to the scathing tone in Devon's voice. "I couldn't leave one because we were never in one place long enough. We didn't have a choice. Tate had to move the tour up and get me out in the public."

"Well, your adoring public seems to know more about you than I do," Devon snapped. "Since when are you getting too big for your britches to make a person-to-person phone call?"

"Devon, I've hardly had five minutes to myself." Except for that one night in Omaha, Kelsy reminded herself. "And if you'd stay home long enough, I wouldn't have to talk to the answering machine."

"Stay home long enough? Do you have any idea what it's like to go to school and run that stupid coffee shop? It never fails—something either breaks down or someone quits every time I have a paper to write or a test to take. This isn't working, Kelsy. I'm supposed to be managing that coffee shop, not working in it."

"It'll all fall into place. Once you find some good help, you won't have to worry—"

"Worry? That's all I ever do now. Over my grades. Over keeping that place running. Over that ice machine. Has it ever occurred to you I could be worried about you, too? Finding out in the newspaper that your only sister was seriously injured in a surfing accident isn't exactly a good time."

"Seriously injured? I didn't even have stitches."

"Well, right now I hardly care. You want to know what I think?" Kelsy was silent, knowing Devon didn't need an answer; she just needed to get it out of her system. "I think that what with all the fame, glory, and money, you're letting the whole shebang go to your head. And yes, I'm getting a little disgusted shoving coffee at leering truck drivers while you're lying on the beach and playing in the ocean."

One word caught Kelsy's attention and she mentally ticked off her known customers. "Leering? Who's leering?"

"That Sam Whatshisname."

"Oh, he always does that," Kelsy scoffed. "Just ignore him. He's so married, his conscience wouldn't let him do anything else."

"Thank God."

"And, Devon?"

"Yes?"

"I'm not doing any lying on a beach. I've been so busy I don't have the foggiest notion what time it even is in Minneapolis when I call. In the last two weeks, I think I've hit four different time zones. Or is it five?" She sighed, sinking onto the bed beside her open suitcase. "I just got in an hour ago and we're resuming shooting tomorrow at the crack of dawn."

"Well, dear, I'm sorry about your long hours, but as you're enjoying your glamorous day of shooting, think of me getting up at the crack of dawn to fill a coffeepot and argue with the driver who brings the Danish."

"Devon, if the coffee shop isn't working out — "

"It's working out just fine. Just fine," Devon snapped again. There was a pause, as if she were reevaluating her position. "Look. You know I was never made to be a waitress. I hate it. I hate every blessed minute of it. I'm practically counting the days till you're out of that contract and my life can go on again. I know I agreed to manage this thing, but — "

"Devon, I don't think you understand," Kelsy said carefully, twisting the phone cord between her fingers. "My life with Redheads doesn't exactly expire when the contractual year is up."

"What? What, exactly, is it you're saying?"

Kelsy slumped against the wall and ran a hand over the back of her neck. The tension and stress of placating everyone was twisting her muscles into one big block of pain. "You know, Dev, maybe you need a break. Put Cass in charge. I mean, we can afford it."

"Sure, out of your salary."

"Hey, you should be thankful I've got this job—it's what's putting you through school."

"Yes, and I'm beginning to feel like a kept relative. Besides, this wasn't the way we first agreed to do it."

"How was I supposed to know what was going to happen back then? At the time, you were more than happy to have me work the coffee shop so you could go to school. Sure, you helped out when you could, but it was a logical arrangement at the time. But I was doing the bulk of the work and I wasn't complaining. Now the parameters have changed a little, that's all."

Across the thousands of miles that separated them, Devon's sniff could be plainly heard, and Kelsy's frustration grew. Devon was being unreasonable, just like when they were kids. Kelsy was weary of giving in to her demands, and she refused to do so now, especially since she'd found something that had come to mean so much to her. She refused to argue over her future, though she wasn't above placating Devon.

"Look, this call is costing too much for either of us to spend time arguing. We're both tired. And you need a vacation. I'm sure for a price Cass'll watch the coffee shop. How about if I send you a plane ticket to come over and join me? Then you can really see how much lying about I'm doing."

Devon hesitated. "Will I get to meet Daniel Marston?"

"Meet him? I'll fix you up with him. Now will you forget this other nonsense and just come?"

"Are you sure you want me to? I mean—"

"Of course I want you to! Then maybe you'll understand this job isn't nearly as glamorous as it seems."

"Well . . . all right. Really, Kels, I am happy for you and I never meant to jump all over you. It's just that I hate that coffee shop. I never wanted that. I wanted to have my own office with my name on the door."

"I know. Hang in there, girl. Give me another few months and we'll manage it."

"Thanks. Oh, and Kels? One other thing. Is there anything special I should bring to wear? You know, if you can arrange this Marston thing? I mean, does he like the sporty look, or ruffles and lace, or . . ."

Kelsy was amused. She couldn't quite imagine her businesslike sister being taken in by Marston's muscles and projected sex appeal. "Heavens, I wouldn't know."

"But you work with him."

"That's right. That's *all* I do." Reaching over, Kelsy pulled the apricot gown from the suitcase, rubbing the lace between her fingers and thinking of the last romantic interlude with Tate.

213

After Tate, she couldn't imagine ever wanting to look at another man again. But since Marston didn't do a thing for her hormones, maybe the chemistry would be right for Devon. If nothing else, it would keep Devon's mind occupied.

"Jeez," Devon said dreamily, "meeting him'd be great. And he's such a hunk on your commercials. If he makes a poster, will you get me one?"

"Right," Kelsy agreed. "One more thing to do."

Gene called a meeting that night. Kelsy likened it to a debriefing. Tate reported on the success of the tour; Gene confirmed it through his other sources. The tour had made an impact; sales for Redheads Only were skyrocketing, particularly in the cities they'd visited.

Cobb and Marston had gotten a lot of background work done and come up with some fresh new ideas for the campaign. Filming would proceed as scheduled the following morning; Tate would be in charge of crowd control.

"Crowd control?" Kelsy repeated, disbelief strangling the question.

In stunned silence, she listened to Cobb describe how several crew members had been badgered for information on the shoot. Not only were the locals interested, a few tourists were willing to sacrifice a few hours of their vacation for a glimpse of the Redheads stars. Worse, the media had already requested access for feature stories on the pair.

"What have we gotten ourselves into?" she asked, almost choking on the magnitude of the situation.

"A money pit," Gene replied happily, not at all troubled by all the other implications. "And we're sinking smack-dab into the middle of it. With enough to go around for everyone. Ah, it's glorious, isn't it?" He settled back against the chair, his hands linked behind his head. "Not only are we selling product, we're getting a wealth of free advertising. A businessman's dream," he chortled. "And the tabloid's ignored our suit so far, but the media's had a heyday with it. Everything's working out just like it's s'posed to."

"Suit?" Kelsy frowned, looking to each of the men around her.

"Elsethe Industries has slapped *The Noisemaker* with a three-million-dollar lawsuit," Gene explained.

"A lawsuit?"

"For the typical stuff. Slander, libel, defamation of character . . ." Gene raised his hands as if he'd had no other alternative, and didn't it make him ecstatically happy.

Cobb snickered and got to his feet, mashing the end of his cigar between his teeth. Marston pushed back from the table, still grinning. "See you guys in the morning," he said, following Cobb out the door.

But Kelsy sat immobilized in her chair. "I don't get it," she said finally. "Defamation of character? Can that apply to an industry?"

"Under the circumstances, Kelsy," Tate said, "we're particularly concerned with how the public views you."

"So?"

"So," Gene explained, "you're co-petitioner in the suit."

"I'm what?" Stricken with surprise, she half rose from the chair, then plopped back down again. Blood yammered through her veins. "I don't go around suing people."

"On behalf of Elsethe Industries—"

"Elsethe Industries? This is Kelsy Williams talking. I don't go slapping indiscriminate lawsuits around!"

"This is certainly not indiscriminate," Gene replied.

"But I didn't authorize any such thing!"

"In your best interests—"

"I decide my best interests," she emphasized, looking to Tate for support. "We both know that what they printed was an outright lie. But I don't want my name dragged through the court system. Why, it could end up a household word."

"It already is."

Kelsy spluttered, irked by Tate's calm response.

"I just want to lead a nice, normal little life. I'll pose for pictures, kiss babies, sell a little shampoo. But I never counted on being in the middle of a media war, my name bandied about on the six-o'clock news because someone questions the legitimacy of my red hair. This is ridiculous! A three-million-dollar lawsuit because *The Noisemaker* thinks I'm something less than a redhead?"

"We're going to show them you're a lot more than a redhead, girl. We're going to show them you're a redhead with conviction, principles. We're going to show them we don't allow anyone to take punches at you or our product and get away with it."

"He's right, Kelsy," Tate said quietly, pinning her with his solid gaze. "We have to do this. It protects us all in the long run. It puts you in a good light, and it ultimately defends the reputation of the company."

"You knew about this all along, didn't you?" she said, pointing a finger at Tate's broad chest, the chest on which she'd laid her head only hours ago.

"I assumed this would be the end result, yes."

"And you never mentioned it?" Dismay crept into her voice. He'd probably known about it all along, yet hadn't told her. She felt . . . deceived, betrayed.

"I didn't know it would make a difference," he shot back, his voice rising.

217

"Well, it does! You should have told me." She paused, then went on angrily, "Why don't the two of you just go off and file your little lawsuits and leave me out of it? I didn't give anyone permission to bring me into this nightmare. I'm going to come off looking like a temperamental, self-centered spotlight chaser."

Gene sighed, leaning like a referee between two prizefighters. "Would you two kids stop your bickering?"

Kelsy and Tate sank back in their chairs and glared at one another.

"Now this is the way it is. Yes, lawsuits are distasteful. No, considering there's so much at stake, we can't get around them. I'm sorry, Kelsy, but it's written in the contract. Elsethe Industries has the inherent right to do everything within its power to protect the product, as well as your image. If we have to force a lawsuit to do it, then that's what we're going to do. Personally I don't think this is going to go very far. But until we know, everyone's going to attend to his or her business—and they're going to leave the legal ramifications to the legal department. Now," he said, looking at each of them, "let's part friends."

Her life was a mess. She was riding a wave to stardom, carrying a wallet stuffed with traveler's checks and a suitcase full of new clothes. She had her personal hairdresser and makeup artist.

Yet, her sister was annoyed with her, she was exhausted, and she was in the middle of a lawsuit she didn't even sanction. Worse, when she'd left Tate at the elevators, they were both tight-lipped and stone-faced, and barely able to manage a good night to each other.

It had been a rotten way to get back to filming, and she hadn't slept much because of it. But there'd been no way to stop the 5 a.m. wake-up call. The first horrible glance in the mirror gave her half a notion to call the local paper and say, "You want to get a real photo of the ravages of being a redheaded superstar? Come on over and I'll give you an exclusive interview."

If nothing else, it was a nice fantasy while she brushed her teeth.

But she'd stoically carried on until she got to the set and saw Tate. Or, rather, didn't see Tate.

He was cool, aloof, and managed to look busy enough to avoid her. That hurt more than anything. She may have still been seething over the lawsuit, but she was smart enough to know it wasn't worth jeopardizing what they'd discovered.

She loved her job, she loved the changes it demanded. Sure, the tour had been difficult, even arduous, but she'd seen more in two weeks than she'd seen in a lifetime. She remembered frilly-dressed babies whose only hair was a bit of downy fuzz and whose mothers pleaded, "Don't you see that touch of red in her hair? I do think she's going to be a redhead." She'd learned how hospitable the Texans were, how sturdy and frugal the Nebraskans were. She'd learned Chicago truly was the windy city, and how the St. Louis arch looked like a manmade rainbow. It had been brief, it had been beautiful, and she wouldn't have changed it for the world.

She even loved getting up at an ungodly hour in the morning, looking like a sad sack of pulpy leftovers while Bruce and Jean worked their artistry on her. Why, she loved everyone she worked with. Jean was the listener. She knew everyone's secrets and, if she trusted you, she shared them with you. From Bruce you could expect the unexpected. Gene was boisterous and fun, and all business. Cobb was a real character. Marston was the neutralizing force that constantly worked for harmony. And then there was Tate.

Tate. Tate, who was always on top of things. Tate, who was always dressed right for the occasion. Tate, who smiled and made the world swoon. Tate, whose determination overshadowed his good nature and good will. Tate, who held babies while their mothers purchased Redheads Only shampoo. Tate, who poured champagne while sitting in a heart-shaped hot tub . . .

In the greater scheme of things, she cared about Tate. Admitting it diminished her enthusiasm for the filming, making her feel as if she were starting a new project with unfinished business still hanging over her head. She didn't want to fight with him; she wanted to resolve their differences.

But over and over again, the same few words kept repeating themselves in her head. The ones she'd said to him last night, the ones he had no answer to. The ones that had driven a wedge between them.

You should have told me.

But he hadn't, and in some respects that single neglectful act was more demoralizing than the lawsuit itself. Had it been intentional or an oversight? Would it make a difference if she'd known?

If she appeared quiet on the set, it was because the conflict over the matter was raging inside her. If she was ambivalent about the new colors Jean tried on her eyes, it was because the change like the modelling industry she'd become involved in appeared only temporary. If she snapped at Bruce, it was, she told herself, because he probably deserved it.

"My, aren't we getting testy?" he said, slapping the top back on the can of hairspray.

"I'm getting tired of it always getting in my eyes. You seem to forget I have a face under here."

He looked unruffled. "Nobody's supposed to notice it. They're supposed to be looking at your hair."

"Fine," she answered sweetly, pulling the cape

off her shoulders and dropping it in his hands. "When my eyelashes are glued shut and I can't even see the camera, let alone smile into it, I'll refer Cobb to you."

Kelsy marched onto the cordoned-off set ready to do business. She matter-of-factly went over the blocking with Cobb, studied her half-dozen words, and adjusted the high-thigh cut of her new lime green swimsuit. Then she stretched out on a deep-dyed beach towel next to Daniel Marston.

No one said a word about her hair, but it took fifteen minutes for them to get the towel right. If the wind wasn't turning over a corner, it puckered from the sand or rippled unappealingly from their body impressions. Cobb was incensed that the only contrary response on his set came from an inanimate object.

Kelsy settled the matter by spilling a few grains of sand on the corners and moving with the lithe ease of a jungle cat. Cobb was eternally grateful; the camera was placated. Tate was inwardly apoplectic with jealousy.

The extras they had hired, two long-legged, dark-haired beauties who were chosen for the way they filled out scanty swimsuits, were directed to walk a carefully blocked path within Marston's line of vision. While Marston and Kelsy lay on the towel the two extras experimented with every form of ambulatory movement known to man.

They strolled.

They sauntered.

They pranced.

At any rate, it was a disaster, and Cobb called a halt before they could hit their stride and everyone forgot what the focus of the commercial really was. With Marston still snickering beside her, it wasn't all that difficult to shoot the next scene—that of Kelsy jabbing him in the ribs.

She got in a good three pokes before Cobb was satisfied. They did two more shots just to give themselves some options. Kelsy felt vindicated.

Unfortunately, Marston's scripted reply to Kelsy's elbow-poking—"Not to worry, I've got eyes for Redheads Only"—changed slightly each time he said it. From teasing to adoring. From gentle to boyish. When he hit a combination of all four, Cobb called it a wrap.

"Not to worry, I've got eyes for Redheads Only," Marston repeated, his voice an outrageous falsetto as he mimicked his own performance.

Kelsy, who had been on and off a towel for more than six hours, looked up and grinned, only to see Tate holding open a cover-up for her. "Me, too," he mouthed when she struggled to her feet.

Something inside her crumbled; she ignored Marston's antics and moved toward Tate. An apologetic smile quirked his face when he extended the cover-up. She half-turned, her mind a swirl of emotion, her fists jabbing for the sleeves. When he smoothed the silk over her shoulders, turning her back to overlap the front and possessively tie the belt, he winked, and it had a strange uncertain quality. At that moment he'd never looked more vulnerable, and she knew instantly he'd been worried she'd rebuff him.

Taking a deep breath, he paused to fluff the ends of her hair and tuck a finger inside and against her neck to free a curl. "Better?"

"Relieved, actually," she said, hoping he caught her dual meaning.

He led her away to meet a few of the fans congregating outside the roped-off area. He was beside her when she signed autographs, and when she saw his lips lift at one of her outlandish responses to a question, she knew their differences were behind them.

Chapter Thirteen

Devon shed her businesslike demeanor the moment she touched ground in Hawaii. Instead of taking a hard, critical glance at everything she saw, she tittered and beamed. If Kelsy hadn't known better, she'd have thought her sister was a magnificent cross between a Cheshire cat and a setting hen.

"This is the sister who antagonizes you?" Tate whispered as Devon made small talk and gazed over her pineapple drink at Marston.

"The plane trip must have thrust her into a personality warp. I've never seen her so mellow."

He smiled, sliding a hand beneath the table to her knee and giving it a small possessive squeeze. "You mean she's not nearly as laid-back as her sister?"

"Laid-back? Should I read a little more into that?"

His hand slid higher, barely skimming beneath the hem of her skirt. "Smart woman."

They'd started to come together, like the private times between man and woman called for. It was natural and age old, as if they needed to explore the parameters of what intrigued them about one another. She wanted to watch the way his eyes twinkled, his left eye dropping closed a tad farther than the right; he wanted to watch her twirl a lock of her hair, maybe just so he could have an excuse—saving it from her unconscious habit—to thread his own fingers through it.

But Marston interrupted them, pulling them apart with a question. Had they been to the Polynesian Cultural Center yet? No, but who cared? they silently said to themselves, their minds elsewhere.

Yet the four of them discussed all the mundane aspects of living and traveling and working in the islands. Some of it was tinged with humor; some simply a way to extend the conversation a little further into the evening. Eventually Tate picked up Kelsy's hand, displaying it like a trophy.

"I've got to get this little lady to her room. No long nights for her. She's got a shoot in the morning, and we don't want any circles under her eyes."

Both Kelsy and Tate stood at the same time. Devon looked ecstatic; apparently this was the moment she'd been hoping for. "Already?" she asked, feigning disappointment. "I'd hoped we could dance, the music is so good tonight. And it is my first night here." She cast a significant look at the teacup-sized dance floor where several couples swayed together, none of whom were in sync with the music but unabashedly in sync with each other.

Marston visibly withered, but being the master of congeniality that he was, he offered Devon his arm. "Let me supervise your first night of fun in Hawaii," he said. "No one worries about the bags under my eyes."

Devon glowed, linking her arm through his. "We'll see you two party poopers later," she said over her shoulder as Marston led her away.

Tate and Kelsy tarried for a moment, watching from a distance. Devon and Marston didn't dance in the conventional manner, hand to shoulder, hand to waist. Instead Devon clung to his shoulders, leaving Marston no choice but to loop his hands behind her back and pull her close.

"You sure it's safe to turn our backs on this?" Tate asked.

Kelsy rolled her eyes. "Devon usually goes after what she wants. Of course," she added dryly, "I've never seen her quite this ambitious before. And certainly not with a human target."

Tate quirked a brow at her, the rugged planes of his face dissolving into tenderness. "You know," he reminded her, "we've never been on a dance floor together."

"I thought about that."

"Oh?"

"But I thought I'd rather have you all to my-self the first time we dance, without all the on-lookers, without all the speculation."

"It can be arranged. I like private parties."

Someone pounded on the door to Kelsy's room like a battering ram. The room shook, pictures bounced against the wall, and Kelsy shot out of bed, expecting a volcanic eruption.

Fumbling in the semi-darkness for her robe, she stumbled to the door, called, "Who is it?" and heard Devon snap, "It's me! Open up!"

Kelsy obliged and was amazed to see her sister's intensely furious expression. Kelsy had seen that look before, but only twice. Once when she'd painted the cat green for St. Patrick's Day and another time when Devon's high-school sweetheart had been two-timing her.

Kelsy winced, knowing she was in trouble. She moved back to her bed and sat on the edge, twisting her hands. "What is it Devon? What's wrong?"

"You have to ask?" Devon swooped down, playing it to the hilt, her mouth emphasizing each word with mock disbelief. "You mean you don't know?"

Kelsy bristled. "Did he put the make on you?"

"Hah!"

"Hah? What hah?"

"Hah, I should be so lucky." Devon kicked a

pair of Kelsy's new shoes out of the way and threw herself into the room's only overstuffed chair. "Don't you ever—do you hear me?—don't you ever do me any more favors and fix me up with some hunk who has the whole world swooning at his feet."

"What?"

"Don't ever do me any more favors," Devon repeated, spitting the words through clenched teeth. "Because I just humiliated myself, that's why."

Kelsy stared at her, automatically drawing the lapels of her robe closer. "What happened?"

"Well, I sure decided to let my inhibitions fly, that's what. I figured, why not have a good time on this vacation? I deserved it—"

"Devon, what happened?"

"I invited Marston to my room."

"You what?"

"For a last drink. To see that crazy little ruffles and lace muumuu I picked up in that specialty shop near the beach."

"And?"

"And? And he turned me down, that's what." Devon gulped and looked as if she were going to burst into tears, her eyes as bulging and bloodshot as a dachshund's. "He kept making excuses, and then he finally said, and I quote, 'Not many people know this, but if anyone's going to be wearing ruffles and lace it's going to be me.'"

Kelsy's jaw couldn't have fallen farther, as the

meaning of Devon's words slowly dawned on her. So that was why she'd always felt that inexplicable lack of chemistry . . .

"He's gay," Devon muttered. "Gay. How could you fix me up with someone like that and let me embarrass myself? I feel like a fool. An absolute fool. A little dimwit from Middle-America who can't even figure out which way the wind blows."

"I . . . he . . . nobody'd ever—" Kelsy stammered over a dozen plausible theories, but none she could put into words. Finally she breathed, "Nobody'd ever guess."

"And that's just the way he wants it. He told me he figured I was a nice enough girl to keep his secret. He said it could threaten his career, it could—"

"Then why'd he tell you at all?"

Devon sank a little deeper in the chair. "Maybe because I was being a little . . . persuasive."

Kelsy knew what that meant. Devon was being insistent and aggressive, as only she knew how to be. Good Lord, the woman would make a great city manager. If she could make a confirmed gay come out of the closet and reveal his secret, she could work wonders with the pigheaded bureaucracy of city government.

Nobody said anything for a few minutes. Finally Kelsy went to the compact refrigerator and got out two pint cartons of orange juice. She offered one to Devon and they both drank right

230

out of the cartons. It was a far cry from the sparkling stemmed goblets and pineapple-skewered drinks they'd had earlier in the evening.

Devon looked thoroughly dejected when she pulled the carton from her lips. "I think I want to go home."

"Oh, come on. This is a vacation. You can't give up on it so easily." Devon just sat there flipping the orange juice spout open and shut. "Marston's a good guy. Really. I'm sure he wouldn't want you to feel like this. But you can't make him into something he isn't."

Devon's eyes lifted sorrowfully. "Like I've been trying to make you into something you aren't?"

Perplexed, Kelsy sat on the end of the rumpled bed opposite her sister, their knees almost bumping.

"There's always been something in you, Kels. Something special, something unique or different or whatever you want to call it. I never could control it even though I tried. Maybe that's why I've always been so hard on you, always so determined to have my own way where you're involved. But that part that's special, it always kept shining through. Redheads Only saw it. And they bought it."

"Come on. All they bought was some red hair."

"You've got a whole country falling in love with you, and the crazy thing is, you don't even know it."

231

"Oh, Devon . . ." Kelsy helplessly lifted her hand to object, making the juice dribble over the lip of the carton and onto her fingers. She wiped it off on the sheets and thanked God for room service, unprepared for how much Devon's next statement was going to shake her.

"Tate's seeing it, too. He doesn't realize it yet, but it's going to change his life."

Kelsy should have been pleased — she'd just gotten the recognition, the endorsement she'd always craved from her big sister. Instead, she was miserable, and if anyone ever felt foolish, it was Kelsy.

She'd never had any idea how Devon had really felt all those years growing up together. She'd always known Devon was an achiever, but she'd never guessed it was because Devon felt the need to outshine her baby sister.

They'd talked deep into the night, contrasting moments of wrenching empathy with the admission they had never really known how the other felt. Together they figured they'd taken it all too lightly, dismissing their petty squabbles and skipping over their good times too easily, without ever looking deeper. It troubled her, too, to think Devon might have manipulated the coffee-shop arrangement in order to make herself, in the final outcome, more successful, more worldly.

Sure, the bottom line was they'd always looked out for each other. They'd thought they were close. But amicably dividing up the dirty-dish detail didn't equal revealing what was hidden in their hearts.

Their confrontation spurred them into moving to a more honest relationship. But not without a price. Kelsy grieved that things weren't the way she'd always thought them and was up half the night, considering all the aspects of her rapidly changing life. If anyone could be accused of looking at the world through rose-colored glasses, she figured she was a prime candidate.

Her role within the campaign suddenly loomed too large. Larger than any farfetched idea she'd ever conceived. She'd taken the job as a lark and was now stymied, properly stymied, over how much impact a thirty-second commercial and still shots in a few women's magazines could make in her life. Moreover, she experienced a tremendous sense of responsibility, one she hadn't taken that seriously before.

The entire scenario, as well as the questions that nagged her, was top-heavy and unwieldy, almost too great a weight to bear. This was supposed to be a romp, a fun time through the better dress shops, in front of a few cameras, and with a few free trips thrown in. No one ever told her that fame was going to turn her psyche inside out and tromp all over the remains.

Why, there was a vast throng of strangers who

knew her name, who knew what she liked for breakfast, who knew she was discovered in the aisle of a discount store. But she knew nothing about them, not really. It left a void in the pit of her stomach, as if she was letting down her end of the bargain. Could she be responsible enough to do the right thing on their behalf, these unknown "friends," and put her best foot forward in the best interests of the campaign?

Worse, people she'd known all her life—even her sister—looked at her through new eyes, as if her role had changed her and what she'd become. Sure, she'd added a little more finesse to her persona. She could call room service with a flourish, smile until her lips felt like a plaster cast, and wear makeup that withstood hot lights and grueling days—but it didn't really make her any different. Not on the inside.

But no one knew that, did they? They all expected more from her. More maturity, more professionalism, more money, and more of a class act—one she wasn't sure she could continue to pull off. Certainly not indefinitely. And privacy? It was out the door. Jean knew which of her eyebrows needed to be plucked more generously than the other; Bruce knew exactly how to coax the cowlick near her temple into submission; Tate even knew what she wore to bed. The latter, of course, not being so bad, unless you considered the boy who delivered room service gawking each time she was wearing it when Tate was there to share breakfast.

She thought about Tate, too, wondering if he was simply enamored with the image she projected, or if his feelings were genuine. After the unexpected confrontation with Devon, she didn't know about anything anymore. Reminded of his affair with Zadora Kane, she almost physically recoiled. What if this was just another fling with a flash-in-the-pan model? What if she were putting more into this than he could return?

It wasn't hard to figure he was torn over the same things. Yet she knew he was capable of trying again, and not just because she was the Redheads model, but because she had touched him on a level more profound than that of a common employee of Elsethe Industries.

She was definitely feeling brittle and worn-out when Tate stopped by early the next morning to escort her to the shoot. He fixed himself a cup of coffee, waiting while she slipped into skimmers and chose a matching pair of earrings for her outfit. Now that people were gathering near the filming location, she couldn't risk being seen in anything less than flattering. When they'd first started filming, she'd simply pulled on a pair of jeans and a comfortable top, knowing wardrobe would provide her with the appropriate clothes on the set. But those days, like everything else, were over.

Fiddling with the earring back, she glimpsed

Tate from the corner of her eye. He was sipping the coffee and watching her get ready. He seemed to like watching her this way. Quietly, unobtrusively, from the sidelines, just like when they were filming.

"I had quite a night last night," she said, picking up the other earring, knowing she had to talk to him, yet making a conscious choice not to tell him about Marston. Not yet, anyway. She needed time to think about it.

"Oh?"

"Devon came over to unwind after they decided to call it a night. We were up, talking late into the night."

He arched a brow at her. "You know you really need your sleep for this filming thing. It wouldn't have hurt for you to send her back to her room."

She finger-combed the ends of her hair loosely about her ears so the glow of the earrings would show. "The little sister doesn't get to do that, don't you know?" She waited for him to smile. Knowing he would. "We talked about a lot of stuff. She's pretty unhappy about the coffee shop. I don't think she realized how much work it really was for me. And she was a bit shocked that this whole campaign has moved so quickly. She said it blew her away to see my face surface for ten seconds during Murphy Brown."

"She can join the ranks. It blew us all away."

"She was also a little upset to learn Elsethe Industries is pursuing that lawsuit." His eyes closed to slits, and his lips tightened, but he remained silent, merely setting his cup aside and opening the door for her, expecting her to be ready. Grabbing her carryall, she walked past him and into the hall. "But she understands why, maybe more than I do. Still, it's made me do a lot of thinking. About how I always end up in the middle."

He merely jammed his hands in his pockets and walked with his head down, as if the nap of the hotel carpet held tremendous interest. If Kelsy hadn't known better, she'd have thought he was looking for loose change. But knowing Tate, she knew it was his way of listening, of considering. They were halfway down the hall when Kelsy offered him the insight that turned his head.

"I just don't know about this campaign, Tate. See, I had a wicked night last night. It was good to be honest with Devon. I know it brought us a lot closer. But it was hard to look at what's happening to me. This campaign's turning my life upside down. Nothing's the same anymore. Things are changing between me and my sister, things are changing within me. Nobody sees me as the person I was, now it's the person — or the persona — I am. Even this lawsuit with *The Noisemaker* has me scared silly. I don't know how I ever found myself in the middle of such a thing."

"Simple," he said, steering her away from the elevators and into the gardenlike setting outside the hotel. "Consider it self-defense on your part."

"But I feel like I've lost control of my life. Like I signed it away the same day I signed the contract with Redheads Only."

"You know the lawsuit is designed to protect you and to protect Elsethe Industries. It's being done for no other reason. Certainly not the money. We'd rather have a marketable product with a flawless reputation."

"I know." She leaned into his arm, still not looking convinced.

"As far as your sister is concerned, I think she's old enough to take care of herself." Stopping beneath a flowering tree, he lazily tipped a branch down to tickle her nose. "You guys made a deal about the coffee shop, just like you made with Redheads. But you know how it is with business—there're always ways to renegotiate."

She knew she shouldn't do it, but she plucked a tiny blossom from the branch and studied it, tracing the fragile petals. "I told her I wasn't very happy about the lawsuit."

"You know, Kels, you've had a lot of over-whelming things happen in your life lately. I hope you won't let them sway you from pursuing this thing, even though it's all a little rocky now."

She said nothing, sandwiching the tiny blossom within his shirt pocket, making it look like a miniature boutonniere. It reminded her of the first time she'd seen him, wearing a stylish wide-lapeled suit and sporting a pocket square. There was something gratifying about his leaving the tiny blossom in place.

"When I found out you were working at a coffee shop to help your sister get her master's, I could hardly believe it. That's a big commitment. One that few little sisters would undertake. This is your opportunity, Kels. Don't be afraid to take it. It's lying right there at your fingertips, just waiting to take off. Don't turn your back on a satisfying professional life because things have temporarily shot out of control."

"They really have, you know," she said. "It wasn't supposed to turn out like this." Beseeching him to understand, her emerald eyes grew troubled. "This was supposed to be a fling. I was going to work hard, put in my time, and hope, like the rest of you, that Redheads would be successful. No one ever told me it would swallow up my life."

"It's because you're so sweet," he gently teased. "It's because you're so sweet the whole world just wants to swallow you up and spit you back out for a return engagement." His lips moved closer to her own, beckoning. "Just like me."

She put her hand on his chest to stop him just as he lowered his head for a kiss. "I told her to do what she wanted about the coffee shop. I told her that, no matter what, Redheads comes first." He inched lower. "It's the same with the lawsuit," she whispered. "No matter what, you can count on me to ride this thing out."

Devon's departure from Hawaii was bittersweet. Tate drove them to the airport, standing a discreet distance away as the two sisters said their goodbyes. The hug Devon offered made Kelsy realize that theirs was more than a temporary parting; it was a way of saying that their lives had become divergent, but that she accepted and respected Kelsy's venture into a new, untried world.

They'd had a second chat the previous night, and Devon confided she found it hard to believe her little sister was growing up. Yet after observing Kelsy as she worked each day, she realized Redheads Only had given her a new level of sophistication. That awareness prompted Devon to promise she'd try her darnedest to give Kelsy the independence she deserved, too. No more fuming over missed phone calls or tedious complaints about the coffee shop, she declared.

"I suppose now I'll have to send my redheaded sister a pair of dark sunglasses for her birthday," she said, her touch still lingering on Kelsy's shoulders.

"Save your money. We've only got one more

commercial to do in Hawaii, then we're off for some other stuff."

"I wasn't thinking about protecting your eyesight and saving you wrinkles. I was thinking more along the lines of a disguise to keep your adoring public at bay." Devon tilted her head toward the stares they had already drawn.

"Don't worry about that. It comes with the territory."

Devon nodded, giving her a last squeeze before slipping a surreptitious glance toward Tate. "And what about him? Does he come with the territory, too?"

Kelsy thought about the man who made her heart dance and her blood grow impatient. Even when he was standing across a crowded airport terminal, she felt his presence. Just knowing he was nearby was a comfort, like the knowledge that he'd always be there for her, whether they agreed on how to do a shoot or whether they disagreed on how much jewelry she should wear during a public appearance. It didn't matter whether the differences between them were great or small; it only mattered that they were heading in the same direction.

Taking a deep breath, she mustered a sly, conspiratorial smile. "Under the circumstances, I like to consider him part of a joint account — one that goes hand in hand with my career."

Chapter Fourteen

She'd planned a quiet evening, so it really didn't matter if she spent it in her room or in Gene's suite. His family was terrific, and his wife, Ann, an angel. Kelsy could see why Gene adored her. His pride was Tommy, an eleven-year-old charmer who did nothing but talk of sports; his joy was Sherry, a dainty four-year-old who pranced on the hotel balcony in leotard and tap shoes.

Tom and Sherry were two very good reasons to offer to fill in as a baby-sitter when Gene's scheduled sitter canceled and his plans for a last night out with his wife looked squashed. It didn't seem like a very rough assignment anyway. Tommy had already tuned in to a basketball game and Sherry was spending hours fussing with the little hairdressing kit Tate had given her. In the first thirty minutes, she'd already snapped dozens of barrettes into Kelsy's hair, creating every style imaginable.

"How about if I stretch out and you work your

magic?" Kelsy suggested, sliding down on the couch with her hair trickling over the arm. "Fix me up pretty while I rest a minute, okay?"

"Okay. It'll be a surprise."

"Great," Kelsy agreed, feeling another barrette slide into place near her temple as the drone of the television lulled her. It had been a long day and she wanted to rest as much as possible for the final commercial. While she wasn't sure what Tate had planned for her after that, she was looking forward to the change. No matter how successful the shoot had been, and how sad it would be to leave the crew, she was ready to move on.

The click-clack of barrettes and the constant movement of little fingers in her hair made her drowsy. At one point the whispery slide of kid's scissors near her ear made her eyes flutter open, but just barely. She yawned and, settling herself more comfortably on the couch, tried to remember what she'd been dreaming about. She must have lain there for another fifteen minutes or so, dozing while Sherry fiddled with her hair.

Finally, squinting at the clock, Kelsy realized she'd slept half an hour past Sherry's bedtime. Tommy hadn't changed position, still intent on the game. "Come on, pumpkin," she said, groggily rolling up to a sitting position and rubbing her eyes, "time to get you in bed."

The hairdressing kit was all neatly put away and laid aside. Good, she thought, one less thing for her to clean up. But Sherry surprised her even more when she agreeably lifted her arms and slipped into the nightwear Ann had laid out.

Sherry was tucked into bed and Kelsy was back on the couch flipping through a magazine in record time. Why hadn't kids been this congenial when she'd been baby-sitting in high school?

It was early, only ten, when Gene and Ann came back, flushed from a few drinks. Gene swayed lightly on his feet, humming a fifties tune and impressing the women with a few tricky dance moves when Ann, laughing at her husband's antics, rolled her eyes at Kelsy. Then she stopped cold.

"Oh, my Lord!" she said. "What on earth happened to your hair?"

"What?" Kelsy ran a hand over the top of her head, expecting to find a few misplaced barrettes.

Gene stopped moving and stared at her in horror, his eyes focusing squarely on a spot above her ear. "Call Tate," he told Ann, "Tell him to get his butt over here right now."

"Oh, my goodness. She really—" Ann whapped a hand over her mouth as if to stop herself from saying more.

Kelsy whirled to the mirror, and then she saw it—the gaping hole near her temple. The spot where four inches of hair had been hacked away. The hair that had been nurtured and mollycoddled, shampooed and conditioned, layered and set. A few good snips from a pair of snubbed-nosed scissors had gouged a hole in Bruce's handiwork and done irreparable damage to the Redheads Only campaign.

Kelsy knew the yelling was about to begin, and, everything considered, guessed all the fingers would be pointing at her.

Tate stared at her with eyes like burning coals. Otherwise he was devoid of color—unless you wanted to call ashen a skin tone. "What were you doing?" he demanded.

"Sherry was putting barrettes in my hair, and I . . ." Kelsy rightly surmised this was going to be a long, painful night. "I fell asleep. I never expected her to—" she gulped "—to do some creative trimming."

Tate slapped a hand on the table, not even flinching at the pain. But Gene bellowed. He bellowed so loud Kelsy feared someone would summon hotel security. Tate turned to the open patio doors and slammed them shut.

"What the hell are you coming down on Kelsy for, Alexander? What were you thinking of, anyway. Giving my kid something like that? Don't you know what a stupid gift that was?"

"Me?" Tate pivoted like an incensed basketball player. "If you know so much, then why'd you let her have it in the first place?"

Gene's jowls puffed up and he looked like a lion ready to pounce. "You know what your trouble is?" he shouted, shaking a clenched paw. "You just need a few kids of your own and then you wouldn't be asking such dumb questions."

Tate stared at him as if the question was so far

off the beam it really hadn't registered. "Right," he said. "That's just what I need right now. One more monkey wrench in the works."

Kelsy felt bad for both men. But, strangely, neither of them blamed her. Tate was truly tormented over her hair. Gene was panic-stricken, his gut reaction inciting him to blame someone or something else. And besides, Tate was the only other person in the room. Ann had gone into the children's bedroom.

Still, everything they pitched at one another was the stuff of silly, rhetorical arguments. It was ridiculous, the kind of fluff that was laughable, if you thought about it. But every shot drew another volley of accusations, and finally Kelsy had had enough and stepped between.

"Are you two finished?" she calmly asked, picking up a handful of macadamia nuts and popping one in her mouth. The chewing noise she made echoed in stunned silence. For a moment she wondered if they'd forgotten all about her. "The damage is done. Now it's time to figure out what to do." Dumping the nuts back in the dish, she brushed the crumbs from her hands and tried a teasing smile before lifting the remaining locks at the side of her head to her temple. "Personally, I thought you guys could come up with something creative. Like pulling my hair back with a barrette . . ."

"Don't even mention barrettes," Tate hissed.

"Or putting a hat on me."

"We're trying to show off your hair, not hide it!"

Gene snapped.

"Or maybe a new camera angle, like we did after the surfboarding thing? After all, it seems the one thing you're both forgetting is that this is only temporary. My hair will grow back."

Tate grumbled; Gene growled. But they looked back at her with a heightened degree of speculation. Then their gazes collided, the blinders dropped into place, and they glared. She wished the shorn locks of her hair hadn't been discovered in the wastebasket and squarely placed on the table between them. The reminder was too painful.

"I think we ought to think about this," Tate muttered.

"Yeah," Gene grudgingly concurred. "Let's sleep on it."

But the decision about what to do with her hair took more than a night's sleep. Filming was suspended and the resumption repeatedly pushed back. The waiting made everyone restless. Finally, Kelsy was summoned to a brainstorming session.

Bruce, looking put-upon, was sitting in the center of the room, making it appear he was holding court. He didn't choose to examine her hair up close, but instead studied it from a distance. Kelsy found his imperious manner more threatening than Gene's harrumphing.

"Okay," Tate began, "we're at a stand-off, and we decided, under the circumstances, to let everybody have their say."

"Concerning her hair or anything in general?" Bruce dryly inquired. "As far as I'm concerned, every time I look at it I think I'm having an extended nightmare."

Tate didn't bother to address that. "We've talked about canceling this commercial altogether. We're planning to stagger the release dates, anyway, so it can be done later. But, obviously, Elsethe wants to avoid the added expense of recalling the crew."

Cobb pulled a cigar from his pocket and started unwrapping it. "I think I can shoot around it. But we're not going to get the same effect as we'd originally intended. If we put a floral headpiece on her, then it's going to change how Marston approaches her. Obviously no man's going to give her a hug if he's got baby's breath waiting to stick him in the eye. And, hell, that kind of crud's so goddamned awkward to film. It'll fall off. It'll make her look like she's got shrubbery sticking out the side of her head, and Marston'll be trying to work around it. Hell, I can give you a dozen reasons to give up on the headpiece."

"But you can film around her hair?" Tate asked.

"Sure."

"I really think I could manage with the headpiece," Marston quietly argued, for the first time sounding almost petulant about his abilities before the camera.

"No, I want the audience to figure it out," Gene said, doodling on a piece of paper while he listened. "That was the whole point of these commercials, audience reaction and involvement. I

248

don't want it spelled it out for them."

Tate studied Kelsy and the plan was beginning to brew in his head before he ever thought it out. "What can you do with her hair, Bruce?"

"Considering what's left of it?" His lips flattened out as if they'd been pinched together. Pushing back from the table, he allowed the chair to totter on its two back legs. "Considering we're discussing the chain-saw massacre, not a whole helluva lot. There's not enough left to blend in. I'd have to get rid of the length all around to make it look right. Otherwise we'll end up with a waterfall effect, something that's going to make your audience wonder if she didn't get half of it caught in a fan."

"So?" Tate prodded.

"So the best I can do is cut it. Drastically. Over the ears and cropped at the back of the neck."

Tate pitched a glance at Kelsy just as her horror-stricken eyes locked with Marston's. Something wrenched inside him. She should've looked at *him* like that. He remembered all the times Marston's hand had twined in her hair, all the takes they'd done of his pinky wrapped in a soft, spiraling tendril. It made the bile rise from his belly; it made him want to gag. He'd seen just about enough of Marston's hands in her hair. Even before this tragedy it had chafed at him.

"It's got to stay soft," Gene warned, looking up from his paper.

"It will."

Tate rapped his knuckles on the table, and the

effect was like a gavel in a courtroom. Either that, or a death knell. "Done. We'll dismiss the crew and postpone the shoot till tomorrow. That gives you this afternoon to do your magic, Bruce."

"Wait a minute," Kelsy implored, her hand catching Tate's sleeve. "Don't I have anything to say about this?"

"Guess not." His sleeve slipped through her fingers when he slapped his portfolio shut.

"You think you're cutting my hair?"

"It's our best alternative."

"Not on your life," she said vehemently, standing her ground and half rising out of the chair. "I'm not going under the blade for the second time in twenty-four hours."

"Kelsy. You said it yourself — your hair's going to grow back." Secretly, he was content he held the cards this time. His ulterior motive, the petty jealousy he wouldn't admit, could be resolved with a simple haircut.

"It won't work."

"She may be right. The commercial's focus is on the changing relationship of our redhead and her honey," Gene theorized, oblivious to Tate's scowl at his choice of words. "We're not into promoting the hairstyle-of-the-month. Some drastic off-the-wall haircut could make her look like a Martian. Not the image we've presented so far."

"But as the relationship matures, so would her looks," Tate argued. "Give her something more than a sexy smile, a tumble on the sand, and a head of hair a man wants to put his hands into.

250

Give her some substance, for cryin' out loud."

"That's crazy," Kelsy said. "Just because I fall in love with my leading man, I have to get my hair cut to a more practical, businesslike style? Absolutely not. That's like saying blondes have no brains."

"Well?" Bruce said drolly, propping a finger to his cheek.

"Besides," Kelsy went on, ignoring him. "The public's not going to go for that. You're messing with a good thing. The public likes the illusion you've presented thus far, and I think you're playing with fire if you go changing it on them. We're projecting the romance of a relationship, the beauty of it, and if that means something as sensuous as a knockout smile, a backdrop of surf and sand, and the touch between a man and woman, then so be it. Let them have their fantasy, too. Don't pare my hair like you're paring the top of some carrot."

Tate's hand trembled. The scene she drew bore too much resemblance to the night they'd spent on the beach together. He remembered the gentle curve above her waist and the irresistible little habit she had of standing on tiptoe to kiss him, even though she didn't need to. It always made him feel like she wanted to be closer, to be just as close as she possibly could to his heart, to his life. Dammit, he didn't want Marston to feel, or even know, those same intimate things about her.

Gene scribbled out the drawing he had been laboring over and threw the pen aside. "She's making sense. Why do we want to take a chance with a sure thing? This has been working before, why mess it up now?"

"So what're we going to do instead?" Tate charged, as ruffled and riled as a rooster.

The answer came from the most unexpected of places. But all heads swiveled when it was offered, and a thoughtful expression settled into the eyes of the men of experience. Kelsy very carefully folded her hands, resting her chin atop them, and her voice, when she spoke, commanded great calm.

"Nobody's cutting my hair," she said. "Not even Bruce. But I do have an idea. One I think's going to work."

The scene was set and she'd memorized her lines.

The filming was different in that they were actually working inside for once. Daniel had done his few seconds at her door, the knock, the wait. But blocking her opening of that door, with the bottle of Redheads Only shampoo visible in the background and beside the flowing wedding dress was a bit more difficult. Especially since she was wearing nothing more than a skimpy towel and holding a smaller one against her freshly shampooed head. Specifically blotting it against the spot where a sizable length of hair was missing.

"You're not dressed?" Marston said, appearing slightly surprised.

"No. And you're pushing your luck to see me

now."

He'd merely laughed, tugging at the towel she'd pressed to her temple, saying, "I'm the luckiest man in the world. Hey? Didn't you once tell me redheads never wear white?"

The camera angle had reverted to Kelsy as Marston lifted a corner of the towel to swipe a trickle of water from her temple. Picking up the bottle of shampoo, she'd snapped closed the cap, moved closer to him, tapping him on the chest with it and slyly commenting, "On certain *rare* occasions we make exceptions."

Everyone in the crew was ecstatic about the results. Bruce was puffed up because of the way he'd kept her hair wet and shiny and artfully arranged. Jean swore no one could ever have guessed she was missing a hunk of hair over her ear. Of course, the cameraman had done some delicate sidestepping to keep her at just the right, most attractive angle.

The hotel had been magnanimous, letting them give an autograph party in the lobby after the commercial was finished. Tourists and hotel visitors couldn't help but notice the linen-draped table that had been set up in their honor or the specially painted poster inviting the public to meet the Redheads Only stars, Kelsy Williams and Daniel Marston.

When eventually Kelsy went down to the lobby, she wore an expensive muumuu and had orchids pinned in her hair over the bare spot, and fortunately it was over the ear Hawaiian tradition decreed for single girls. Marston met her wearing a Hawaiian print shirt and a lei. They signed autographs, shook hands, and posed for pictures. But when the crowd was thickest, he drew forth a lavish lei, sensuously lowering it over her head.

When he gave her a chaste peck on both cheeks, Kelsy thought the teenyboppers in the crowd were going to swoon. She didn't doubt there was one woman present who didn't want to be in her place. She saw it in their eyes: they, too, were waiting for their knight in shining armor to sweep them off their feet. She saw it in the pinched lips of the long-married women, their lips visibly softening as they remembered younger, more carefree days. In the little girls, she saw a curious twist of the brow, as if they were wondering if that was how it really was. Was every hero really that big, really that gentle? Did every heroine always smile as if she hadn't a care in the world, and all because she'd discovered love?

The thought made her lift her eyes to Tate. At that moment she knew how it was to be a heroine and to fall hopelessly, desperately, in love with a dashing cavalier — one that was always chasing rainbows and dreams. She knew how it was to fall for a man whose ambition charged his demeanor with drive and intensity.

Yet she looked into his eyes and knew right then where he, too, wanted to be standing. She saw it in his narrowed gaze and the hungry tilt of his mouth. His feet were spread, his legs braced. His stance was one of appraisal.

It was good the public appearance was coming to a close because she ached to be whisked away and held in his arms. They needed to talk. There'd been little time for that since they'd returned from the mainland. Maybe it was time to find out where they were going; maybe it was time to explore where their relationship fit into the campaign.

She was relieved when Tate gave her the nod to make her exit. It was always difficult to detach herself from a crowd, but she was becoming more adept at it, appearing reluctant to say goodbye, pausing to chat with one more mother, bending to pat a small red head. But Marston made it even easier, his bulk guiding her through the crowd and finally between the stainless steel doors of a waiting elevator.

"The hotel's ecstatic," Gene said, beaming when the doors finally closed. "The overflow crowd went into the bar."

Marston grinned, dropping his hand from the small of her back and moving away the moment the elevator started moving.

Tate moved in, his arm possessively circling her shoulder. "Next time don't kiss her in front of a bunch of people," he said gruffly, criticism hot in his voice. "It didn't look natural. It looked contrived."

Marston reacted with surprise, every movement defensive. Then he laughed. "Are you suggesting I need an acting coach?"

"I'm just suggesting," Tate said evenly, pushing

Kelsy ahead of him as the doors opened, "that—"

"Can it, Tate," Gene boomed. "The event was a success. A couple of pecks on the cheek can't ruin it." He toddled off to his room without another word, leaving Marston and Tate, with Kelsy directly in the middle, staring at one another.

Marston frowned, his gaze skimming over the possessive hold Tate had on Kelsy before an illuminating light danced through his eyes. Tate made his rebuttal by sidling even closer to her; Marston answered by pumping up a little muscle. Even in Tate's shadow Kelsy felt dwarfed. Worse, she was anxious, and she didn't have the slightest idea how to defuse the situation.

"I knew you two were getting thick, Tate, but I didn't know it was that serious. Sorry. Look, I won't step on your toes where Kelsy's concerned, not if you don't want me to." Marston lifted his ham of a shoulder, his lips curling. "But you decide to give her up, you let me know. A man can't work that close to a woman and not know she doesn't have some possibilities worth exploring."

Tate tensed, the cords in his neck standing out, the muscles in his shoulders bunching up. With his head lowered, he looked like a bull ready to charge. At his first tentative step out of the elevator, the flutter-light motion of Kelsy's hand stopped him.

"Hey, Tate," Marston cajoled, moving out of the elevator, "this is just between us—with a compliment thrown in for the lady. Don't get hostile."

The elevator doors started to close; Tate thrust

his arm between them, stopping them. Kelsy unsuccessfully tried pulling it back, but her gesture was futile, only making him more determined, it seemed.

"Tate," she hissed, succeeding only in pulling his sleeve up his forearm, exposing his watch. "Tate. Come on!"

"Yeah?" Tate hollered out through the charging elevator doors. Like a mechanical wonder they kept ramming against him, hopelessly urging him to withdraw. "You're the real reason I held out for getting Kelsy's hair cut. We never could do a take without you sticking your fingers in it. All along I thought it looked pretty damned stupid."

Kelsy gasped and yanked harder.

Marston smirked, before sliding an assessing eye to Kelsy. She was horror-stricken, her eyes wide, her mouth pinched, as if she were swallowing a secret. But it didn't bother Marston. Instead his answer was cryptic. "You underestimate me, Tate," he said smoothly. "I know for a fact I can put on a very convincing performance. Now take good care of my leading lady and know your greatest accomplishment may be just what's hanging onto your arm tonight."

Tate was still straining for battle, his hands balled into fists, a vein popping out on his forehead. But Kelsy's insistent struggle had been numbed, and self-consciously she drew back just as the elevator closed. Uncomfortably she hugged the rail, crossing her arms, and tapping the carpeted floor.

"You didn't need to do that," she said finally, stepping out of the elevator when they'd reached their floor. "Remember the night the four of us went out for dinner?"

Tate nodded grimly and walked with her down the hall.

"I told you Devon stopped by that night? What I didn't tell you was how upset she was over her night with Marston."

"She was in seventh heaven when we left her."

"Yes, well, the bottom dropped out for a straight descent into hell. Actually, she described it as a mortifying experience."

Tate waited in confusion. It was pretty obvious Devon had enjoyed her evening with Daniel Marston. The man hadn't ruined it by telling her he had eyes for his leading lady, had he?

"Apparently Marston turned down her invitation for some—" Kelsy cleared her throat, hesitating over her choice of words "—quality time."

"Quality time?"

"I think Marston would call it 'exploring possibilities.' "

They'd reached her door, and Tate's eyes narrowed to dangerous slits. But he said nothing.

"He turned Devon down. And with a very good excuse."

Tate tensed, waiting. "What?"

"He's gay."

Tate stopped in midstride. "I don't believe it," he said flatly.

"He keeps it very quiet."

Tate looked at Kelsy and realized it was the truth. "Omigod." He slapped his forehead and sank against the door frame to her room. "I can't believe I said all that stuff to him."

"But you didn't know."

"But the way he . . ." With his head tilted back, his eyes drifted closed. "I always thought there was this . . . this thing between you."

"Sorry. There wasn't. Ever. That's what made the whole thing so unbelievable. The audience response, I mean. We've both put on an incredible acting job."

"Omigod," he said again, raking a hand through his hair. "Something like this could jeopardize the campaign, it could—"

"It could ruin his career. At least that's what he's afraid of. That's why there's the big macho act. That's why he lives a double life, and why he doesn't want anyone to know."

Tate cupped her shoulder, pulling her closer. She rested her forehead against his chin, and he traced the petals in her hair before investigating the warmth at the back of her neck. With their heads tipped together it seemed like a communion of minds.

"Leave it to you to think of the person behind the problem," he said softly. "I never would have guessed. About any of it."

"He's done a lot for this campaign."

"I know. If we're careful, and if we comply with his wishes, that won't have to change. It's just . . ." He shook his head, closing his eyes as the

259

revelation tumbled around inside his head. "I can't believe this," he finally said. "All this time. All this time seeing him look at you, touch you, talk to you, and here I was thinking . . ." He wrapped an arm about her. "This is ridiculous."

"What, Tate? What's ridiculous?"

"Here I was thinking that I didn't want you to smile like that for him. I kept thinking I didn't want you to share those crazy scripted quips with him. I didn't want to share you. Any of you. I didn't want you to poke him in the ribs like you had a handle on what made him tick. I wanted it to be me you poked. And maybe I was a little jealous because he kept making me see myself, and what I wanted for me."

"Well, then," Kelsy said, wrapping her arms about his middle and burying her head against his shoulder to avoid being recognized by a couple of passing tourists, "it looks like I'm all yours."

She was in his arms only briefly. For what he needed to say haunted him. Yet he needed to say it for her best interests as well as his own. He might have made a fool out of himself only minutes ago, but he couldn't let her go on thinking things were any different than they were before. He'd laid out the game plan months ago in Minneapolis; he couldn't change it now.

He wanted her, yes, but they still had responsibilities—and none of them included each other. They still had a long haul with Redheads, and Kelsy would soon find her work even more demanding. He couldn't ask her to give any more of herself. He couldn't afford to splinter her attention with the uncertainty of a romance.

"Not for long," he said gently, straightening and holding her at arm's length. "I've arranged for you to fly to New York to do a still shoot with one of Zadora's favorite photographers. I've got a ton of promotional work I need to arrange. The fact is, Kelsy, I don't know when we're going to see each other again. This could be our last night together."

Chapter Fifteen

Tate didn't return to his room that last night. He spent the night with her, in her room, making love and waking to the roar of the surf and the pinkish haze of dawn. They made love again that morning, but it wasn't the impassioned kind of the previous night. Instead their lovemaking, though gentle and tender, was overshadowed by the uncertainty of their future together.

He lifted her, cupping his hands beneath her arms and allowing the weight of her breasts to drag against his chest and against his palms. He suspended her thus, idolizing her, tempting her with thrusts and wet kisses. Kisses that trailed from her mouth, to the lobe of her ear, to the thrumming hollow of her throat, and back down to the translucent flesh covering her heart. They were both impatient.

Perhaps it was because they knew their separation was imminent. Perhaps it was because they knew their love needed to be tempered with a heavy dose of self-control. No matter. It was no less sweet, no less memorable. There was only frustration that the number of minutes they could hold one another was dwindling—and that there was nothing they could do to stop it.

Maybe that was what made her pull away and draw the silk wrapper over her shoulders as she gently accused him of trying to get rid of her. "I can't believe you booked me a four-o'clock flight. Why, we have to check out in a little over two hours. You *are* trying to send me on my way, aren't you?"

"Don't be silly," he said, throwing his legs over his side of the bed as he reached for his boxers.

The shorts were intriguing because they were silk and because they were emblazoned with gold coins. Somehow that was appropriate. All his clothes, including his underwear, made a statement. In a fit of antagonism she wondered what he'd do if she gave him a pair depicting cartoon characters. Considering their imminent separation, the Road Runner carried a lot of appeal. She didn't want their interlude to end but she didn't know how to stop it, either. She couldn't believe he'd made arrangements for her to fly to New York so soon.

"Silly?" she repeated, picking up her slip. "You're the one who made all the arrangements. I'm just telling you how it looks to me. If we only could've had a day to—"

"The photographer isn't at our beck and call. This works best for him. I had to take what I could get. Besides," he said, pulling on one stretched-out sock and refusing to look at her, "I have other things that need my attention, too."

Kelsy grew hot and whirled back to him, unaware that the lapels of her robe were loosened, that they buckled to her middle and sagged, exposing the curves of her body. "Then this morning was just something that needed attention?"

"It was my way of saying goodbye . . ."

Kelsy's stomach did a flip-flop, her features stiff, brittle. "Goodbye? I'm sorry, I guess this sort of thing was never in my repertoire." She wadded the expensive slip and threw it into a suitcase. "I've heard about the quickie romances that happen on a shoot, but I—"

"Kelsy?" He swung from the bed, looking bewildered and more than a little concerned, his hair standing endearingly on end. "I don't want this separation any more than you do. But we'll see each other back in Minneapolis. This is only temporary. You do know that, don't you?"

"No," she shot back, focusing on pulling her underwear out of a dresser drawer and tossing it in beside the slip. "I only know that I take your instructions and go where you send me. I only know that I've achieved instant fame, everything a girl could ever dream of, and I'm miserable."

"Come here."

"Why?"

"I thought you always followed my instructions."

Her head turned away from silky panties and lacy bras. She studied him from the corner of her eye and conceded he looked a lot less imposing wearing only one sock as he was. Maybe even kind of appealing. Vulnerable.

"Come here."

She threw two pairs of panty hose on top of the mess in her suitcase before she did his bidding. Facing him, she stiffened when his hands gripped her shoulders. She refused to cave in when he tipped his forehead against her own. "What?"

"It's hard to say goodbye."

"No kidding."

He bit his lip and sighed at her bitter response. As he pulled his head back, his eyes lighted on the ragged ends of her hair. He paused to stroke them, tucking them behind the curve of her ear. "I'm sorry, Kelsy. But it wouldn't have been any easier if we'd had six hours or six days. I can't promise you what's going to happen. But I can promise you this isn't some fly-by-night affair."

Maybe his touch lulled her somehow, luring an involuntary smile. Maybe she just didn't want to fight. Either way she softened. "Oh? Really? It felt like it. At least last night—and this morning—I thought I was soaring," she said dreamily, lifting her head for his kiss. . . .

That was the moment she remembered when she said goodbye at the airport, boarding with

Bruce and dreading the loneliness, anticipating the antagonism she'd feel at his cutting remarks and crude ways. She'd desperately wanted Tate with her, to neutralize everything, to guide her through the inevitable.

But it wasn't to be. Now she was in New York with Bruce, who was needed to work with her hair for the shoot. She'd do as much work as she could before he'd have to trim it. There was no alternative, not for the session they had in mind. Things were rolling and she was the hub of it all; she couldn't be anything less than cooperative. Not this time. There was too much to lose; there was everything to lose.

Even Tate.

If someone said, "Smile," she couldn't think about Tate or how much she missed him. She couldn't put herself first. She had to put the campaign first. Everything came before her feelings. This time, it had to. Logically, she knew that; her heart just wouldn't listen.

But Tate's infectious grin and crooked nose were with her as she posed during the shoot. Staring into blinding lights, she thought about the first luscious night he'd kissed her, making her feel as though they were castaways on a tropical island. She thought about the wacky day they'd scoured the tourist shops, each trying to outdo the other in finding the most outrageous souvenir. She wondered if she'd ever have the chance to wear the grass skirt.

Through it all, Bruce was merely fussy. But on one particular day—the day he had to cut her hair—he was a tyrant, an absolute tyrant. She couldn't wait to get away from him.

Running into Zadora in the corridor outside the photographer's, Kelsy saw the familiar face as a relief, almost forgetting that Zadora and Tate had shared more than an interest in the industry. She even forgot Jean had said the woman was self-serving and coldhearted. Just answering all of her questions about Tate and the campaign made her feel better.

"So this campaign has really taken off, hasn't it?" Zadora said, pulling a key ring with an attached vial of perfume from her pocket. She twisted off the stopper and dabbed a generous amount beneath the bangles on her wrists. A pungent, almost breathtaking scent filled the hall. "Every time I read about you in the papers I can't believe it. You really struck it rich, girl."

"We aren't so pleased with all the publicity," Kelsy admitted.

"Oh, that thing about your hair color? Not to worry. Knowing Gene, I think he'll make *The Noisemaker* pay." Zadora dropped the key ring back into her pocket. "So where you off to next?"

"We're staying in New York for a while. Bruce has contacted some salons and wants to meet the distributors."

Zadora nodded sympathetically and, after

chatting for several more minutes, dashed off. If Kelsy hadn't stepped on the tiny vial, she'd never have noticed it had fallen to the floor. The jump ring holding it had separated. Must have happened when Zadora was putting it back in her pocket. She noted the scent — Z Woman. Slipping it in her pocket, and knowing she and Zadora traveled the same path, she figured she'd return it later. The only thing troubling her about the conversation was that Zadora had been strangely silent about Tate.

Had the industry grapevine reached her? Were the stories out that Tate and Kelsy were more than just employer-employee? Or had she guessed? Kelsy decided it didn't really matter.

After spending nearly three weeks in New York with Bruce, Kelsy was ready to go home to Minneapolis. They'd toured a number of salons while Bruce touted Redheads Only and Kelsy shook hands, let people touch her hair, and smiled a lot. She got used to the smell of permanent-wave solution and the sight of zippered uniforms. But at the end of their stay, and apparently to make up for one unusually trying day, Bruce escorted her to the theater. She didn't enjoy the performance nearly as much as his efforts to apologize. It even lapped over into the flight, especially when he said, "Uh, you don't have to mention that little thing at the Pompadour to Tate. He doesn't understand the kind of networking, showmanship, that a salon like that appreciates."

She'd only lifted an eyebrow at him, and turned her attention back to the fashion magazine she was reading. She doubted networking included the kind of insults she'd had to parry. They'd pulled it off, making the salon managers think theirs was nothing more than a good antagonistic relationship.

Thank God Tate had promised her three vacation days; she fully intended to savor them. Her only regret was that he was traveling and wouldn't be with her to make the most of them.

But only forty-eight hours had passed when he called her to come in to the office. She was in the middle of her favorite game show, wearing her worn-out jeans and eating an ice-cream cone, when the summons came. She didn't even take the call. Devon took it for her, saying he'd cut his trip short and wanted to see her immediately.

She was at the office in record time, more anxious to see him than to find out what the powwow was about. There was no secretary on guard outside his office, so she knocked before peeking inside. "Hi! This is a surprise . . ." Her face was wreathed in smiles as she anticipated a warm embrace.

But when he pulled his head up from the paperwork, his eyes were cold. He tossed a newspaper on the center of his desk, making it thwack the surface. "Quite a surprise. One I don't need right now."

"I thought . . ." She hesitated, scarcely over the threshold. "I thought you wanted to say hello. I've been back for a couple of days and—"

"I know."

"Tate?"

"This," he said, lifting the paper, "is what brought me home."

If his carpet had been made of eggshells Kelsy couldn't have been more uneasy crossing it. His gaze never wavered as she reached for the Minneapolis paper, but she wondered if he could tell her fingers were trembling. A multitude of possibilities assaulted her. She wondered if Bruce had outdone himself insulting people in New York; she wondered if the photographer had broken the story about how he'd photographed her with a half a head of hair. She even wondered if Devon had done something stupid, like say Daniel Marston was gay.

The article was on an inside page, and the bold headline read: Redheads Only Contest Sham. Beneath, the copy alleged that the "Redheaded Baby Beauty" contest inspired by Gene was a hoax, and that the thousands of entries Elsethe Industries had received from parents who hoped their child would win a four-year scholarship was merely a method of recruiting customers for a targeted market share. There would be no college scholarship.

Kelsy grew weak when she thought of the implications. Coupled with the tabloid story, this could do real damage to the product, as well as the company. She knew why Tate was incensed.

"They quote a 'reliable source,' " Tate pointed out. "Was it you?"

"Me? I'd never do that."

"You're always patting the little redheads on the head and telling their mothers to send their pictures in."

"That's part of my job, Tate."

"This story is totally erroneous, and there has to be a reason for it. I want to know what it is."

"I can't tell you."

"You've been unhappy with your contract."

"That's not true. I love working for Redheads."

"What about all that stuff you told me back in Hawaii? You kept saying you wondered what you'd gotten yourself into, how it was messing up your life."

"For a while, yes, it was overwhelming."

Tate rose from behind his desk and leaned across it, his penetrating gaze reaching into her soul. "It's occurred to me that if you destroy the product, you'd have an out with your contract."

Kelsy's face drained of color. Her knees went weak and her ankles wobbled. Grasping the edge of the desk, she held on more for support than to challenge Tate. "You can't believe I'd do something like that. You can't. Not after what we shared."

Agony glimmered in his eyes, and his chin jutted forward just enough to make her realize he already regretted his accusation. "Tate," she said softly, "if I did that, I'd be hurting you. This is your life. It's part of you. But the best of it was that you made me a part of it, too. I couldn't do anything to hurt you. Not ever."

He drew a deep rasping breath before his lips thinned and indecision flitted through his eyes. He stood a little straighter but his shoulders heaved and, on the desktop, his hands were splayed, every joint tense.

"I just never knew what a commitment Redheads Only would be, Tate." She gently rapped his knuckles with the paper before laying it aside. When he didn't withdraw, she knew he was pushing away the old doubts. "That's what I was talking about in Hawaii. You can't blame me for my shock when I realized how the campaign would change my whole life. None of us, not even you, expected the results."

He focused his gaze back on the paper. "But Kelsy, they had to have a source. This is a reputable paper—they didn't just make it up."

"It wasn't me."

"Then who was it? It's almost as if someone's trying to sabotage this campaign."

Kelsy slowly shook her head. In all honesty, she couldn't think of one person who'd want to do in Redheads Only. There wasn't one person on the crew who wasn't pulling for the success of the product. Even the photographers she'd worked with, the salons they'd visited, were all particularly welcoming, generous. "I just don't know. When I was in New York, a few people mentioned it. But I never seriously thought about the contest, other than occasionally handing out an entry form to a customer."

When she lifted her eyes again, they were troubled, shadowed. "I don't know anything about big business, so this may sound stupid, but—" she shrugged helplessly, as if she, too, were plucking at straws "—have you thought about the competitors? Could they . . . ?"

He stopped to consider the suggestion, hesitating long enough to flip the paper in half, covering up the damning headline. "It would be a risk. I don't like to think that. If that's the case, it would be something we couldn't fight without another lawsuit. These kinds of accusations are hard to fight—it could ruin us."

His hostility toward her had evaporated; she could see it in every move. Suddenly she realized he wasn't nearly as concerned about someone else's involvement as he was hers. Still, she was disappointed he could even believe for a moment she'd do such a thing. Suddenly, from what Jean had told her, she realized it was the kind of trick Zadora would pull. Maybe he just hadn't gotten over his belief that all models were cast in the same mold. Maybe, if she gave him time, her sincerity would outweigh that belief.

"Kelsy, look, let's get out of here," he said, sliding his paperwork aside and coming around to give her a light, almost apologetic kiss. "I need to clear my head with a breath of fresh air. How about lunch?"

Kelsy willingly agreed. They traveled down the freeway talking of general things: the photography and promotional sessions in New York, Bruce, Tate's trip to see his parents in Wisconsin.

But she was totally unprepared for their lunch stop. It was a lavish condo in Edina—and it was where he lived. The place had the traditional look of old money, with perfectly painted white detail, bay windows, paned glass, and different-colored doors, each one embellished with brass kickplates and exquisite door knockers. "This doesn't look like you," she finally said, staring at the oversize arrangement of silk flowers framed by heavy pulled-back draperies at the bay window. "It's so unlike your office."

"A decorator did my office." Switching off the ignition, he regarded the two-story structure and thought of the three empty bedrooms upstairs and the neat little-used patio in back. If Kelsy were with him he wondered, would they buy a gas grill and lawn chairs? He'd never had time before. "Here, I do what I like and I don't worry about image."

"Really?"

He ignored the note of disbelief in her voice, instead walking her up to the front door as if he were a real estate agent showing her a home, trying to persuade a buyer this place was special, just what she was looking for.

He didn't know why the silly comparison surged in his head as he fumbled with his house key. But, suddenly, inexplicably, he wanted her to like it. Throwing open the door, he tried passing off the impulsive invitation, ushering her in as if he expected her to accept the marble tile in the hall, the oil painting hanging above the umbrella stand, and the oriental carpets in the formal dining and living rooms. He knew she got a glimpse of the eighteen-light brass chandelier, and suddenly wished it didn't seem so ostentatious. He'd bought it for dinner party atmosphere, not because it was practical.

"I always keep sandwich makings in the fridge. I hope that's okay." Guiding her to the bar in the kitchen, he winced when he saw he'd neglected to load the dishwasher again.

Fifteen glasses and half a dozen plates littered the bar top. The trash was overflowing again, too. Crushed fast-food boxes and frozen-food cartons sat among wadded napkins and pieces of junk mail. Near his favorite bar stool was a stack of newspapers, his pocket calculator and checkbook, loose change, the remote control for the VCR, and a rental video. Compared to the immaculate interior of the rest of the house, it was pretty obvious which room he lived in. Snapping open a paper bag he swept the counter free, dumping everything in and carrying it to the broom closet. He tossed it in and slammed the door shut.

Kelsy grinned as he matter-of-factly wiped the counter down with a wet paper towel, snatching up the nearby wall phone when it rang. The caller made him stop rubbing the dried drop of gravy. Instead he poked at it with a fingernail and watched Kelsy take in the adjacent family room. As he talked, she studied the framed family photos.

Tate turned his back to Kelsy, as he continued to reply to his caller's assault of questions.

"Tate? Do you hear me?"

"Yes."

"Well?"

"I'm thinking it over."

"Did you know about the article?"

"It was brought to my attention."

"And that's not all — word's out she was a tyrant during the session. You know Al. He's already saying Kelsy was difficult and demanding during the shoot. It wouldn't surprise me one bit if you'd never get another decent photographer for her again. You should look into this. Why, nobody'll have a thing to do with her."

"This is unexpected. I wouldn't have guessed."

"I know you're—" Zadora hesitated, as if choosing the right word, yet detesting it "—fond of her, Tate. And I'm not trying to interfere. You know I love you too much to do that. But it's only because we had something together once that I'm so concerned. I know what this campaign means to you. I'm only telling you these things for your own best interests. That, and Elsethe Industries."

"Of course. I appreciate it."

"I know she seems like a nice girl, but the talk is hot. If you'd want me to find out any more, or if—"

"Can I return your call?"

"That'd be great. If there's anything I can do . . ."

"I'll keep it in mind."

"Love you, Tate. You know I just don't want to see a repeat of the last time."

"Sure."

Tate hung up the phone and looked into Kelsy's innocent eyes. How the hell could she be a tyrant? You didn't go on location for months, interrupt it for a grueling promo trip, dazzle the crew, and then top it off with a temperamental spree in New York.

The only item he hadn't factored in was Bruce. He knew he and Kelsy could be impatient and testy with one another. They had been since the beginning. Could he have punched her buttons? Maybe gotten a little reaction out of her to liven up the atmosphere?

He rummaged in the refrigerator and came back, slapping two packages of deli-shaved lunch meats on the counter and unceremoniously dumping the bread next to it. "So what happened in New York?"

"The usual," Kelsy answered, pulling open the package of turkey slices. "We spent one day doing some neat location shots. But I thought you arranged that. You know, fountains, the Statue of Liberty, some crazy shots inside museums and on busy street corners. It was great."

"So how'd things go? Otherwise?"

"Fine. But I think Bruce trimmed too much off my hair. What do you think? You haven't said anything yet." Kelsy turned slightly, letting him see the shorter haircut. Just below her ears it feathered into classic disarray, the kind of thing Bruce was good at. "I thought you'd say it was too short."

"It is. But I don't imagine he had much choice."

She shrugged, seemingly unbothered. "Probably not. But I realized it looked good for the museums. Makes me look more professional, sophisticated, don't you think?"

He didn't answer. "What did you say when he cut it that short?"

"What was I going to say? It was too late then."

"So was Bruce a good boy for the whole trip?" Tate asked, handing her a luncheon plate. "With those salons, I was concerned—" He stopped when Kelsy avoided his look. "What happened, Kelsy?"

"You really ought to ask him."

"I'm asking you."

"He kind of got into it with the guy at the Pompadour because they weren't set up for us, and then he got upset with me. He tried to smooth it over, though." She fussed with putting mustard on her sandwich. "He had one hard day at the photographer's. But that was because it was drizzly out and the photographer wanted to shoot outside, even though it made my hair go limp. You know how Bruce likes everything to be perfect. Oh," she said, pushing her plate aside to rummage in her purse, "that was the day I ran into Zadora. Would you return this to her?" She offered Tate the tiny vial of perfume. "It fell off her key chain."

Suddenly, she turned wide, disbelieving eyes to Tate. "Oh, Lord," she whispered, the animation on her face replaced by dark, brooding horror. "She was being so nice—she kept asking me all about the campaign. That's all she wanted to talk about. She even asked about the baby contest."

Together they reconstructed Kelsy's run-in with

279

Zadora. Tate, suspicious of Zadora's motives for phoning him anyway, began to make sense of things. It was he who suggested the meeting was no accident. But when he told her Zadora habitually dabbed perfume on her wrists when she was nervous, Kelsy was grateful she at least had proof of the meeting. To Kelsy's benefit, Zadora had neglected to cover herself by telling Tate they'd spoken.

Tate speculated that the entire scenario was orchestrated by Zadora. He wondered if Bruce was implicated. Kelsy suffered the full gamut of emotions: relief, indignation, anger, outrage. Tate tempered her response. But each time he did, she felt worse. She felt as if she'd let him down, betrayed his trust.

The entire situation was sad. Life had handed her a bowl of cherries and stuck a silver spoon in her mouth, but Zadora had come along with the intention of ramming the whole thing down her throat. She was tired of the push-pull agony. She was weary of choking on wealth and good times. She simply wanted a few small bites and the opportunity to savor them.

But Redheads wouldn't allow that. It was all or nothing. Feast or famine. Dreams or disaster.

It was late when Tate finally picked up the phone to call Zadora. Kelsy didn't know whether to cling to his elbow or retreat to a distant corner.

"Zee? Hi. Yeah, I looked into that little matter you mentioned." He lifted an anticipatory brow to Kelsy, motioning her to come closer. "No kidding?" A pause. "Say, you didn't happen to run into Kelsy when she was in New York, did you? No? Oh, I was just wondering. She could really learn a lot from someone like you, Zee," he said. "The thing is," he went on, lifting the vial of Z-woman to the overhead light and examining the amber liquid before shifting his glance to Kelsy, "Kelsy wanted me to return your vial of Z-Woman. She picked it up in the hall outside the photographer's studio after it came off your key chain."

He held the phone slightly away from his ear so Kelsy could listen. The wires buzzed, intensity thrummed, but Zadora was strangely quiet. She'd been trapped in the first lie. She'd claimed she hadn't run into Kelsy in New York. But Kelsy had the little vial to prove that she had.

"Tate . . ." Zadora began hesitantly, "I did see Kelsy in New York, that's true. But it was only a chance meeting. I guess I'd forgotten it . . ."

"No kidding?"

"Well, it's not like it seems . . ."

"Explain it to me." With their heads together, and the phone cradled between, Kelsy and Tate waited.

"Tate. We just talked about the campaign, that's all. I wanted to see how things were going."

"Why would you care?"

281

"Why? Well, because . . ." Zadora's voice momentarily faded. "Look. Kelsy's shot to fame is a kind of a blow to those of us who've worked so hard. I mean everyone has to pay their dues. Some of us are sitting back and wondering how she managed it. Surely you don't begrudge me a few questions?"

"I don't think that's why you asked them, Zee."

"Knowing you, you would have been mad if I hadn't asked. I mean, what's the harm? I was only being polite."

"You asked her about the baby contest, didn't you?"

"So?"

"So how come there's an interesting accusation in the Minneapolis newspaper about the same thing? It reads like another tabloid article."

"What would I know about that?" she huffed.

"Maybe you'd know about it because you'd rather destroy a job than see someone else have it."

There was dead silence on the other end of the telephone line. Zadora spoke first.

"I really wanted that job, Tate. It should have been mine. I told you at the time I'd do anything for a chance at that Redheads job. Instead I ended up pushing some moron's creations in podunk towns I'd never even heard of. After all I did for you, I figured you owed me that much."

"Did you break the story, Zee?"

"You mean you don't know? You're only guessing?"

"It isn't hard to figure."

The voice at the other end of the line was small, almost ashamed. "No, I suppose it isn't."

"Are you going to make me do some digging? I can get a court order and find out where that call to the paper originated from. I'd bet anything it came from your apartment."

More silence hummed over the phone lines. Then "You'd do that?"

"I don't have any choice. Elsethe Industries has a multimillion-dollar investment in this project."

"Okay, okay." Zadora cleared her throat, obviously stalling for time. "I called the paper and gave them the story, and I made it look like it came directly from Kelsy."

"Aw, Zee . . . how could you?"

"Because I—I kept thinking of how when we met you were working on that crazy Redheads project and I knew it would be perfect for me. I just knew it. Why do you think I first dated you, you stupid jerk? It wasn't for your great ambitions or one brilliant idea. It was for me. It was for me all along. I really thought if you cared for me you'd have given me that job." She hesitated. "And when I found out from Daniel where you were staying, I phoned and canceled your reservations in Omaha just to be spiteful.

God, I'm sorry, Tate. I know it seems callous, but I just . . ."

Kelsy stiffened and pulled slightly away. She shouldn't be hearing this. This was between Zadora and Tate. Worse, she figured his ego would suffer quite a bruising from Zadora's forced confession. Aware of his reaction, she noted the clench he had on the receiver, his set jaw, and the livid skin around his mouth.

At last he dropped the receiver back in the cradle. As if that wasn't enough to break the connection, he matter-of-factly pulled the cord from the wall outlet.

"I shouldn't have heard all that," she said uneasily. "Maybe I'd better go."

"No. Don't." He drew her into his arms and between his legs as he straddled the barstool. "My mind just needs to muddle through this."

"You could muddle better if I wasn't here."

"I don't think so." He closed his eyes and dropped his head so that his temple and ear rested against the soft cushion of her breast.

She wondered if he could hear her quickened heartbeat. Zadora's vicious acts had been so appalling! Yet when Tate held himself against her, he and his feelings were all that mattered. While Kelsy was profoundly disillusioned at finding herself the victim in an elaborate scheme of vindictiveness, she began to see what mattered, and what did not.

"I think," she said gently, tracing the fine lines

of his haircut with her fingertips, "that when the roller coaster stops I want to get off. This is all too much for me. It started out as a lark — and look how it's ended up." He said nothing, but his fingers slightly tightened about the flesh above her elbow. "We're all hurting each other. You. Zadora—"

His head lifted, his gaze defiant. "She hasn't hurt me!"

"But look what's happened to everything. To the campaign. To the company. To us . . ."

He struggled to sit up, but Kelsy could see that the real struggle for Tate was resolving the fact that Zadora had once again interfered in his life. "Look," he said, "the only thing that's hurtful is how Zadora Kane tries to manipulate everything around her. But this time she's failed. The campaign, the company's going to survive — *we're* going to survive. I know she's a witch, I knew that years ago. That's why I broke it off with her, that's why—"

"You broke it off?"

"You didn't think I'd let *her* have the pleasure, did you?"

"But I though—" she paused "—that's why you were so cautious of me, that's why you were always so distant."

"I wasn't going to let it happen a second time, no."

The vehemence in his voice sent a ripple of panic through Kelsy. What was he telling her?

That this would remain a comfortable, uncommitted relationship? That scared her. It scared her more than the tabloid lawsuit, the fight with Zadora, the magnitude of the campaign, everything. Tate had become the most important thing in her life, whether or not she was willing to admit it to him.

She didn't want to slog through the rest of her life on a maybe. She wanted the whole thing, the whole dream, with Tate smack-dab in the center of it. He was the hub around which the rest of her world revolved.

"Kelsy, I know this has been rough on you," he said carefully, wedging his fingers between her own and pressing the joints together for a slight squeeze, "but the worst is over. Now we can refute everything Zadora's done. We can deal with the issues, and the campaign can go back to what it was before."

She ached to say, "And what about us?" She ached to demand an answer, an explanation. But her pride wouldn't let her. They'd suffered enough. This wasn't the time, nor the place. But his next sentence rocked her, making her question how they could ever splice the pieces back together.

"After tonight we'll each go back to our own lives, to the way it was before. We'll put this behind us. Because I no longer care about Zadora, she can't hurt me. Because you understand about the past, it's not going to hurt you or your career. Sometimes I think you're unstoppable, like this was all destiny or fate or. . . . Well, never mind, it'll work out, you'll see. Because, if nothing else, I promise you that."

He didn't say anything about the fateful end result of their own relationship — only the company's. If she was down and discouraged when he took her home, it wasn't because her success with Redheads Only had been jeopardized; it was because she was falling in love and didn't know what to do about it. After all, love didn't fit into the company-approved game plan.

Chapter Sixteen

It had been three weeks since they learned Zadora orchestrated the mess surrounding Redheads Only. As Tate promised, they'd managed to pull themselves free of the muck. The scholarship had been awarded to a precocious little redhead from Topeka, Kansas. Best of all, the story made national news when Gene announced that the six-year-old would be offered a bit part in an upcoming commercial. Elsethe Industries was redeemed; Tate was jubilant.

Only Kelsy had trouble rolling out of bed each morning to face the multitude of engagements Tate had scheduled for her. She'd been staying close to home, visiting department stores and salons all within a comfortable radius of the Twin Cities. Tate had busied himself with a new project for Redheads. Kelsy felt so discouraged about how little she was seeing him, she didn't even bother to ask about it.

Devon must have sensed something was amiss. She insisted Kelsy ask Tate for dinner, her treat.

Knowing Devon's aversion to working in the kitchen, Kelsy was impressed and felt she had to offer Tate the invitation. Even when he accepted, she couldn't work up much enthusiasm for the evening.

Things seemed to be happening exactly as he'd predicted: they were each going on with their own lives. Only she felt like the poor little rich girl, with a great big void right in the middle of all the fuss and excitement. On her worst days she thought the campaign had been bigger than both of them and, because of it, they'd let the other down. On her good days, she merely experienced a horrible sense of loss over the relationship.

"Kels?" said Devon the morning of the dinner party.

"Yeah?"

"You got a phone call."

Pulling the pillow from over her head, she wished the world would take a hike. "Take a message."

"C'mon. It's Gene."

Kelsy groaned. "Tell him I'm in the shower. Tell him not to worry, his little redhead is going to go out and glow for her ten-o'clock appointment."

"You know I hate lying for you."

Kelsy kicked the covers, thinking about Tate. "I'm not lying about the glowing part."

"Right."

When Devon returned to the bedroom, she told her Gene had called a private meeting and expected her promptly at his office at noon. The brisk, no-nonsense way Devon delivered the message made Kelsy shiver. Gene never summoned anyone to his office. If he wanted to do business he did it over a plate of doughnuts or a game of golf. Apprehension goaded Kelsy into wearing her most appealing outfit, but it didn't dispel the anxiety that hung over her like a shroud.

It was indeed a private meeting. The secretary held her captive in the waiting room, telling her—*snarling* might have been the more apt word, Kelsy thought—that Gene and Tate were behind the same forbidding doors she was expected to enter and had left strict orders they didn't want to be disturbed.

She waited an agonizing fifteen minutes, and each time the minute hand made another revolution, she wondered if she were being dismissed, if she'd go back to being Kelsy Williams, scorned lover and coffee shop manager. What a combination, she thought sourly.

Heavens, what would Devon say? After all that had happened, she would probably regret seeing her redheaded sister back in the coffee shop working her buns off—huh, strike that. Working a truckload of Danish off. As it was, Devon was volunteering to go in and work, even when she didn't need to. Why, anymore she'd just tuck her books under one arm and claim the old coffee klatch gang was getting together to crab about city government. The topics were getting hot; Devon figured she couldn't afford to miss it.

While she waited, Kelsy fiddled with a loose button on her jacket; she would have twisted her hair, too, just for comfort's sake, but Bruce had cut it too short. Now there were only cropped ends curling over her neck. She was turning them like pinwheels when Tate opened the door. The grooves in his cheeks deepened, the way they always did when he accused her of doing something sexy.

Self-consciously, she gripped the handles of her purse, imagining she must have looked like a little old lady. The fleeting thought of aging crossed her mind, making her speculate that Gene and Tate would really come unglued when the first few strands of gray mingled with the red in her hair.

But that was being premature. Right now she was just concerned with staying out of the unemployment office.

"Come on in," Tate said. "We wanted to get some loose ends tied up, and it took a little longer than we expected."

Rising, Kelsy smoothed her skirt and searched for some glimmer of hope in Tate's face. Nothing. It appeared he was keeping himself and his emotions carefully in check. Was it for Gene's benefit? The secretary's? Or hers? Devon's dinner was that evening — how could she look across the table to his stoic reserve?

Gene was calmly looking over a stack of paperwork. He was wearing glasses, new ones Kelsy had never seen before. He wasn't actually looking through them, because they were perched to the end of his nose and he seemed to be tipping his head so they wouldn't get in his way. "Kelsy, come on in," he said, indicating with the papers which chair she should take. "I was just looking over your contract."

Kelsy's stomach sank as quickly as her body did into the chair. The chair seat stopped her body's descent; her stomach kept plummeting.

"I wanted to see how this worked what with the tabloid thing and all." He pursed his lips, scanning a few more lines on her contract. "Well, first things first . . ." He sat straighter and looked at her. "Word has it you want to quit."

She pitched slightly forward, her eyes widening. "I — I haven't said anything like that, Mr. Theis. I hope you'll consider that only a rumor."

"Still, this campaign's taken quite a toll on you."

It wasn't a question, it didn't demand an answer, yet Kelsy felt she owed him an honest one. Tate, one hip wedged against the credenza, appeared to be taking the whole thing casually.

"I guess it has. I didn't think it would be like this. The instant recognition, the demands. Of course, I've enjoyed it, but . . . it has put strain on everything. My relationship with—" she first thought of Tate, but rebelled against laying out his name before Gene "—my sister, with the people I work with. Of course, we've worked that all out."

"And the other things haven't been easy for you," Tate commiserated, "the lawsuit, the surfing accident." He grinned a little wickedly, his features nicely set in mock sympathy before adding, "the haircut."

"Some of those things were unavoidable," Kelsy said quietly, fumbling for the right words. "You know," she said finally, darting a look between Tate's impassive face and Gene's curious one, "I don't want to quit. I've got another six months left on my contract, and I intend to fulfill them."

"Speaking of contracts, Kelsy," Gene said, digging in his pocket. "We want to keep up our end of the deal, too." He flipped her two quarters and she caught them easily. "Here's fifty cents. The lawsuit over the tabloid is settled. Go buy yourself a cup of coffee."

Kelsy stared at the quarters, trying to make some sense of Gene's dismissal. So he *was* firing her. *Go buy yourself a cup of coffee,* he said, and the words rang singsong through her head. They were telling her she hadn't failed as the Redheads Only representative, but she'd somehow failed Elsethe Industries. It wouldn't be long before she'd be back at the coffee shop, mopping down the countertop and seeing her image on the television screen.

What was happening? Had she really not met their expectations?

Her legs were unsteady, but she struggled to rise from the chair, the strap of her purse crumpling as she pushed away on the armrests. Gene frowned at her movement; Tate moved closer. "Thank you," she said feebly, "no matter what happened, it was a good experience."

"I don't think you're listening," Gene said as Tate's hands settled on her shaking shoulders.

Gently Tate pushed her back in the chair. He bent over so that his cheek grazed her own, his lips only inches from her flawlessly groomed hair and the dazzling gold earring he'd once insisted was perfect for her. "If you love me," he whispered, "you'll stick around long enough to listen." She glared at him in astonishment.

"Now, as I was saying—" Gene coughed, resuming when he seemed sure she was going to stay seated "—we've learned Zadora was behind the mess with *The Noisemaker*, too. She made a tidy bundle off that piece of fiction."

Pulling a chair close to Kelsy's, Tate dropped into it, picking up her hand and winking at her. "*We* didn't do as well."

"Not necessarily," Gene corrected, beaming. "Think of all the free advertising. Kelsy, you just got your half. We settled for a dollar."

"A what?" She stared at the two quarters in her hand.

"A dollar, and a retraction. The media's just picking up on it—I expect it to be on the six-o'clock news."

Tate chuckled. "Zee's frantic. They've named her as the main contributor to the story—and just when she's ready to go to contract with a major cosmetics company. She's seeing a lifetime of deceit and treachery take wings, just in time to fly away with her career."

"We've been through thick and thin together, Kelsy," Gene said expansively, tucking his thumbs into his waistband the way he always did when he was extraordinarily pleased. "Tate and I have spent the morning looking over your contract. We'd like to extend it for another six months. We've got a couple of little perks we think you're going to like. We'll talk about some of them now, and Tate'll wrap up the rest later tonight."

Dinner turned into a victory celebration. It was, considering Devon was the cook, a culinary feast. She'd prepared prime rib, a Caesar salad, orange-glazed muffins, baby carrots, and pea pods, then topped it all off with a French Silk pie. But in the end she only set places for two, because she was heading over to the coffee shop. The ice maker had broken down again and the repairman said he'd come late to fix it.

Kelsy suspected Devon was beginning to enjoy

handing the man his wrenches. Besides, every time she mentioned getting a new machine now that they could afford it, Devon kept dodging the issue, saying that since they'd paid for the service contract they may as well get some use out of it. Kelsy decided it was a small price to pay—especially since she'd be getting an evening alone with Tate.

He'd brought over his favorite disks and she'd put them on her new player, savoring the warmth of a house filled with the smells of cooking and the thrumming beat of good music.

Tate must have felt the same because he pulled her into his arms. "Dance?" he asked, wrapping both arms about her waist and pulling her near. Without waiting for her answer he started moving, his touch gliding up her spine before spreading over her shoulder blades and dipping near the sensitive softness beneath her arms.

Kelsy tingled as he drew nearer, increasingly aware of the thickness of his pelvis as he cradled against her, hollowing into the cushion of her abdomen. He tilted his head and their foreheads touched, the perfect cut of his hairline grazing her temple. He smelled sweet, fruity, like the cooler full of pineapple drinks he'd brought with him. When he nuzzled her cheek and the curve of her jaw, tremors rippled through her, making her cling to him, making her think of all the glorious Hawaiian days and nights.

It was over, but the memory, the illusion, was

bright. She'd been with Tate for just six months, but she couldn't imagine working next to him for another year. It would be agony . . . yet it was all she had left. Beside him, the job's importance diminished. Now it was simply a vehicle to keep her close to him. To do her best for him. To cheer him on when life looked ragged or like it was coming apart at the seams.

His lips wandered close to her ear, whispering a kiss inside the outer rim. Her heart quickened, matching the cool, sensual beat. Her body seemed to melt, lost in the warmth of his arms.

Inexplicably, he chuckled. "You're awfully quiet tonight. Don't tell me," he speculated, leaning back from the waist to study her. "I suppose you're thinking about your big settlement from *The Noisemaker.*"

"Nope." Regretfully, she smiled, refusing to admit she was more concerned about the outcome of their relationship than the unexpected settlement of the law suit. "Fifty cents barely buys a cup of coffee anymore."

"Disappointed?"

"No, not really," I'd rather have you, she thought. I'd rather have you than a five-million-dollar contract and two closets full of new clothes and an on-location shoot. "If I could just get my personal life in order," she said softly. "I'd consider fifty cents a windfall."

"Devon's been better?"

"Oh, she's been great. Even understanding.

The coffee shop isn't even an issue anymore."

"So . . . ?"

Kelsy paused and stopped moving to the music, wondering how much she should say, wondering how much he'd accept. After his last unhappy exchange with Zadora, she'd come to believe he'd absented himself from her because of the similarities, because of the pain. Had he used the excuse of work to keep himself from her because of those very same reasons? "I've loved it all, Tate. The travel, the security . . . And you gave me something I never could have purchased—confidence. I step into a crowd now and I feel good about myself, good that I have something to share, good because I give them a few moments of fun. But I've paid the price, too."

"And that is?"

"The trade-off is that occasionally I miss being anonymous, able to get lost in the crowd. I miss being just a regular person. It scares me sometimes, because I've come to know how fleeting all these friendships are. And I'd rather have one solid relationship with one good man."

He paused, apparently debating, his gaze skimming her lips, the breezy innocence of her tumbled hair, the pearl studs he'd bought her in Hawaii. "Someone like me?" he asked huskily, his voice cracking.

"Just like," she said softly, strength burgeoning in her reply.

"You know, you'll never be anonymous again," he warned. "Redheads guarantees it."

"I know."

"You've become a recognizable public figure — the all-American success story that hard work and diligence pays off."

"That, and a hank of red hair," she said dryly, conscious only of the fact they were talking about her career again, not about the feelings that ran between them.

"I've been pretty busy these past few weeks, Kelsy. Getting the tabloid thing settled and taking care of the loose ends with the kids' contest. But you were always in the back of my mind, always nudging me to think about how much influence you've made over this campaign and what we, as a company, could do to make you an attractive offer. One that'll make you stay. See, I know it's been hard on you, more difficult than anyone could've imagined. But you've come through like a real trouper."

Kelsy gave him a hard, proud smile, one that said she appreciated his concern, but that she'd keep her chin, as well as her spirits, up.

"Kelsy, the foundation of this campaign is solid. And it's been well-received. I figure if you'd only work a few weeks out of the year after your contract expires, just to supplement the advertising with some stills and an occasional commercial, you could keep a particularly well-paying job in the family."

Kelsy sighed, frowning while she rested her elbows against his shoulders and her fingers picked at the top button of his shirt. It wasn't hard to figure he was still talking about maintaining that delicate balance of working and getting Devon through school. "It's not that easy. The coffee shop . . ."

"Coffee shop?" He look bewildered, then smiled. "If you have to keep that, we'll just hire the help."

"We'll just do what?"

"I hadn't thought about it, but celebrities have their own restaurants all the time. Why can't Kelsy Williams have a coffee shop? Sure, we can do that. If that's what you want."

"What's all this 'we' stuff? If I can live comfortably working for Redheads Only for a few weeks a year, and if Devon wants out, then—"

"We? The 'we stuff' is for us. The Redheads formula is going to make us a lot of money, Kels. But I'm talking about keeping a second well paying job in *my* family," he emphasized. "When I said that I wasn't thinking of your pushing coffee at the ten o'clock regulars."

She stared at him, wondering if she'd correctly interpreted what he'd just said.

Apparently sensing her indecision, he gazed at her. Then he grew businesslike, as if he needed to prove these were logical choices for both of them. "Look, I've worked it all out. We need some time together, and we'll have it now that the baby shampoo for Redheads is ready for the market."

Kelsy felt her world spinning out of control, accelerating so quickly she couldn't comprehend all the changes Tate was offering. She should be asking what he meant about keeping the coffee shop and spending more time together. Instead, she focused on the only tangible thing he'd referred to.

"Baby shampoo? Is that why you contracted that little girl from Topeka?" Suddenly it all made sense—the long hours, his preoccupation with work. "No one ever told me you were bringing out another product. You never said a word."

"I never had time because we had to act quickly. People have been inundating us with requests for kids' products. You ought to see the mail room. Gene's secretary is quietly going nuts because he left instructions that every letter should get a personal reply."

"So that's why she was snarling at me."

"She'll be okay. She's only temporarily annoyed." He squeezed her. "If this kid from Topeka works out, it'll take some of the pressure off you. Of course, there'll still be personal appearances, but once we get rolling, we'll be putting in just as much time on the kids' campaign."

"But I'll never see you," Kelsy protested, giving him a quick shake, as if she'd like to bring him to his senses. "Anyway, I don't think you'll work well with a child actor. Remember what Gene said after Sherry cut my hair about you needing a few kids of your own?"

He grinned down at her. "That was one of his better ideas—I may have to get some." He tweaked a loose curl. "We could work on that soon. You know, get into practice so everything's a go when your contract expires. That's only a year away."

"You really do plan ahead, don't you?" At his nod, she said, "But you've neglected one thing—a full-time wife. One that takes a few weeks off each year to promote her husband's passion, his creation, Redheads Only. It really should be a family project," she insisted, "because she's as proud of it as he is."

He kissed her full on the lips, making it a promise, sealing it with commitment. "You do drive a hard bargain. I'll consider that a once-in-a-lifetime proposal. One I'll have to accept. For a businessman like me, I don't have any other choice." He pulled her close, loving her, needing her. "I love you, Kels. And," he chuckled, the glint in his eye baiting her, "when we have those babies, can you make them redheads?"

"You take what you get," she rebuked, kissing him on the cheek and looping her arms about his neck. "And let me tell you right now, no matter what color their topknots, none of them is going into this modeling racket. When we have those babies I want us to settle down, because most of all I love you, and I want us to be together." She paused, cocking her head to the side. "You know that wedding dress we used in the last shoot? According to my contract it becomes my personal property. I'd like to see it go down the aisle for real once."

"Just once?"

"Just once. How soon do you think that can be arranged?"

"Like anything else with this campaign—as soon as possible."

CATCH A RISING STAR!

ROBIN ST. THOMAS

FORTUNE'S SISTERS   **(2616, $3.95)**

It was Pia's destiny to be a Hollywood star. She had complete self-confidence, breathtaking beauty, and the help of her domineering mother. But her younger sister Jeanne began to steal the spotlight meant for Pia, diverting attention away from the ruthlessly ambitious star. When her mother Mathilde started to return the advances of dashing director Wes Guest, Pia's jealousy surfaced. Her passion for Guest and desire to be the brightest star in Hollywood pitted Pia against her own family — sister against sister, mother against daughter. Pia was determined to be the only survivor in the arenas of love and fame. But neither Mathilde nor Jeanne would surrender without a fight. . . .

LOVER'S MASQUERADE   **(2886, $4.50)**

New Orleans. A city of secrets, shrouded in mystery and magic. A city where dreams become obsessions and memories once again become reality. A city where even one trip, like a stop on Claudia Gage's book promotion tour, can lead to a perilous fall. For New Orleans is also the home of Armand Dantine, who knows the secrets that Claudia would conceal and the past she cannot remember. And he will stop at nothing to make her love him, and will not let her go again . . .

SENSATION   **(3228, $4.95)**

They'd dreamed of stardom, and their dreams came true. Now they had fame and the power that comes with it. In Hollywood, in New York, and around the world, the names of Aurora Styles, Rachel Allenby, and Pia Decameron commanded immediate attention — and lust and envy as well. They were stars, idols on pedestals. And there was always someone waiting in the wings to bring them crashing down . . .

Available wherever paperbacks are sold, or order direct from the Publisher. Send cover price plus 50¢ per copy for mailing and handling to Zebra Books, Dept. 4112, 475 Park Avenue South, New York, N.Y. 10016. Residents of New York and Tennessee must include sales tax. DO NOT SEND CASH. For a free Zebra/Pinnacle catalog please write to the above address.